To Dear Decca
Lots of Love
From
Great Grandma 1991

x x x

GRIMMS'

FAIRY TALES

Translated
by Vladimír Vařecha
Illustrated
by Luděk Maňásek

CATHAY BOOKS

First published 1979 by
Cathay Books
59 Grosvenor Street
London W1
Reprinted 1981
Translated by Vladimír Vařecha
Graphic design by Jiří Schmidt
© Artia, Prague 1979
ISBN 0 904644 96 0
Printed in Czechoslovakia by PZ Bratislava
1/18/02/51-03

CONTENTS

THE FROG PRINCE

In the old days when wishing could still cast a spell, there lived a King whose daughters were all beautiful, but the youngest was so lovely that the sun itself, which had looked on so many things, was amazed whenever it shone on her face. Near the King's castle was a large dark forest, and in that forest there was a well under an old lime-tree. When the day was very warm, the King's youngest child would go out into the forest and sit down on the edge of the cool fountain. And when she felt bored she took a golden ball, threw it up in the air and caught it again, and that was her favourite pastime.

Now it so happened one day that the golden ball did not drop back into her little hand stretched out to catch but bounded away on the earth and rolled straight into the well. The Princess followed the ball with her eyes but the ball disappeared, and the well was deep, so deep that the bottom could not be seen. Then she began to cry and cried louder and louder, and there was nothing to comfort her.

As she was thus lamenting, someone called out to her. "What is the matter, Princess? The way you are lamenting would move a stone to pity." She looked round to see whence the voice was coming and saw a frog poking its thick, ugly head out of the water. "Oh, it's you, old water-splasher?" said she. "I am crying for my golden ball which has dropped down the well."

"Be quiet and stop crying," answered the frog. "I have a way of helping you, but what will you give me if I recover your plaything and bring it up again?"

"Anything you wish to have, dear frog," she said, "my clothes, my pearls and diamonds, even the gold crown which I am wearing."

"I do not care for your clothes, your pearls and diamonds, or your gold crown, but if you will love me and let me be your companion and play-fellow and sit by you at your little table, eat out of your little golden plate, drink from your little cup, and sleep in your little bed; if you promise me all this, then I will go down and fetch your golden ball again."

"Oh yes," she said, "I promise you all you wish, if you but bring back my ball." However, she thought to herself, "What is this silly frog babbling about? He sits and croaks in the water with his mates, and cannot be a human being's companion!"

As soon as the frog received the promise, he dived his head under the water, sank down, and after a short while came swimming up again with the ball in his mouth and threw it onto the grass.

The King's daughter was overjoyed when she saw her lovely plaything again, picked it up and ran away with it.

"Wait, wait," called the frog. "Take me with you, I can't run as fast as you!" But what use was it for him to cry "Croak, croak!" after her as loudly as he could? She did not listen to him, hurried home, and soon forgot all about the poor frog who had to descend into his well again.

The next day, when seated at the dinner-table with the King and all the courtiers, she was eating from her little golden plate, something came creeping splish, splash, splish, up the marble staircase, and when it got to the top it knocked at the door and cried, "King's daughter, the youngest, open the door for me." She ran to see who was outside, but when she opened the door and saw the frog sitting there, she banged the door to as fast as she could and went and sat down again at the dinner-table, though she was quite frightened. The King saw plainly that her heart was beating fast and said, "My child, what are you afraid of? Is there a giant outside the door wanting to carry you away?"

"Oh no," she answered, "it is no giant, but an ugly frog."

"What does the frog want with you?"

"Oh, dear father, yesterday as I was sitting at the well playing with my golden ball, it fell into the water. And because I was crying so bitterly, the frog brought it up again for me and, as he begged and insisted on it, I promised him he should be my companion. But I never thought that he could come out of the water. But he is here now and wants to come in here to me."

Meanwhile, the knocking and shouting started again.

"Youngest daughter of the King,
Open the door to me.
Don't you remember what yesterday
You said at the cool well-water?
Youngest daughter of the King,
Open the door to me."

Whereupon the King said, "As you have made a promise you must keep it. Just go and open the door to the frog."

She went and opened the door, and the frog hopped in following her footsteps as far as her chair. There he sat and cried, "Lift me up." She hesitated till at last the King ordered her to do so. The moment the frog was on the chair, he wanted to sit on the table, and when he was sitting there he said, "Now move your little golden plate nearer that we may eat together." She did this, but it was plain to see that she did not do it willingly. The frog made a hearty meal, but not so the Princess: nearly every morsel stuck in her throat. At last he said, "I have eaten my fill, and I am tired. Carry me now into your little room and make your silken bed ready that we may lie down and sleep."

The Princess began to cry, and was frightened of the cold, clammy frog which she did not dare to touch and which was now to sleep in her pretty clean little bed. But the King lost his temper with her and said, "He who helped you when you were in need shall not later be despised."

So she took the frog with two fingers, carried him upstairs, and put him in a corner. But when she was lying in bed, he crept towards her and said, "I am tired and want to go to sleep as well as you. Lift me up, or I will tell your father."

She flew into a rage, picked him up, and threw him with all her might and main against the wall, shouting, "Now you shall be quiet, you hideous frog!" But when he fell down he was no frog but a king's son with beautiful, kind eyes.

Her father's wish was that he should become her beloved companion and husband. He told her that he had been changed by a wicked fairy into a frog, and no one could have delivered him from the well but she herself, adding that tomorrow they would go together to his kingdom.

Then they went to sleep, and next morning when the sun wakened them a coach came driving up with eight white horses, with white ostrich feathers on their heads and harnessed with golden chains. And behind stood faithful Henry, the young King's body-servant. He had been so grieved when his lord and master was changed into a frog that he had three iron bands placed round his heart lest it should burst with grief and sadness.

The coach was there to carry the young King into his kingdom. Faithful

Henry helped both to get in, and once again took his stand behind overjoyed about this deliverance.

When they had driven only a little way, the Prince heard something crack behind him as if something had broken. He turned round and cried:

"Henry, the carriage is breaking."
"No, sir, it's not the carriage
But a band from my heart is in twain
That for long was great pain,
While you sat inside a well
A frog by a bad witch's spell!"

Once more and then again there was cracking on the way. The Prince thought it must be the carriage breaking, but it was only the bands which were springing from faithful Henry's heart because his lord and master had been delivered and was happy.

FAITHFUL JOHN

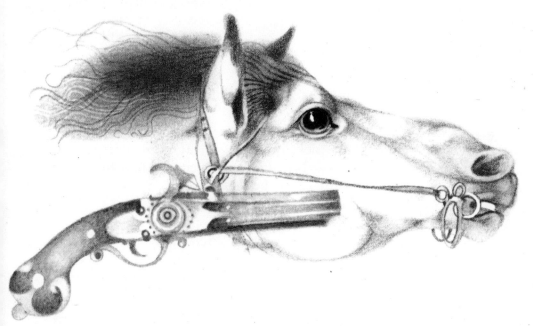

There was once upon a time an old King. He was ill and thought to himself, "It may be that I am lying on my deathbed." Then he said to one of his attendants, "Tell Faithful John to come to me."

Faithful John was his favourite servant and was so called because he had been faithful to him all his life. When he came to the bedside, the King said to him, "Most faithful John, I feel I am approaching the end of my days, and the only thing I am worried about is my son. He is still of a tender age, and does not always know what to do for the best. Unless you promise me to instruct him in everything that he ought to know, and to be his foster-father, I shall not be able to close my eyes in peace."

Then Faithful John answered, "I will not leave him, and will serve him faithfully, even if it costs me my life."

Hearing this, the old King said, "Now I can die in peace." Then he went on, "After my death, you must show him the whole castle, all the chambers, halls and vaults, and all the treasures deposited in them. But you must not show him the last chamber in the long passage, where the picture of the daughter of the King of the Golden Roof is hidden. If he sees that picture, he will fall passionately in love with her and will drop down in a swoon, and will expose himself to great dangers for her sake. You are to guard him against that."

And, when Faithful John had once more given the old King his hand on it, the King fell silent, laid his head on the pillow, and died.

When the old King had been carried to his grave, Faithful John told the young King what he had promised his father on his deathbed. "I will certainly keep that promise, and be as faithful to you as I was to him, even if it costs me my life."

When the days of mourning were over, Faithful John said to the young King, "The time has come for you to see your inheritance, I will show you your castle."

He led him about, up and down, and showed him all the riches and the magnificent chambers. Yet there was one chamber which he did not open — the one which held the fateful picture. The picture was placed in such a manner that when the door opened one looked straight at it. It was so magnificent-ly painted that it made you think it breathed and lived and that there was nothing more charming and beautiful in the whole world.

The young King noticed, of course, that Faithful John always passed a certain door by, and asked, "Why don't you ever open it for me?"

"There is something inside," he answered, "that would harm you." But the King answered, "I have seen the whole castle, now I want to know what's in there." And he went and was about to force the door open.

Then Faithful John held him back and said, "I promised your father before his death you should not see what that chamber holds. It might turn into great misfortune for you and me."

"Oh no," said the young King, "if I don't get in, it is sure to torment me. I should know no rest by day and night till I have seen it with my own eyes. I shall not move from the door till you have unlocked it."

Then Faithful John saw that he could no longer prevent him and, with a heavy heart and many sighs, picked out the key from the big bunch. When he had opened the door, he went in first hoping to cover the picture from the King who was behind him, but what use was that? The King stood on tiptoe and saw it over his shoulder. And when he looked at the portrait of the maiden which was so resplendent and sparkling with gold and jewels, he fell down in a faint.

Faithful John lifted him up, carried him to his bed, and full of sorrow thought, "The misfortune has befallen us. What will it all come to?" Then he revived the young King with wine till he was himself again.

The first words he said were, "Oh, that marvellous painting. Whose portrait is it?"

"It is the daughter of the King of the Golden Roof," Faithful John replied.

Then the King spoke again, "My love for her is so great that if all the leaves on the trees were tongues, they still could not express it. I will risk my life to win her. You are my most faithful John, and must help me."

The faithful servant pondered within himself a long time how to go about it at all, for it was hard even to come into the presence of this beautiful daughter. At long last he did think of a way and said to the King, "Everything she has about her is of gold – tables, chairs, dishes, bowls, and all household utensils. Your treasure comprises five tons of gold. Have one ton wrought by the goldsmiths of the kingdom into all manner of vessels and utensils, into all kinds of birds, game and wondrous animals. She will find pleasure in them, and we will travel there with these things and try our luck."

The King summoned all the goldsmiths, and they had to work day and night till at last the most magnificent things were ready. When everything had been loaded on to a ship, Faithful John dressed as a merchant, and told the King to do likewise to disguise himself. Then they sailed across the sea and sailed till they arrived in the city where the daughter of the King of the Golden Roof dwelt.

Faithful John bade the King stay behind aboard the ship and to wait for him. "Perhaps I shall bring the Princess back with me," he said. "Therefore see that everything is ready, have the golden vessels displayed and the whole ship decorated."

Then he gathered up all kinds of gold things in his apron, went on land and straight to the royal palace. When he reached the palace courtyard, a pretty girl was standing by the well. She had two gold buckets in her hands and was drawing water. She was just about to carry away the sparkling water when she turned round and saw the stranger and asked who he was.

"I am a merchant," he replied, opened his apron and let her look in.

"Oh what beautiful gold things!" she cried and put her buckets down, and looked at the things one after the other. "The Princess must see these! She is so delighted by such gold things that she will buy them all from you." She took him by the hand and led him upstairs, for she was the Princess's chambermaid.

When the King's daughter saw the wares, she really was delighted and said, "They are so beautifully wrought that I will buy them all from you."

But Faithful John said, "I am only a rich merchant's servant. What I have here is nothing compared with what my master has on board his ship. Indeed, they are the most artistic and most precious jewels that have ever been wrought in gold."

The Princess would have liked everything to have been brought up to her, but he said, "That would take days. There are so many things and it would need so many halls to display them in. I am afraid your palace has not enough room to accomodate them all."

This roused her curiosity and desire even more so that she finally said, "Guide me down to the ship. I will go there myself and view your master's treasures."

Then Faithful John led her down to the ship and was most happy. And when the King saw her, he found her beauty even greater than it had been represented on the portrait, and his only feeling was that his heart would burst with love for her. She went on board, and the King escorted her in. However, Faithful John stayed behind with the captain and ordered the ship to weigh anchor, saying, "Set all the sails, so that she may fly like a bird in the air!"

Below decks, the King was showing the Princess the gold utensils, the dishes, beakers, bowls, birds, wild beasts and the wondrous animals. Many hours passed while she inspected everything and, in her delight, she failed to notice that the ship was moving. Having looked at everything she thanked the 'merchant' and turned to go home, but when she came to the ship's side she saw that they were far from land on the high seas, and speeding full sail along. "Oh," she cried terrified. "I have been tricked, I am kidnapped and in the power of a merchant. I would rather die!"

But the King took her by the hand and said, "I am no merchant, I am a king, and of no lower birth than you are. I have captured you only because I love you so much. The first time I saw your portrait in my castle I fell to the ground in a swoon."

When the daughter of the King of the Golden Roof heard this, she was comforted and her heart inclined towards him so that she willingly consented to become his wife.

But it so happened that while they were on the high seas, Faithful John, who was sitting near the bows of the ship playing a tune, suddenly saw three seabirds flying through the air towards the vessel. He stopped playing and listened to what they were saying to one another, for he well understood their speech.

One of them cried, "Yes, he is bringing home the daughter of the King of the Golden Roof."

"Ah," answered the second, "But he has not got her home yet."

"Well, he has her, hasn't he?" cried the third. "She is sitting beside him in the ship."

Then the first seabird cried again, "When they come ashore, a chestnut horse as red as a fox will gallop up to meet them. The King will want to mount it and, if he does so, it will spring away with him and into the air and he shall never see his maiden again."

The second said, "Can nobody rescue him?"

"Oh yes," said the first. "When someone else quickly mounts it, takes out the gun that is sure to be in the saddle, and shoots the horse dead, the young King will be saved. But who knows that? And, if anybody knows and tells it to him, he will be turned to stone from his toes to his knees."

Then the second seabird said, "I know still more. Even if the horse is killed, the young King will not keep his bride. When they enter the castle together, there will be a bridal shirt ready on a table and it will look as if

it is woven of gold and silver. Yet it is nothing but sulphur and pitch. If he puts it on, it will burn him to the very bone and marrow."

The third asked, "Is there no way at all of rescuing him?"

"Oh yes, there is," answered the second. "If someone gets hold of the shirt with gloves and throws it into the fire so that it burns up, then the young King will be saved. But what's the use? Whoever knows this and tells him will turn to stone from his knees to his heart."

Then the third seabird spoke saying, "I know still more. Even if the bridal shirt is burnt up, the young King will not have his bride. After the wedding when the ball begins and the young Queen is dancing, she will suddenly turn pale and fall down as if dead. And, unless someone lifts her up and draws three drops of blood from her right breast and spites them out again, she will die. But if anyone who knows this discloses it, his whole body will be turned to stone from head to foot."

Faithful John had understood everything but from that moment he became quiet and sad. If he was to conceal what he had just heard from his master, the latter would suffer misfortune and, if he were to reveal it to him, he himself would have to sacrifice his life. In the end, however, he said to himself, "I shall save my master, even if it costs me my life."

Now when they landed, everything happened as the seabirds had foretold. A magnificent chestnut horse, as red as a fox, came springing up. "Come on!" said the King, as he was about to mount it. "He shall carry me to the castle!"

But Faithful John was quicker, swung up on to the horse, drew the gun from the saddle and shot the chestnut dead.

Then the other servants, who were none too fond of Faithful John, cried, "What a shame to kill such a fine animal that was to have carried the King to the castle!" But the King said, "Be quiet and leave him alone. He is my most faithful John, who knows what it may be good for!"

They went into the castle and there in the hall was a table and the perfectly wrought bridal shirt lay on it looking no less than as if it were made of gold and silver. The young King came up to it and was on the point of taking hold of it, when Faithful John pushed him aside, seized it with gloves on and carried it quickly to the fireplace. There he let it burn up.

Once again the other servants began to murmur, "Lo and behold! Now he is even burning the King's bridal shirt!" But the young King said, "Who knows what it may be good for. Leave him alone, he is my most faithful John."

The wedding was celebrated. The ball began and the bride started dancing. Faithful John was on the lookout and kept an eye on her face. All of a sudden, she turned pale and fell down to the ground as if dead. He quickly rushed up, lifted her and carried her into a chamber. There he laid her down, knelt and sucked the three drops of blood from her right breast, and spat them out. At once she breathed again and recovered.

But the young King witnessed all this and didn't know why Faithful John had done it. It made him angry and he cried out, "Off with him to the dungeon!"

Next morning, Faithful John was condemned to death and led to the gallows. And, as he stood there and was about to be executed, he said, "Everyone who is to die is allowed to say his last words before his end. May I also have this right?"

"Yes," answered the King, "the privilege shall be granted to you."

Then Faithful John said, "I am wrongfully condemned, and have always been faithful to you." Then he recounted how he had overheard the seabirds talk while at sea, and he had been forced to do all those things to save his master.

Then the King cried, "Oh, my most faithful John! Mercy, mercy! Bring him down!" But as Faithful John uttered his last word, he had fallen down dead and become a piece of stone.

The King and Queen were sorely grieved over this, and the King said, "Oh, how ill I have repaid such great loyalty!" And he had the stone figure picked up and moved into his bedchamber beside his bed. Whenever he looked at it he would weep and say, "If I could but bring you back to life, my most faithful John!"

Some time passed and the Queen gave birth to twins, two little boys, and they grew up and were her joy.

Once, when the Queen was at church and the two boys were sitting beside their father playing, the King once again looked sadly at the stone figure, sighed and said, "Oh, if only I could bring you back to life, my most faithful John!"

Then the stone began to speak and said, "Yes, you can bring me back to life if you use what is dearest to you to bring it about."

Then the King cried, "I will sacrifice everything I have in this world for you!"

The stone went on, "If you, with your own hand, cut off the heads of your two children and smear me with their blood, I shall come back to life."

The King was horrified when he heard that he would have to kill his dearest children with his own hand, but he thought of Faithful John's great loyalty and how he had died for him. So he drew his sword and with his own hand cut off his children's heads. And when he had smeared the stone with their blood, life was restored to it, and Faithful John stood hale and hearty before him.

He said to the King, "Your loyalty to me shall not go unrewarded."

Then he took the children's heads, put them on, and rubbed the wound with their blood. They were whole again that instant, skipped about, and went on playing as if nothing had happened.

The King was overjoyed, and when he saw the Queen coming, he hid Faithful John and the two boys in a big cupboard. When she came in, he asked her, "Did you pray at church?"

"Yes, I did," she answered, "but all the time I was thinking of Faithful John and of what misfortune had befallen him on our account."

Whereupon he said, "Dear wife, we can give him his life again, but it will cost us our two children, we must sacrifice them to do that."

The Queen turned pale and terror seized her heart, none the less she said, "We owe it to him for his great loyalty."

Then the King was glad that she was of the same mind as he had been. He went and opened the cupboard, brought out the children and Faithful John, and said, "God be praised! He is freed from the spell, and we have our two little sons back again," and he told the Queen how it had all happened.

And then they lived happily together to the end of their days.

BROTHER AND SISTER

A little boy took his little sister by the hand and said, "Since mother died we have not had a happy moment. Our stepmother beats us every day and, when we come near her, kicks us out with the toe of her boot. The left-over hard crusts of bread are all we get to eat. Why, the little dog under the table is better off than we are, for he often gets a choice morsel thrown to him. God forbid that mother should know of this. Come, we will go forth together into the wide world!"

So all day long they walked over the meadows, fields and rough stones, and when rain came the girl said, "It is heaven and our hearts weeping together." Towards evening they waded into a large forest and, tired with misery, hunger and the long wandering, they lay down in a hollow tree and fell asleep.

When they woke up the next morning the sun, already high in the sky, was shining nice and warm into the tree. The little boy said, "Sister, I am thirsty. If I can find a little brook, I will go and have a drink. I think I can hear one gurgling."

The brother got up, took his sister by the hand, and they set out to look for the spring. However, the wicked stepmother was a witch and had seen the children go away. She had sneaked after them stealthily, the way witches do, and cast a spell over all the springs in the forest.

When they found a spring gushing and sparkling over the rocks the boy made to drink out of it. But his sister heard it murmuring, "Who drinks of me shall turn into a tiger."

Then the sister cried, "Pray, dear brother, don't drink the water, or you will be a wild beast and tear me to pieces!"

So the brother, though he was so thirsty, did not drink, saying, "I will wait for the next spring."

But when they came to the next brook this, too, was saying, "Who drinks of me, shall be turned into a wolf."

The sister heard it and cried out, "I beg you, brother, don't drink the water, or you'll become a wolf and gobble me up."

The brother did not drink the water either, and said, "I'll wait till we get to the next spring but then, no matter what you say, I must drink, I am far too thirsty."

When they reached the third small fountain, the sister heard it say in between the rushing, "Who drinks of me shall be a roe, who drinks of me shall be a roe."

The sister cried, "Don't drink the water, dear brother, I beg you, or you'll be a roe and run away from me."

But the brother lost no time in kneeling down by the spring, bent over it and drank, and when the first drops touched his lips, he lay there changed into a fawn.

Now the sister wept over her poor bewitched brother, and so did the little roebuck sitting, oh so sad, by her side. Finally, the poor maiden said, "Don't weep, my little fawn, I will never, never leave you." Then she untied her golden garter and put it around the little roebuck's neck and, pulling up some rushes, wove them into a soft cord. She put the little animal on the leash and led it on, and went deeper and deeper into the woods. Thus they walked for a long, long time till they came upon a cottage. It was empty and so the girl thought, "Here we can stay and live."

Then she went to gather leaves and moss and made a soft bed for the roe, and every morning she would go out and gather roots, berries and nuts, and for the fawn she always brought some soft grass. He ate it out of her hand, was content and scampered merrily around. In the evening the sister was tired, and having said her little prayer, laid her head on the roebuck's silky back that was her pillow, and softly drifted off to sleep. If only the brother had his human shape it would have been a glorious life.

Thus they were living alone in the wilderness for some time. But as it happened, one day the King of that country held a big hunt in the forest. Through the trees came sounds of horns blowing, of dogs barking and merry shouts of the huntsmen. The fawn heard it and would fain have joined in the sport. "Oh, let me out to join the hunt," he said to his sister, "I can't stand it any longer."

"But mind," she told him, "you come back home in the evening. I will lock the door against the wild huntsmen, and that I may know it is you, you will knock and say, 'Sister dear, let me in here.' And unless you speak just this, I will not unlock the door."

Then the fawn leapt out and felt so happy and gay in the open air. The King and his huntsmen saw the fine animal and pursued him but could not overtake him, and even when they were certain they had him, he leapt away over the bushes and was gone.

When darkness fell, he ran to the cottage, knocked at the door and said, "Sister dear, let me in here." Then the little door opened, and he leapt in, and rested himself on his soft bed the whole night.

Next morning, the hunt was on again, and again the fawn heard the bugle call and the "heigh, heigh" of the huntsmen. He became restless and said, "Please, sister, open the door, I must get out."

His sister opened the door for him and said, "Mind you are back here again by the evening, and say your little piece."

When the King and his huntsmen again spotted the fawn with his golden collar, they gave chase, but he was too swift and nimble for them. Thus it went all day, but in the evening the huntsmen surrounded the animal at last, and one of them wounded it a little on the foot so that it ran slowly away limping. A huntsman stalked it all the way to the cottage, and heard it say, "Sister dear, let me in here." The door opened for it and immediately shut again. The huntsman remembered all this well and went to the King and told him what he had seen and heard. Whereupon the King said, "Tomorrow we shall hunt again."

The sister, however, got a dreadful fright when she saw that her fawn had been wounded. She washed the blood off the wound, laid herbs on it, and said, "Now go to bed, dear fawn, that you may get well again."

But the wound was so slight that next morning he did not even feel it any more. And when he again heard the merry sounds of the chase outside, he said, "I can't stand it, I must be there. No one shall catch me so easily."

The sister cried, saying, "This time they will kill you, and I'll be here alone in the forest, forsaken by all the world. I will not let you out."

"Then I shall die here of misery," replied the fawn. "Every time I hear the bugle, I feel as if I should jump out of my skin."

Though with a heavy heart, the girl could do nothing but open the door, and the fawn, sound and gay, leapt out into the woods.

When the King saw it, he said to his huntsmen, "Now pursue it all day long until nightfall but be careful none of you does it any harm."

The moment the sun had set, the King said to the huntsman, "Come and show me the forest hut." And when he stood at the door, he knocked and sang out, "Sister dear, let me in here." Then the door opened and the King stepped in, and there he saw a maiden more lovely than he had ever seen. The girl was frightened when she saw it was not her fawn but a man with a golden crown on his head. But the King looked at her kindly, gave her his hand and said, "Would you come to my palace with me and be my dear wife?"

"Yes, I would," answered the girl, "only the little fawn must come along. I will never forsake him."

The King said, "It shall stay with you as long as you live, and never lack anything."

Meanwhile, the fawn came springing in. The sister put him on the rush leash again and, taking it in her hand, led him out from the cottage in the forest.

The King put the fair maiden on his horse and led her into the palace, where the wedding was celebrated in all pomp and splendour. Now she was Queen and they lived happily together for a long time. The fawn was cherished and tended carefully and skipped about in the palace garden.

The wicked stepmother who was to blame for the children's going out into the world was quite certain that the girl had been torn to pieces by wild beasts, and that her brother, transformed into a fawn, had been killed by the huntsmen.

Now that she heard they were so happy and well off, her heart racked by envy and jealousy gave her no peace. She could think of nothing but how she might contrive to bring misfortune upon the two.

Her own daughter, who was one-eyed and exceedingly ugly, reproached her saying, "I ought to have become Queen; that luck should have been mine!"

"Just keep quiet," said the old witch soothingly. "I shall be on hand when the time comes."

Time passed on and the Queen brought a fine little boy into the world.

The King happened to be out hunting, and so the old witch assumed the shape of a waiting woman. She entered the chamber where the Queen was lying and said, "Come, the bath is ready. It will do you good and refresh your strength. Hurry up, before it gets cold!"

Her daughter was also at hand, and they carried the weak Queen into the bathroom and put her into the tub. Then they locked the door and ran off. But they had made a proper hellish heat in the bathroom, so that the beautiful young Queen soon suffocated.

When this was done, the old witch took her daughter, put a nightcap on her head, and made her lie down in place of the Queen. She even gave her the Queen's figure and looks, but what she could not make good was her lost eye. So that the King should not notice it, she was to lie down on the side

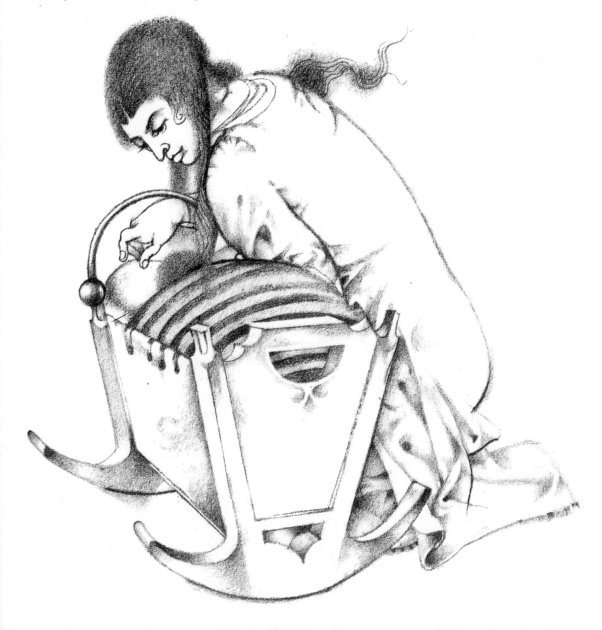

where she had no eye. When the King came home in the evening and heard that a son had been born to him, he rejoiced in his heart and desired to go to his dear wife's bedside to see how she was.

But the old witch exclaimed quickly, "Not on your life! Keep the curtains drawn, the Queen should not be exposed to light, and must have quiet."

The King went away without knowing that an impostor was lying in the Queen's bed.

Midnight came and everybody was asleep. Suddenly, the nurse sitting by the cradle in the nursery and being the only one still awake, saw the door open and the real Queen come in. She took the baby out of the cradle, laid it on her arm and suckled it. Then she shook up its little pillow, put the child back again, and covered it with its little quilt. Nor did she forget the fawn, but went into the corner where he was lying and stroked his back. Then, without saying a word, she went out through the door again.

Next morning the nurse asked the guards if anyone had entered the palace during the night, but they answered, "No, we did not see anybody." Thus the Queen came many nights and never spoke a word while there. And every time the nurse saw her, but did not have the pluck to tell anyone anything about it.

Some time passed in this way, when one night the Queen began to speak saying,
"How is my baby? How is my fawn?
Twice more I will come and then never again."

The nurse made no answer, but when the Queen was go ie again she went to the King and told him everything. The King said, "Oh God, what is this! Tonight I will watch the child myself." In the evening he went to the nursery, and at midnight the Queen reappeared and said,
"How is my baby? How is my fawn?
Once more I will come and then never again."

She nursed the baby and was gone again. The King did not dare to address her, but kept watch the next night again. Once more she said,
"How is my baby? How is my fawn?
I have come this time but never more."

Then the King could not restrain himself, sprang towards her and said, "You can be none other than my dear wife."

And she answered, "Yes, I am your dear wife." And at that very moment through the grace of God she was restored to life, becoming fresh, rosy-cheeked and whole again. Then she told the King of the mischief done to her by the evil witch, and her daughter.

The King had them both taken before the judge and the sentence was pronounced against them. The daughter was led into the forest where wild beasts tore her to pieces, but the witch was cast into the fire to burn to a miserable death. And no sooner had she been burnt to ashes than the fawn was transformed back and received his human form again. The brother and sister then lived happily together until the end of their days.

RAPUNZEL

There was once a man and his wife, and for a long time they had been longing for a child, but in vain. At last, the woman was in hope that heaven would grant her wish. At the back of their house there was a little window overlooking a magnificent garden full of the most beautiful flowers and herbs. However, a high wall surrounded the garden, and no one dared to enter it, for it belonged to a witch who was very powerful and of whom the whole world stood in awe.

One day the woman was standing at this window looking down into the garden, when she noticed a bed which was planted with the finest rampion. It looked so fresh and green that it made her mouth water and she was possessed by the desire to eat some. This craving grew from day to day, but she knew she never could get any. So she began to pine away and looked pale and miserable. Her husband, in great alarm, asked her, "What ails you, my dear?"

"Alas," she replied, "if I can't eat some of the rampion from the garden behind our house, I shall die."

The husband, who loved her, thought, "Rather than let your wife die, you shall fetch her some of the rampion, cost what it may." So when dusk came, he climbed over the wall into the witch's garden, hurriedly cut a handful of rampion, and took it to his wife. She at once made it into a salad and ate it up with great lust. She found it so tasty, so very tasty, that her desire grew three times as strong the next day. If it was to be stilled, her husband once more had to climb over into the garden. So at dusk, he let himself down again but just as he had clambered over the wall, his heart stood still, for there was the witch confronting him.

"How dare you come into my garden like a common thief and steal my rampion?" she said eyeing him angrily. "This shall cost you dear."

"Alas," he answered, "temper justice with mercy, it was from dire necessity that I resolved to come. My wife has seen your rampion from her window and her longing is so strong that she will die if she does not get some to eat."

Thereupon the witch's wrath abated, and she said to him, "If it is as you say, I will let you take home as much rampion as you like. Only I make one condition. You must give me the child that your wife is going to give birth to. It will be well off and I will care for it like a mother."

In his anguish the man agreed to everything, and the moment the wife gave birth the witch appeared, christened the child Rapunzel (rampion), and took it away with her.

Rapunzel grew up to be the most beautiful girl under the sun. When she was twelve years old, the witch shut her up in a tower in a forest. It had no stairs or doors, only a little window quite high up at the top. When the witch wanted to get in, she stood down below and called, "Rapunzel, Rapunzel, let down your hair."

Rapunzel had magnificent long hair, as fine as spun gold. When she heard the witch call, she loosened her tresses and wound them round a hook by the window. She let them fall down, and the witch climbed up by Rapunzel's braids.

It came to pass a few years later that the King's son, riding through the forest, came close to the tower. Suddenly, he heard someone singing. The

voice was so charming that he stopped to listen. It was Rapunzel who in her loneliness amused herself by letting her sweet voice resound. The Prince wanted to climb up to join her and sought for the tower door but there was none to be found.

He rode home, but the singing had touched his heart so deeply that he went out into the forest every day and listened. Once, as he was standing behind a tree, he saw the witch come near and heard her call, "Rapunzel, Rapunzel, let down your hair."

Then Rapunzel let her braided hair fall down and the witch climbed up.

"If this is the ladder by which to come up," he thought, "I will try my luck once myself."

The very next day, when dusk began to fall, he went up to the tower and cried, "Rapunzel, Rapunzel, let down your hair."

Presently the plaits came down and the King's son climbed up by them.

At first, Rapunzel was terribly frightened when a man came into her room, for she had never set eyes on a man in her life. But the Prince talked to her most kindly telling her that his heart had been so deeply moved by her singing that he knew no peace and had to come to see her. Then Rapunzel lost her fear, and when he asked her if she would take him for her husband, and she saw that he was young and handsome, she thought, "He will love me better than old Mother Gothel," and she said, "Yes", and laid her hand in his.

She said, "I would be glad to go with you, but I do not know how to get down. Will you bring a skein of silk every time you come? I shall weave it into a ladder, and when it is ready, I will come down, and you will take me on your horse."

They arranged that meanwhile he should always come to see her in the evening, for the old woman came by day.

Nor did the witch discover anything until Rapunzel broached it one day and said to her, "Please tell me, Dame Gothel, how is it that you are much heavier to pull up than the young Prince who will be here before long?"

"Oh, you wicked child," yelled the witch, "what do I have to hear from you? I had thought I cut you off from all the world, and yet you have deceived me!"

In her rage she clutched Rapunzel's lovely hair, wound it several times round her left hand, picked up a pair of scissors with her right, and snip, snap the lovely tresses lay on the ground. She was merciless and took poor Rapunzel into a wilderness, where she was forced to live in greatest wretchedness and sorrow.

Yet on the very day she had cast Rapunzel away, the witch fastened the plaits she had cut off to the window hook. When the Prince came again he cried, "Rapunzel, Rapunzel, let down your hair."

Then the witch lowered the hair. The Prince climbed up, but above he found not his beloved Rapunzel but the witch, who looked at him with evil and venomous eyes.

"Oh ho," she cried mockingly, "you have come to fetch your dearly beloved, but the pretty bird sits no longer in her nest, and she can sing no more, for the cat has snatched her away, and it will scratch your eye out for you, too. Rapunzel is lost to you, you shall never set eyes on her again."

The Prince was beside himself with grief and, in his despair flung himself down from the tower. He escaped with his life, but had his eyes scratched out by the thorns among which he fell. He wandered about in the forest blind and feeding on nothing but roots and berries. He could do nothing but lament and weep over the loss of his most beloved Rapunzel. Thus he roamed about in utter misery for some years and, at last, found himself in the wilderness where Rapunzel had been living in dire poverty with the twins that had been born to her, a boy and a girl.

He heard a voice and it seemed to him very familiar, so he went on in its direction. When he got there, Rapunzel recognized him and fell on his neck in tears. Two of them wetted his eyes and, at once, his eyes grew quite clear and he could see as well as ever.

He took her and their twins to his kingdom, where he was joyfully received, and they lived long in happiness and contentment together.

HANSEL AND GRETHEL

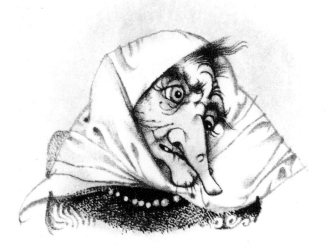

There was once a poor woodcutter living near a big forest with his wife and two children. The boy was called Hansel and the girl's name was Grethel. They were poor and had very little to eat and once, when a great dearth fell on the land, he could no longer manage to earn their daily bread.

One night, tossing about in his bed worrying over his troubles, the woodcutter sighed and said to his wife, "What shall become of us? How are we to feed our poor children when we have nothing left for ourselves?"

"You know what, husband," answered the wife, for misery had hardened her heart, "tomorrow quite early in the morning we will take the children out into the wood where it is most dense. There we shall make them a fire, give each another a piece of bread, go about our work, and leave them alone. They won't find their way back home, and so we'll be rid of them."

"No, wife," said the man, "that I will never do. How could I have the heart to leave my children in the wood all by themselves. Soon wild animals would come and tear them to pieces."

"Oh, you fool," said she. "Then we must starve to death, all four of us. You may as well start planing the planks for the coffins." She gave him no peace till he gave in. "But I pity the poor children all the same," he said.

Nor had the two children been able to fall asleep for hunger and they heard what their stepmother said to their father. Grethel wept bitter tears and said to Hansel, "This is the end of us."

"Be quiet, Grethel!" said Hansel. "Don't be sad. I will find some way out of this."

When the parents had gone off to sleep, Hansel got up, put on his little coat, opened the back door, and stole out. The moon was shining bright, and the white pebbles lying before the house glittered like so many new silver coins. Hansel bent down and put as many of them into his coat pocket as it would hold.

Then he went back to Grethel and said, "Don't worry, dear sister, and go to sleep. God will not forsake us." And he went to bed again.

At the break of day, even before the sun had risen, the woman came and woke the two children. "Get up, you lazy-bones, we're going to fetch some wood from the forest." Then she gave each a little piece of bread, saying, "Here's something for your dinner, but mind you don't eat it before, you shall get no more."

Grethel put the bread in her apron, for Hansel had the stones in his pocket. Then they all set out together for the forest.

When they had gone a little way, Hansel stopped, and gazed back towards their little house, and did this over and over again.

His father said, "Hansel, why do you keep looking back and falling behind? Take yourself in hand and don't forget to use your legs."

"Oh father, I am looking at my white kitten, it's sitting on the top of the roof and wants to say good-bye to me."

"Fool," said the woman. "That's not your kitten, it's the morning sun shining on the chimney."

But Hansel was not really looking at the cat. He always dropped one of the shining pebbles from his pocket on to the road. When they reached the middle of the forest, the father said, "Now gather some wood, children. I'll make a fire so that you will not feel cold."

Hansel and Grethel gathered some brushwood and made a pile of it. The wood was kindled and, when the fire was blazing, the woman said, "Now, children, lie down by the fire and rest a while. We're going further into the forest to cut some wood. When we're ready, we'll come back and fetch you."

Hansel and Grethel sat by the fire and, when it was noon, they each ate their piece of bread. They heard the blows of an axe and thought that their father was nearby. Yet it was no axe, it was a branch he had tied to a withered tree and the wind blew it to and fro. They had been sitting for a long time till they got weary and their eyes began to close and, before long, they were fast asleep.

When they awoke, it was dark night. Grethel burst into tears and said, "How shall we get out of the wood now?"

Hansel comforted her saying, "Wait a little till the moon rises, then we shall quickly find our way."

Then the moon rose. Hansel took his sister's hand and followed the pebbles which, shimmering like newly coined silver, showed them the way. They walked the whole night and by daybreak were back at their father's house.

They knocked at the door and when the woman answered it and saw

Hansel and Grethel she said, "Wicked children, why did you sleep so long in the wood? We thought you didn't want to come back ever again." But the father was very glad to see them, for it grieved him to have left them all alone.

Not long after this, want gaped at them from every corner, and the children heard the stepmother at night in bed say to their father, "Everything is eaten up again and we have only half a loaf of bread left. The children must go. We will take them deeper into the forest and they won't find their way out again. Otherwise there is no hope for us."

The father's heart was heavy and he thought, "Better if we share our last crust with the children." Yet his wife would listen to nothing he said, but scolded and reproached him. But one step leads to another and, since he had given in the first time, he had to do so the second time as well.

Again the children were still awake and heard what was said. When the parents had fallen asleep, Hansel got up, and was going out to pick up pebbles as before. But the woman had locked the door, and Hansel could not get out. But he comforted his sister saying, "Don't cry, Grethel. Just go to sleep. The dear Lord is sure to help us."

Early in the morning the woman came and got the children out of bed. Again they were each given a piece of bread, yet even smaller than last time. On their way to the forest Hansel crumbled his up in his pocket and, stopping every so often, each time dropped a crumb on the ground.

"Hansel, why do you keep stopping and looking back?" asked the father. "Look where you are going."

"I am looking at my little dove who is sitting on the roof and wants to say good-bye to me."

"You fool," growled the woman, "that's no dove but the morning sun shining on the chimney."

But Hansel gradually dropped all the crumbs, one by one, on the path. The woman led the children even deeper into the forest, where they had never been before in their lives. Again, a big fire was made, and the woman said, "You children stay here and when you are tired, you can have a little nap. We're going into the forest to cut wood and, in the evening when we are ready, we'll come and fetch you."

At midday Grethel shared her bread with Hansel who had crumbled his and scattered it on the way. Then they fell asleep. The evening passed but no one came to call for the poor children. They did not wake till it was pitch-dark, and Hansel comforted his sister by saying, "Wait awhile, Grethel, till the moon rises. Then we shall see the breadcrumbs I have scattered along the path. They will show us the way home."

When the moon rose, they set out but found no crumbs, for the thousands of birds which fly about in forest and field had pecked them up.

Hansel said to Grethel, "We shall soon find the way," but they did not find it. They walked the whole night and yet another day from morning till evening, but did not get out of the wood. They were very hungry, for they had had nothing to eat but a few berries that grew there. And so tired were they that their legs would not carry them any further. So they lay down under a tree, and fell asleep.

Now it was the third day since they had left their father's house. They started walking again, but they only got deeper and deeper into the forest. If no help came, they were doomed to die.

At midday they saw a beautiful snow-white bird sitting on a branch. Its song was so sweet that they stopped to listen to it. When the singing was done, the bird spread its wings and flew ahead of them. They followed it till they came to a little cottage where it alighted on the roof.

When they got quite close to it they saw that the little house was made of gingerbread and covered with cakes. The windows were of barley sugar.

"Now we will set to and have a proper meal," said Hansel. "I will have a piece of the roof and you, Grethel, can have a little bit of the window, that should taste nice and sweet."

Hansel reached up and broke off a piece of the roof to see what it tasted like and Grethel stood near the window-panes and nibbled at them.

Then a soft voice called out from inside,
"*Nibble, nibble, little mouse,*
Who is nibbling at my house?"

The children answered,
"*The wind, the wind,*
The heaven-born wind,"

and went on eating. Hansel, who found the roof much to his taste, broke off a big piece of the roof for himself and Grethel pushed out a whole round window-pane, sat down, and ate it with great relish.

Just then, the door suddenly flew open and a woman as old as the hills came sneaking out, hobbling on crutches. Hansel and Grethel were so frightened that they dropped what they had in their hands. But the old hag only shook her head saying, "Oh, you dear children, who ever has brought you here? Do come in and stay with me, no harm shall befall you."

She took them both by the hand and led them into her cottage. There they were given a nice dinner of milk, pancakes, sugar, apples and nuts. Then two little beds were covered with clean white linen and Hansel and Grethel lay down in them and felt they were in heaven.

The old woman had only pretended to be friendly and kind. She was really a wicked old witch who lay in wait for children and had built the gingerbread house only to lure them to her. When one came into her clutches, she cooked it and ate it and made a feast day of it. Witches have red eyes and can't see very far, but they have a good sense of smell like animals and notice when humans approach them. When Hansel and Grethel came into the forest near her house, she gave an evil laugh and crowed, "I have got these two, they shan't get away from me."

Early next morning before the children were awake she got up and, when she saw them both resting peacefully with their full red cheeks, she muttered to herself, "They will make a tasty morsel." She seized Hansel with her shrivelled old hand, carried him off into a little stable with a grilled window and shut him in. He could shriek for all he was worth but it would do him no good. Then she went to Grethel and shook her to rouse her and cried, "Get up, lazy-bones, fetch some water and cook something good for your brother. He sits in the stable, and has got to be fattened. When he is fat, I shall eat him."

Grethel began to cry bitterly but it was all in vain, she had to do as the wicked witch had ordered. The best food was cooked for poor Hansel but Grethel got nothing but crab-shells.

The old hag sneaked out to the little stable every morning and cried, "Stick out your finger, Hansel, that I may feel if you're fat enough."

Hansel stuck out a little bone and the old witch, whose eyes were dim, could not see properly and thought it was Hansel's finger. So she was much astonished that he was not getting at all fat.

Four weeks passed and Hansel was still as thin as ever. Impatience got the better of her and she would wait no longer.

"Hola, Grethel," she cried. "Look sharp and fetch the water. Fat or thin, tomorrow I will kill Hansel and cook him."

Oh, how his poor little sister lamented when she was forced to fetch the water and how the tears rolled down her cheeks.

"Dear God, please, help us," she cried. "If only the animals in the forest had devoured us, at least we should have died together."

"Stop that bawling," cried the old woman, "it will help you not a whit."

Early next morning Grethel had to go out, hang up the cauldron with water in it and light the fire.

"We shall bake him first," said the old witch. "I have heated the oven and kneaded the dough." She pushed poor Grethel towards the oven, from

which flames were already leaping and said, "Creep in and see if it is properly heated that we may put in the bread."

Once Grethel was in, she meant to shut the oven, roast and eat her. But Grethel saw what she was up to and said, "I don't know how to do it. How do I get in?"

"Stupid girl," cried the witch. "The opening is big enough, you can see I could get in myself."

She hobbled up and stuck her head into the oven. That moment Grethel gave her a push that drove her far inside, shut to the iron door and bolted it.

"Oohoo," she began to howl quite horribly. But Grethel ran away and the wicked witch burned to death miserably.

Grethel ran straightaway to Hansel and opened the little stable, crying, "Hansel, we are saved! The old witch is dead!"

Hansel flew out like a bird out of a cage when you open the door. How happy they were. They fell into each other's arms, kissed and danced about. As there was nothing to fear now, they went into the witch's house and found chests of pearls and precious stones in every corner.

"These are much better than pebbles," said Hansel as he put as many in his pockets as they would hold.

Grethel said, "I must bring something home, too," and filled her apron.

"Now we'll have to get going," said Hansel, "if we are to get out of the bewitched forest."

They had not been walking many hours when they came to a great expanse of water.

"We can't get across," said Hansel. "I see no plank and no bridge."

"And there is no boat either," answered Grethel. "But there's a white duck swimming. I'll ask her if she will help us get across." So she cried,
"Little duck, that cries quack, quack,
Here poor Grethel and Hansel stand.
Take us across on your white back,
There is no plank nor bridge at hand."

And indeed, the duck did come up to them and Hansel got on its back and told his little sister to sit next to him.

"No," said Grethel, "we will be too heavy for the duck. She must take us over one after the other."

This the good bird did and, when they were safely across and had walked awhile, the wood seemed to grow more and more familiar to them till at last they espied their father's house from afar. They began to run and burst inside and fell on their father's neck. The poor man hadn't had a single happy hour since he had left the children behind in the forest. And, since then his wife had died.

38

Grethel shook out her apron so that the pearls and precious stones bounced about all over the room and Hansel threw one handful after the other out of his pockets.

Then all their troubles were over and they lived most happily together.

My tale is out, there runs a mouse and, whosoever catches it may use it to make a big cap out of its fur.

THE FISHERMAN AND HIS WIFE

Once upon a time, there was a fisherman and his wife who lived together in a hovel close by the sea. Every day the fisherman went out fishing and he fished and fished.

Once he sat angling and gazing into the bright water; he sat and sat.

Then his hook suddenly went to the bottom, deep down below and, when he pulled it up, he brought out a large flounder. Then the flounder said to him, "Listen fisherman, I pray you, let me live. I am not a real flounder but an enchanted Prince. What help will it be to you that you kill me? Why, I wouldn't even taste good. So put me in the water again and let me swim away."

"Well," said the man, "you do not need to talk so much. A flounder that can talk I should have let swim away anyhow."

With this he put it back into the clear water and the flounder swam down to the seabed, leaving a long stream of blood behind him. The fisherman got up and went to his wife in the hovel.

"Husband," said the wife, "Didn't you catch anything today?"

"No," said the man. "I just caught a flounder who said he was an enchanted Prince, so I let him swim away again."

"And didn't you make a wish first?" said the wife.

"No," said the man, "what should I have wished for?"

"Oh," said the wife, "it is terrible to have to live forever in this hovel. It smells and it is disgusting. You might have wished for a little cottage for us. Go back at once and call him. Tell him we want to have a little cottage. He is sure to do it for us."

"Ah," said the man, "why should I go there again?"

"Well," said the woman, "because you caught him and let him swim free again. He is sure to do it. Go on!"

The man didn't really feel like going, neither did he wish to act against his wife's advice. So he went to the sea once more. When he got there, the sea was quite green and yellow and not at all as clear as before. So he stood there and said,

"Flounder, flounder in the sea,
Come, I pray you, here to me.
For my wife, my Ilsebill,
Wills not as I should will."

Then the flounder came swimming up to him and said, "Well, what does she want?"

"Oh," said the man, "when I caught you, my wife says I ought to have wished something for myself. She no longer likes living in a hovel. She would like to have a cottage."

"Just go there," said the flouder, "she will have it all."

So he went home and there his wife sat no longer in the hovel; there stood a little cottage instead and his wife was sitting outside on a bench. Then she took him by the hand and said, "Come in and see how much better it is."

So they went in and there was a little porch in the cottage, a pretty little living room and bedroom where their bed stood. There was a kitchen and pantry, with all the finest utensils made of tin and brass, all that a kitchen should have. And behind the cottage, there was a little yard, with chickens and ducks and a trim little garden with vegetables and fruit in it. "See that," said the wife, "isn't it nice?"

"Yes," said the husband, "and so it shall stay. Now we shall live quite content."

"We'll see about that," said the woman. With that they had something to eat and went to bed.

So all went well for about a week, then the woman said, "Listen, husband, the cottage is far too narrow and the yard and the garden are so small. The flounder could have given us a bigger house. I should like to live in a big stone castle. Go to the flounder, tell him he should give us a castle."

"But wife," said the husband, "the cottage is good enough as it is. Why do we need a castle to live in?"

"Ah, be off with you," said the woman. "Go to him, the flounder can do this quite easily."

"No, wife," said the man, "the fish has given us the cottage. I have no mind to go to him again, the flounder might get offended."

"Go all the same," said the woman. "It's well in his power and he'll be glad to do it. Just go and see him!"

The man did not feel like going, his heart was so heavy. He said to himself, "It is not right," but in the end he went.

When he came to the sea, the water was purple and dark-blue, grey and thick, but calm enough. Then he stood there and said,

"Flounder, flounder in the sea,
Come, I pray you, here to me.
For my wife, my Ilsebill,
Wills not as I should will."

"Well, what is it she wants?" said the flounder.

"Ah," said the man rather troubled, "she wants to live in a stone castle."

"Just go home," said the fish. "She is standing before the door."

The man went off and thought he would be going home to the cottage. But when he got there, there now stood a big stone castle. His wife was standing on the steps about to enter and she took him by the hand and said, "Come in."

Then he went in with her. There was a great hall with a marble floor and lots of servants everywhere who quickly opened the great doors. The walls were hung with lovely tapestries and, in the chambers, nothing but golden chairs and tables, crystal chandeliers hanging from the ceilings, and carpets covering all the floors. Food and the choicest wines were on the tables which looked as if they would break under the load.

Behind the house was a big courtyard with stables and cowsheds and the most splendid coaches. There was a magnificent garden with the loveliest of flowers and fine fruit-trees and a pleasure-grove, quite half a mile long. There were stags and roes and hares, indeed, all that a man's heart could ever desire.

"Well, now," said the woman. "Isn't it nice?"

"Ah yes," sighed the man, "and so it shall stay. Now we shall live in this fine castle and be content."

"We'll see about that and sleep on it," said the woman. And with that they went to bed.

Next morning, the wife was the first to wake up. It was just before daybreak and from her bed she saw the glorious land lying before her. The man was still stretching himself, so she dug him with her elbow, and said, "Man, get up and take a look out of the window. Look, we could be King and Queen over all that land. Go to the flounder, and say we would like to be King and Queen."

"Oh, wife," said the man. "Why should we be King and Queen. I have no wish to be King."

"Well, if you won't be King, I will. Just go to the flounder and say I wish to be King."

"Oh, wife," said the man. "What do you want to be King for? I simply can't ask him for that."

"Why not? said the woman. "Go there straightaway. I must be King!"

The man was in utter distress that his wife wished to be King. "It isn't right, it isn't right," he thought. He did not feel like going there at all, but in the end he went.

When he came to the sea, the sea was all black and grey and the water was boiling up from below. It smelled quite foul. Then he stood there and said,

"Flounder, flounder in the sea,
Come, I pray you, here to me.
For my wife, my Ilsebill,
Wills not as I should will."

"Well, what is it she wants?" asked the flounder.

"Ah," said the man, "she wants to be King."

"Go home, she is King already," said the flounder.

The man went back and when he came to the castle, he saw the castle had become much bigger, like a palace. It had a great tower magnificently embellished, sentries stood before the gate, and there were many, many soldiers with drums and trumpets.

He went inside and everything there was pure marble and gold with velvet coverings and golden tassels. Then the doors of the great hall opened and the whole of the royal court was assembled there. His wife sat on a high throne of gold and diamonds and had a big golden crown on her head. The sceptre in her hand was of pure gold and precious stones and on either side of her stood six maidens in a row, each a head shorter than the one before.

Then he went and stood before her and said, "Oh wife, so now you are King."

"Yes", said the wife. "Now I am King."

So he stood and gazed at her and, having thus looked at her for some time he said, "Oh wife, being King suits you so well. Let us wish for nothing more."

"No, husband," said the woman, growing quite restless. "I am already feeling bored and can't stand it any longer. Go to the flounder. I am King, now I must be made Emperor as well."

"Alas, wife, what do you want to be Emperor for?"

"Husband," said she, "go to the flounder. I will be Emperor."

"Oh, wife," said the man, "the flounder can't make emperors. I can't even say that to him. There is but one Emperor in the realm. The flounder can't make you Emperor. He positively can't do that."

"What!" said the woman. "I am King and you are merely my husband. Go there at once! If he can make kings, he can make emperors. I simply must be Emperor. Go straight to him."

So he had to go.

However, on his way there, he suddenly felt terribly miserable and, as he walked on, he thought to himself.

"This is not right and not a good thing. To ask to be Emperor is too impudent. The fish will get tired of it in the end."

Just then, he reached the sea. The sea was black and thick and had begun to boil from below so that it made bubbles. Then a gust of wind blowing over it made it all frothy and the man got frightened. But he stood there and said,

"Flounder, flounder in the sea,

Come, I pray you, here to me.

For my wife, my Ilsebill,

Wills not as I should will."

"Well, what does she want?" said the flounder.

"Alas, flounder, my wife wants to become Emperor."

"Just go home," said the flounder. "She is Emperor already."

The man went back and, when he came home, the whole palace became one of polished marble with alabaster figures and gold decorations. Soldiers were marching in front of the gate blowing trumpets and beating cymbals and drums. Inside, there were barons and earls and dukes walking about as mere servants. Doors of pure gold opened for him. He entered, and there was his wife sitting on a throne made of one solid piece of gold easily two miles high. She had a large golden crown on her head set with diamonds and carbuncles. In one hand she held the sceptre and in the other the imperial apple. On either side of her stood the life-guards, each shorter than the one before him, from an enormous giant two miles tall, to the smallest dwarf only as big as my little finger. And there were many princes and dukes standing before her.

The man went up and stood among them and said, "Oh, wife, you are Emperor now."

"Yes," said she, "I am Emperor."

Then he stood and gazed at her for quite a long time and afterwards he said, "Oh wife, isn't that nice that you are Emperor?"

"Husband," said she. "What are you standing about there for? I am Emperor now but I want to be Pope, too. Go and see the fish about it."

"Alas, wife," said the man, "what more do you want? Pope you cannot be. There is only one Pope in all Christendom. He cannot make you that."

"Husband," said she, "I will be Pope. Go straight to him, I want to be Pope today." "No, wife," said the man. "That I dare not tell him. That would not do, that's asking too much. The flounder cannot make you Pope."

"Husband, what silly chatter!" said the wife. "If he can make me Emperor, he can make me Pope as well. Go straight to him. I am Emperor and you are merely my husband, so go there at once!"

Then he got frightened and went, but he felt quite faint. He trembled and quaked and his knees and calves shook. A high wind swept over the land and clouds gathered, so that it was dark, like evening. The leaves were falling off the trees and the water rushed as if it were boiling, and crashed against the shore. In the distance ships were firing guns in distress and pitching and tossing on the billows. Yet there was still a patch of blue sky in the middle, but on every side it was as red as before a heavy thunderstorm. Then he went and stood by the edge of the sea, anxious and despondent, and said,

"Flounder, flounder in the sea,
Come, I pray you, here to me
For my wife, my Ilsebill,
Wills not as I should will."

"Well, what is it she wants?" asked the flounder.

"Alas," said the man, "she wants to be Pope."

"Go to her then," said the flounder, "she is Pope already."

He went back and when he got there, there stood a big cathedral with nothing but palaces all around. He pushed his way through the crowd. Inside, everything was lit with thousands and thousands of lights and his wife was dressed all in gold, sitting on a throne much higher than the one before. Three golden crowns were on her head and all around was rich in ecclesiastical splendour. On either side of her stood two rows of lights, the largest so thick and so tall as the highest of towers, down to the tiniest of kitchen candles. Emperors and kings from every land were on their knees before her and kissing her slippers.

"Wife," said the man, and looked at her wonderingly. "You are Pope now, aren't you?"

"Yes," said she, "I am Pope."

Whereupon he stood and looked straight at her, and it was as if he were looking at the bright sun. When he had thus contemplated her for a time, he said, "Oh wife, how nice that you are Pope."

But she looked as stiff as a post, and did not stir.

Then he said, "Wife, be content. Now you are Pope, you cannot go any higher."

"We will see about that," said the wife.

Then they went to bed. But she was not contented. Greed would not let her sleep and she lay awake thinking of what she might still become.

The man slept really soundly. He had done a lot of running the day before. But his wife could not fall asleep at all and tossed from side to side all night long.

At last, the sun was about to rise and when the wife saw the dawn reddening on the horizon, she sat up in her bed, and gazed at it. And when, looking through the window, she saw the sun rise, it occurred to her. "Could I not make the sun and moon rise?"

"Husband," she said giving him a poke in the ribs, "wake up and go to the flounder. I want to be like the good God himself."

The man was still half asleep but he got so alarmed that he fell out of bed. He thought he had not heard aright, rubbed his eyes and said, "Oh, wife, what did you say?"

"Husband," said she, "I cannot order the sun and moon to rise. I can only sit and watch them. I cannot bear it and I know no peace any more, not even for an hour. I must cause them to rise myself."

Then she regarded him with such a terrifying look that a shudder ran through him.

"Go at once to the flounder. I wish to be like God."

"Alas, wife," said the man and fell on his knees before her. "That the fish cannot do. He can make emperors and popes but I beseech you, be sensible and remain Pope!"

Then she got into a rage, her hair flew wildly about her head, she tore open her bodice, gave him a kick and screamed, "I simply cannot and will not bear this any longer. Go right away, will you?"

The man put on his trousers and ran off like a madman.

Outside a storm was raging and it was blowing so hard that he could hardly keep on his feet. Houses and trees were blown over and the hills trembled. Rocks rolled down into the sea and the skies were pitch-dark; there was thunder and lightning and the sea rolled with black waves as high as church steeples with crests of white foam. He couldn't hear his own voice when he cried,

"Flounder, flounder, in the sea,
Come, I pray you, here to me.
For my wife, my Ilsebill,
Wills not as I should will."

"Well, what is it she wants now?" said the flounder.

"Alas," he cried, "she wants to be like God."

"Go to her," said the flounder. "She is back in the hovel again."

And there they are living to this very day.

MOTHER CAREY

A widow had two daughters. One of them was pretty and industrious, the other ugly and lazy. Oddly enough, she was much fonder of the ugly and lazy one, because she was her own daughter and the other, her stepdaughter, was made to do all the work and be the drudge of the house. Every day the poor girl had to sit by a well on the high road and spin and spin till blood spurted from her fingers.

Now it came to pass that once the spool got soaked with blood. She took it and bent over to wash it in the well, but it slipped out of her hand and dropped in. All in tears she ran to her stepmother and confessed what misfortune had befallen her. Her stepmother scolded her severely and pitilessly saying, "If you dropped the spool down, go and bring it up again."

So the girl went back to the well not knowing what to do. In her desperation, she jumped into the well to recover the spool. She lost consciousness and, when she came to again, she found herself in a beautiful meadow. The sun was shining and there were thousands of flowers all around.

She walked across this meadow until she came to an oven full of bread. The bread was crying out, "Oh, take me out, take me out, or I shall burn, for I have long since been thoroughly baked!" So she went up to the oven and with the bread shovel took everything out, one loaf after another.

Then she went on and came to a tree on which many apples were hanging, and it cried out to her, "Oh shake me, shake me, we apples are altogether ripe!" Then she shook the tree till the apples came showering down and until not one apple was left on it. Having made a heap of them, she went on again.

At length she came to a cottage where an old woman was peeping out at the window, but her teeth were so big that the girl was frightened and would have run away. But the old woman called after her, "Why are you afraid, dear child? Stay with me and if you do all the housework properly, you will be well off. Just take care you make my bed right and shake the pillows thoroughly so that the feathers fly about like snow. I am Mother Carey."

As the lady spoke so cheeringly to her, the girl took heart, agreed and became her servant. She took care of everything to her satisfaction and always shook out her pillow so energetically that the feathers flew about like snowflakes. In return she had a good life with the old woman with never a bad word and boiled and roast meat every day.

Now she had been with Mother Carey for quite a while. Suddenly, however, she felt sad. At first she did not know what ailed her. Finally she realized she was homesick. Though easily many thousand times better off here than at home, she had a longing to go back. At last she said to her mistress, "I am homesick and, though my life down here has been fine, I can stay no longer. I must go home again to my family."

"I am glad that you wish for home again," said Mother Carey, "and, as you have served me so faithfully, I am going to take you back up there myself."

Then she took her by the hand and led her to a large gate. The door opened and, just as the girl was standing under it, a heavy shower of gold fell and stuck to her, so that she was covered all over with it.

"This you shall have because you have been so diligent," said Mother Carey. Then she gave her back the spool that had dropped into the well. The gate closed and the girl found herself back on the earth, not far from where her stepmother lived.

As she came into the yard the cock, sitting on the well, cried out,
"*Cock-a-doodle-doo!*
Your golden maiden's come back to you!"

Then she went in to her stepmother and, being covered with gold, was well received by her and her sister, too.

The girl told them everything that had happened to her, and when the mother heard how she had come by such riches, she wanted to procure the same good fortune for the other daughter, the ugly and lazy one. She made her sit down by the well and spin; to stain her spool with blood, the daughter pricked her finger by sticking her hand into a thorn hedge.

Then she threw the spool down the well and jumped in herself.

Like her sister, she came to the lovely meadow and walked on following the same path. When she reached the oven, the bread again called out, "Oh, take me out, take me out, or I shall burn, for I have long since been thoroughly baked!"

But the lazy girl answered, "As if I wanted to make myself dirty for your sake!" and walked on.

Soon she came to the apple tree which was crying, "Oh shake me, shake me, we apples are altogether ripe!" But she said, "What a silly idea! I might have one drop on my head!" And so she walked on.

When she came to Mother Carey's, she was not frightened, for she had already heard about her big teeth and she hired herself out to her at once.

The first day she restrained herself, was industrious and obeyed Mother Carey whenever she was told to do something. She thought only of the heaps of gold Mother Carey would give her. But already on the second day she began her lazy ways and even more so on the third, when she would not even get up in the morning. Nor did she make Mother Carey's bed the way she was expected to and did not shake the pillows to make the feathers fly.

Mother Carey soon tired of this and gave her notice to leave. The lazy girl was only too pleased and waited for the golden rain to come. She, too, was led by Mother Carey to the big gate but, as the girl stood there, a big kettle of pitch was poured out over her.

"That is the reward for your services," said Mother Carey shutting the gate upon her.

Then the lazy girl came home, but she was covered with pitch and, as the cock on the well saw her, he cried out,
"Cock-a-doodle-doo!
Your dirty maiden's come back to you!"

And the pitch stuck to her and would not come off as long as she lived.

LITTLE RED RIDING HOOD

Once upon a time there was a sweet little girl beloved of everyone who ever looked at her. But the one who loved her most was her grandmother and she hardly knew of anything in the world that she would not have given to the child. Once she made her a gift of a hood of red velvet and, as it suited her so well so that she would not wear anything else ever afterwards, she was simply called "Little Red Riding Hood".

One day her mother said to her, "Come, Little Red Riding Hood, here is a piece of cake and a bottle of wine. Go out and take them to your grandmother. She is ill and weak and this will help her to get better. Set out before it gets too warm and, once you are out, just walk like a good little girl and don't run off the path, or you will get lost. When you come to Grannie's room, don't forget to say 'Good morning', and don't go round looking into every corner before saying so."

"I will do everything all right," Little Red Riding Hood assured her mother.

However, the grandmother lived a long way away in the forest, half an hour's walk from the village. And, as Little Red Riding Hood went into the forest, she met a wolf. Little Red Riding Hood did not know what a wicked beast he was and was not afraid of him.

"How are you, Little Red Riding Hood?" the wolf addressed her.

"Very well, thank you, Mr. Wolf."

"Where are you off to so early in the morning?"

"To my grandmother's."

"What is it you're carrying under the apron?"

"Cake and wine. We did some baking yesterday, so my sick and weak Granny could have something nice to eat and get stronger again."

"Where does your grandmother live, Little Red Riding Hood?"

"A good quarter of an hour further on in the forest, under the three large oak trees, that's where her house stands — down below by the nut trees, you surely will know that," said Little Red Riding Hood.

The wolf thought to himself, "What a tender young thing! What a tasty morsel. She will taste much better than the old one. You must go cunningly about it and catch both of them."

He went a short while by the side of Little Red Riding Hood, and then said, "Little Red Riding Hood, see the beautiful flowers all about here. Why don't you look round a bit? I don't think you even hear how pleasantly the little birds are singing. You are walking on as if you were going to school and it is so delightful out here in the forest."

Little Red Riding Hood raised her eyes and, when she saw the sun's rays dancing to and fro through the trees and the many lovely flowers all around, she thought, "I will take Grandma a fresh bunch of flowers, that will also give her pleasure. It is still early in the day, so I will get there in good time."

So she ran off the path into the forest looking for flowers. And when she had picked one, she thought there was one still more beautiful further on and she ran to it and got deeper and deeper into the forest.

The wolf, on the other hand, ran straight to the grandmother's house and knocked at the door.

"Who is there?"

"Little Red Riding Hood, bringing cake and wine," said the wolf. "Open the door."

"Just press on the latch," said the grandmother. "I am too weak and can't get up."

The wolf pressed upon the latch, the door flew open, and without saying a word, he went straight up to the grandmother's bed and ate her. Then he put on her clothes, set her nightcap on his head, lay down in her bed and drew the curtains.

Meanwhile, Little Red Riding Hood had been running about looking for flowers and, when she had picked so many that she could carry no more, she thought of her grandmother again and made ready to go and see her.

She was surprised to find the door ajar and, as she entered the little room, she had a peculiar feeling. She thought to herself, "Oh, goodness, what an uneasy feeling I have today. At other times I am always so happy at grandmother's." Then she called out, "Good morning!" but there was no reply. So she went up to the bed and drew back the curtains. Grandmother lay there with her nightcap pulled far down over her face, and looked very strange.

"Oh, Grandma, what big ears you've got?"

"All the better to hear you with."

"Oh, Grandma, what big eyes you've got!"

"All the better to see you with."

"Oh, Grandma, what big hands you've got!"

"All the better to grip you with."

"Oh, but Grandma, what a terrifying big mouth you've got!"

"All the better to eat you with!"

Scarcely had the wolf said this when he dashed out of the bed with one jump and swallowed up poor Little Red Riding Hood.

When the wolf had satisfied his appetite, he laid himself down in the bed again and began to snore very noisily.

The gamekeeper was just passing the house and thought, "How the old woman is snoring. I must go in and see if she is alright." Then he stepped into the little room and, when he came to the bed, he saw that the wolf was lying in it. "So I have found you here, you old sinner," said he. "I've been looking for you for a long time." And he was about to fire his rifle when he remembered that the wolf might have devoured the grandmother and that she might perhaps still be saved. So he did not fire but took a pair of shears and began to cut open the sleeping wolf's belly.

When he had made a few snips he saw the little red hood gleaming and, with a few more snips, the little girl jumped out crying, "Oh, how terribly scared I was. How dark it was in the wolf's belly!"

Then the old grandmother also came out, still alive, but nearly out of breath. Then Little Red Riding Hood promptly fetched some big stones and they filled the wolf's belly. When he awoke, he wanted to leap off the bed, but the stones were so heavy that he sank down at once and fell dead.

Then all three of them rejoiced. The gamekeeper skinned the wolf and took the skin home; the grandmother ate the cake and drank the wine brought by Little Red Riding Hood and soon revived. But Little Red Riding

Hood thought to herself, "Never again will I run off the path into the forest by myself when Mother has forbidden me to do so!"

The story also goes that one day as Little Red Riding Hood was once again taking some pastries to her old grandmother, another wolf spoke to her and wanted to lead her away from the path. But Little Red Riding Hood was on her guard. She went straight on and told her grandmother that she had met a wolf who had wished her "Good morning". He had had such a wicked look in his eyes that she said, "Had I not been on the path he would have eaten me."

"Come," said the grandmother, "we will lock the door so that he can't get in."

Soon afterwards the wolf came knocking and cried, "Open the door, Grandma. I am Little Red Riding Hood bringing you some pastries."

But neither spoke nor opened the door. The grey-headed wolf prowled round the house a few times and, at last, jumped up on the roof, intent on waiting for Little Red Riding Hood to go home in the evening. Then he would steal after her and devour her in the darkness.

But the grandmother saw what he had in mind. Now there was a big stone trough in front of the house, so she said to the child, "Fetch the pail, Little Red Riding Hood. I made some sausages yesterday, so take the water in which they were boiled and pour it into the trough."

Little Red Riding Hood carried the water until the great, great trough was quite full. Then the smell of the sausages rose up to the wolf's nose. He sniffed and looked down. Finally, he stretched his neck so far that he could no longer hold himself up and began to slip. So he slipped off the roof straight into the big trough and drowned.

Little Red Riding Hood went merrily home and no one did her any harm.

TOM THUMB

One evening a poor peasant was sitting by the hearth tending the fire, and his wife was spinning. Suddenly he said, "What a sad thing that we have no children! It's so quiet in our cottage, and there is so much noise and fun in other people's houses!"

"Yes," answered his wife with a sigh, "even if it were just one, and quite tiny, no bigger than a thumb, I'd be as happy as can be, and we would love it with all our hearts."

Now it so happened that seven month's later the wife gave birth to a child which, though perfect in all its limbs, was no taller than a thumb. Then they said, "Now our wish has come true. It shall be our darling child." And, because of his size, they called the little boy Tom Thumb.

He was given everything in the way of nourishment, but he grew no bigger and remained the same size as he was the first hour he was born. Nevertheless, his eyes were marked with an intelligent look, and soon he was to prove a clever and nimble little creature who succeeded in everything he undertook.

One day, the peasant made ready to go to the forest to cut wood and he said to himself, "I wish there were someone here to bring the cart after me."

"Oh father," cried Tom Thumb, "I'll be sure to bring the cart, you can depend on it. It will be in the forest by the time you need it."

The man laughed and said, "How could you possibly do this, you're far too small even to hold the reins."

"That doesn't matter, father. If mother will harness the horse I will sit in its ear and tell it where it ought to go."

"All right," answered the father. "We'll try it for once."

When the hour came, the mother got the horse ready and put Tom Thumb into the horse's ear. Then the little creature shouted directions to the animal, "Gee gee! Whoa and gee up!" And everything went as well as with a real master carter, and the cart went straight along the right road to the forest. And it happened that just as it turned the corner and Tom shouted his "Whoa!", two strangers came along.

"My goodness!" said the one. "What's that? There's a cart coming along, and a driver is shouting at the horse, yet he's not to be seen."

"There's something peculiar about this," said the other, "we will follow the cart and see where it halts."

The cart went right on into the forest and directly to the place where the wood was being cut. When Tom saw his father he called to him, "You see, father, here I am with the cart. Now please help me down." The father held the horse with his left hand, and with the right he brought his little son out of its ear. Tom sat down quite happily on a blade of straw.

When the two strangers noticed Tom, they didn't know what to do or say, they were so amazed. Then the one took the other aside and said, "Listen, that little fellow could make our fortune if we were to show him in a big town. We will buy him."

They went up to the peasant and said, "Sell us the little man, he'll be well off with us."

"No," said the peasant, "he is my heart's little treasure and is not for sale for all the gold in the world."

But Tom Thumb, when he heard about the deal, climbed by the folds of his father's coat to his shoulder, and whispered to him "Father, don't worry. Sell me. I will soon be back again!"

Then his father sold him to the two men for a large sum of money.

"Where will you sit?" they said to him.

"Oh, just put me on the brim of your hat, there I can walk to and fro, look at the countryside and not fall off."

They did as he wished, and when Tom had said good-bye to his father, they took him away with them.

So they walked until it grew dark, and then Tom Thumb said, "Put me down at once. I must get down."

"Just stay up there," said the man on whose head he was sitting. "Birds let their droppings fall on me now and then. I won't mind if you do, too."

"No," said Tom, "it is not the thing to do. Lift me down at once."

The man took his hat off and put the little one in a field by the roadside. Tom skipped and crawled a little among the clods, then slipped suddenly into a mouse-hole which he had discovered.

"Good evening, gentlemen," he called after them and laughed. "You can go home without me."

They came running up and poked sticks into the mouse-hole but their efforts were all in vain. Tom Thumb crept further and further back and, as it soon grew quite dark, they were forced to go home, angry and with their purses empty.

When Tom saw that they were gone, he crawled out of the mouse-hole again. "It's dangerous walking along the field in the dark," he said. "How easy it is to break one's neck or leg." Luckily, he stumbled on an empty snail shell. "Thank goodness," he said, "I can spend the night in safety here," and he sat down inside.

Before long, just as he was about to fall asleep, he heard two men walking by. One said, "How shall we go about robbing the rich parson of his money and his silver?"

"I could tell you that," Tom interrupted them.

"What was that?" said one of the robbers, full of fright. "I heard someone speak."

They stood and listened, then Tom spoke again. "Take me along and I will help you."

"Where on earth are you?" they said.

"Just look around on the ground, and see where the voice comes from," he answered.

Finally the thieves found him and lifted him up. "You little thing, how are you going to help us?"

"Look here," he answered, "I can creep between the iron bars into the parson's room and hand you out whatever you want."

"All right," they agreed, "we shall see what you can do."

When they came to the parsonage, Tom Thumb crawled into the small room, but at once he shouted with all his might. "What do you want? Do you want everything that's here?"

The thieves got scared and said, "Do speak softly, so as not to wake anybody."

But Tom went on as if he hadn't understood, and shouted, "What do you want? Everything that's here?"

The cook, who was sleeping in the next room, heard him, sat up in bed and listened. In their fright the thieves had retreated a little, but at last they regained their courage and thought, "The little fellow is trying to tease us." They came back and whispered to him, "Now be serious and hand something out to us."

Then Tom cried out again as loud as he could, "I will give you everything, only put your hands inside."

The cook who was listening, heard this quite distinctly, sprang out of bed, and stumbled towards the door. The thieves turned and fled as if wild huntsmen were at their heels. But the cook, unable to see anything, went to light a candle. When she came back with it, Tom Thumb had already slipped away to the barn and the cook, having searched every nook and corner, found nothing.

At last she went back to bed thinking she had been dreaming after all.

Tom Thumb clambered about in the hay and found a pleasant little spot for sleeping. He would rest till morning and then return to his parents. But there were other things he had still to experience! Yes, the world is a sorry place full of woe and tribulation.

The dairy maid got up at the crack of dawn to feed the cattle. Her first steps led her to the barn where she picked up an armful of hay, just the very hay where poor Tom Thumb was lying asleep. But he was so fast asleep that he noticed nothing, and did not wake up until he was in the mouth of the cow which had snatched him up along with the hay.

"Heavens!" he cried. "How did I tumble into this mill!" But he soon realized where he was. He had to be careful not to get between the teeth and so be crushed to death. At last, there was nothing for it but to let himself slide with the hay down into the cow's stomach.

"They forgot to put windows in this little room," he said. "No sun is shining in. Nor is there any light or candle." Altogether he didn't like his new quarters in the least, and, worst of all, there was always new hay coming in at the door, and the place was getting narrower and narrower. Then, in his anguish, he cried as loud as he could, "Don't bring me any more hay, don't bring me any more hay!"

The dairy maid just happened to be milking the cow at the time, and when she heard a voice and saw nobody, she was so frightened that she slipped off her stool and spilt the milk. Then, in great haste, she ran to her master, crying, "Oh dear, parson, the cow has spoken!"

"You're crazy," answered the parson, but he went to the cowshed to see for himself. But scarcely had he set foot inside than Tom Thumb shouted, "Don't bring me any more hay, don't bring me any more hay!" Then the parson himself got scared, thought that an evil spirit had possessed the cow, and ordered it to be killed.

And so the poor cow was slaughtered, but its stomach with Tom Thumb in it was thrown on to the dunghill. Tom Thumb had a lot of trouble in working his way out of it, but at last he managed.

Just as he was about to stick out his head, a new misfortune befell him. A hungry wolf came running by and swallowed the whole stomach at a single gulp. Tom Thumb did not lose heart. "Maybe," he thought, "the wolf will listen to reason." And he called out to him from the belly, "Dear wolf, I know of a magnificent feast for you."

"Where is it to be had?" said the wolf.

"In a house I know. You'll have to crawl in through the drain, but you'll find cakes and bacon and sausages as many of them as you can eat." And he gave the wolf an exact description of his father's house.

The wolf did not have to be told twice. That night, he squeezed himself through the drain into the pantry of Tom Thumb's house and ate to his heart's content. When he had eaten his fill, he hurried to get away again but he had become so big that he couldn't get out through the drain. This was just as Tom Thumb had planned and now he began to make a terrific noise in the wolf's belly, shouting and yelling for all he was worth.

"Will you be quiet," said the wolf, "or you'll wake up the people in the house."

"Eh, what's that to me?" answered the little fellow. "You've eaten your fill, I want to have a little fun now myself." And once again he began to scream as loud as he could.

At last, the noise roused his father and mother. They ran to the pantry and peeped in through a crack in the door. When they saw that a wolf was inside, they ran off, the man fetched an axe and his wife a scythe.

"You stay behind," said the man to his wife as they entered the pantry. "If the blow I give him doesn't kill him at once, then you must cut him down and rip open his belly."

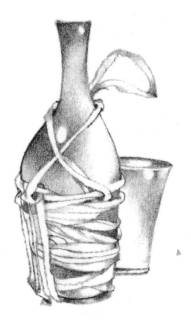

When Tom Thumb heard this he shouted, "Dear father, I am here, stuck in the wolf's belly!"

Full of joy, his father cried, "Thank God, we have found our dear child again!" And he told his wife to lay aside the scythe so as not to hurt Tom.

Then he swung back and dealt the wolf such a blow on his head that made him tumble down dead. Then they brought a knife and scissors, cut open the wolf's belly, and got the little boy out.

"Ah," said the father, "how we have been worrying about you!"

"Yes, father, I have wandered a lot in the world. Thank heavens that I can draw in fresh air again!"

"Why, where have you been?"

"Oh, father, I was in a mouse-hole, in a cow's stomach, and in a wolf's belly. Now I will stay with you."

"And we will not sell you again for all the riches in the world," said the parents, hugging and kissing their beloved Tom.

Then they gave him plenty to eat and drink, and had new clothes made for him, for those he had on had been ruined during his travels.

OLD SULTAN

A peasant had a faithful dog whom he called Sultan. The dog was very old, had lost all its teeth and no longer had a tight grip. One day the peasant standing with his wife in front of the house said, "Tomorrow morning I am going to shoot old Sultan, for he is no good any more."

His wife, who felt pity for the faithful animal, answered, "He has served us for so many years and has been so loyal, we might as well give him his keep for the rest of his days."

"What?" answered the man, "you're out of your senses. There's not a tooth in his mouth and no thief is afraid of him now. He might as well go. He served us well, but was fed for it."

The poor dog, who was lying close by stretched out in the sun, heard everything and was distressed to think tomorrow was to be his last day on earth. He had a good friend, the wolf, and to him he crept out into the wood that very evening and told him of his impending fate.

"Listen, old pal, be of good cheer. I will help you out of your trouble. I've got an idea. Tomorrow, quite early in the morning, your master will go haymaking with his wife and, as there is no one at home, they will be taking their baby with them. While at work they always lay it down behind the hedge in the shade. You lie down close by the child just as if you were guarding it. I will come out of the wood and steal the child. Then you must rush out as if to catch me and recover the child. I will drop it and you will bring it back to its parents. They will think you have saved their child for them and will be far too grateful to do you any harm. On the contrary, you will win full grace and they will never let you want for anything in your life.''

The dog liked the plan very much and the plot was carried out as they had planned. The father screamed when he saw the wolf running off with the child through the field, but was overjoyed when old Sultan brought it back. He patted him and said, "No one shall ever hurt a single hair of your coat, you shall eat the bread of grace as long as you live."

Then he said to his wife, "Go straight home and make old Sultan some porridge of the finest wheaten bread that he has no need to chew and bring the pillow from my bed. I will give him that to lie on."

From that time on old Sultan had as good a life as he could wish for.

Soon afterwards, the wolf came to see him and was glad to hear that everything had gone so well. "But, old pal," he said, "you will no doubt wink an eye if I should carry off one of your master's fat sheep. It's more and more difficult these days to make both ends meet."

"Don't count on that," answered the dog. "I intend to remain true to my master. I can't allow that to happen."

The wolf thought it was spoken in jest and came prowling in the night to carry off the sheep. But the peasant, to whom the faithful Sultan disclosed the wolf's intention, waylaid him and combed the wolf's hair cruelly with the flail. The wolf had to run off but he shouted at the dog, "Just you wait, old rogue, you shall pay for this!"

The next morning the wolf sent the boar and challenged the dog to come out to the forest to settle their differences there. Old Sultan could find no second but the old three-legged cat and, when they went out together, the poor cat limped along sticking up her tail in pain.

The wolf and his second were already on the spot, but when they saw their opponent coming they thought he was bringing a sabre with him, mistaking the cat's erected tail for a weapon. And, as the poor animal hopped along on three legs, they could only think it was picking up a stone every time to hurl at them. So they both got frightened, the wild boar crept into the shrubs, the wolf jumped up into a tree.

The dog and the cat soon came up and wondered that there was no one in sight. The boar, however, had not been able to hide completely, for his ears were sticking out. While the cat was looking carefully about, the boar twitched his ears. The cat, thinking it was a mouse stirring, sprang upon it and bit it heartily. The boar jumped up with a fearful outcry, "Look up in the tree, there sits the guilty one!"

Old Sultan and the cat looked up and saw the wolf who, ashamed of having proved so faint-hearted, agreed to make peace with the dog.

THE SIX SWANS

Once upon a time a King was out hunting in a large forest, and pursued a deer with such zeal that none of his men could keep up with him. When evening came, he made a halt, looked around him, and saw that he had lost his way.

He sought for a way out of the forest, but could find none. Then he saw an old woman with a wobbly head coming towards him who turned out to be a witch. "Dear lady," he addressed her, "can you show me the way through the woods?"

"Oh yes, Your Royal Highness," she answered, "of course I can, but there is one condition. Unless that one is fulfilled, you shall never get out of the forest, and shall starve to death in it."

"What sort of a condition?" asked the King.

"I have a daughter," said the old woman, "she is as beautiful as any girl you can find in the world and well deserves to become your wife. If you will make her your Queen, I will show you the way out of the forest."

Afraid of dying a miserable death, the King agreed, and the old woman led him to her cottage where her daughter was sitting by the fire. She received the King as though she had been expecting him, and then he saw that she was indeed very beautiful. Yet there was something he did not like about her, and he could not look at her without secret dread. He lifted the maiden on to his horse, the old woman showed him the way, and he arrived at his royal palace again, where the marriage was celebrated.

The King had already been married once before, and had seven children by his first wife who had died. He had six boys and one girl, whom he loved beyond anything in the world. Now he was afraid that their stepmother might not treat them well and even do them some harm. So he took them to a lonely castle which stood in the middle of a forest. It lay so hidden, and the way was so difficult to find that he would never have found it himself had not a wise woman given him a ball of yarn of such wonderful property that when he threw it in front of him it unwound by itself and showed him the way.

However, the King went so often to visit his dear children that the Queen found his absence strange. She was curious to know what he was doing all alone out in the forest. She bribed his servants with a large sum of money, and they disclosed the secret to her, and even told her of the ball of yarn which alone could show the way. Now she knew no peace till she had found out where the King kept the ball of yarn. Then she made tiny little shirts of white silk, and as she had learnt witchcraft from her mother, she sewed a charm in each of them. One day, when the King had ridden out hunting she took the little shirts and went into the forest, and the ball showed her the way.

The children seeing someone coming from the distance thought it was their dear father coming to see them, and full of joy ran out to meet him. Then she threw one of the little shirts over each of them, and the moment it touched their body, they turned into swans, and flew away.

The Queen went home pleased with her work, and believed herself rid of her stepchildren, but the maiden had not run out with her brothers to meet her father, so the Queen knew nothing about her. Next day the King came to see his children, but found only the little girl. "Where are your brothers?" asked the King.

"Alas, dear father," she answered, "they are all gone and have left me here quite alone," and she told him how from her little window she had seen all her brothers changed into swans flying away over the woods, and showed him the feathers which they had dropped in the courtyard.

The King was sad, but did not know that it was the Queen who had done the evil deed and, as he feared that the maiden might also be stolen from him, he wanted to take her away with him. But she was terrified of her stepmother, and begged him to let her stay at least one night in the forest castle.

The poor girl thought, "It's not right for me to stay here any longer. I will go and look for my brothers." And when night came she ran away and went straight into the forest. She went on and on throughout the night, and the next day as well without stopping till she was so weary that she could not walk any further.

Then she saw a woodman's hut, went up and found a room with six little beds in it. However, she did not dare to lie down in any of them, but crept under one, and lay down on the hard floor in order to spend the night there. When the sun was about to set, she heard some rustling and saw six swans flying in through the window. They alighted on the floor, and blew at one another's feathers till they blew them all off, and their swan skins pealed off like a shirt. The maiden looked on and recognized her brothers, and full

of joy she crept from under the bed. The brothers were no less pleased to see their little sister but their joy was not for long.

"You simply cannot stay here," they said to her, "this is a robbers' hide-out, when they come home and find you here, they will kill you."

"But can't your protect me at all?" asked their little sister.

"No," they replied, "we may take off our swan skins for a mere quarter of an hour every evening, and during that time we have our human form, but afterwards we turn into swans again."

The sister cried and said, "Can't you be disenchanted?"

"Alas, no," they answered, "the conditions are too hard. Anyone who wants to break the spell must not speak or laugh for six years, and during that time must sew six shirts for us out of starwort. If a single word leaves your lips, then all the labour is lost." And by the time the brothers had finished speaking, the quarter of an hour had passed, and they flew out of the window again changed back into swans.

However, the maiden firmly resolved to save her brothers even if it should cost her life. She left the hut, went into the middle of the forest, settled herself in a tree, and spent the night there. Next morning she went out, and gathered starwort, and began to sew. She did not talk to anyone, and she was in no mood for laughter. She merely sat at her labours.

When she had been there for some time, it chanced that the King of that country was hunting in the forest, and his huntsmen came to the tree on which the maiden was sitting. They called out to her saying, "Who are you?" But she made no reply. "Come down to us," they said, "we will do you no harm."

She only shook her head. When they kept harassing her with questions, she threw her gold necklace down to them hoping to satisfy them by doing so. But they wouldn't stop, so she threw down her girdle, and when this did not help, her garters, and gradually everything she had on that she could dispense with. Eventually she was left with nothing but her shift. However, the huntsmen would not let themselves be put off by this, but climbed the tree, brought the maiden down, and led her before the King.

The King asked, "Who are you? What were you doing up there in the tree?"

She did not answer, however. He asked in all the languages he knew, but she remained as mute as a maggot. However, as she was so beautiful, the King's heart was touched and he fell passionately in love with her. He wrapped her in his cloak, took her on his horse, and brought her to his palace. There he had her clad in rich robes, and she shone in her beauty like the brightness of the day, but no one could make her utter a single word. He made her sit by his side at the table, and her demure behaviour and her modesty pleased him so much that he said, "This is the girl I desire to marry and I shall have no other in the world." And a few days later he married her.

But the King had a wicked mother who was dissatisfied with the marriage and said evil things about the young Queen. "Who knows where the wench who cannot speak comes from," she said. "She is not worthy of a king."

A year later, when the Queen gave birth to her first child, the King's mother took it away from her while she was asleep and smeared her mouth with blood. Then she went to the King and accused her daughter-in-law of being a cannibal. The King did not believe it and would not allow anyone to do her any harm. She sat all the time silently sewing shirts and took no notice of what went on around her.

The next time, when she again gave birth to a pretty boy, the wicked grandmother repeated her cruel plot, but the King did not believe anything against his wife.

He said, "She is too pious and good to do such a thing. If she weren't dumb and could defend herself, her innocence would be proved."

However, when for the third time the old woman robbed the mother of her new-born babe and accused the Queen, who uttered not a word in her defence, the King had no other choice but to hand her over to the court, and she was sentenced to be burnt at the stake.

The day arrived when the sentence was to be carried out. It happened to be the last day of the six years during which she had not been allowed to speak or laugh, and by keeping her silence she had delivered her dear brothers from the power of the spell. The six shirts were ready, only the left sleeve was still missing on the last one. As she was being led to the stake, she laid the shirts over her arm, and when she was standing up there and the fire was just about to be kindled, she looked round, and there came six swans flying through the air. Then she saw that their deliverance was at hand, and her heart was moved with joy. The swans came fluttering towards her and

dropped down so that she could throw the shirts over them; and the moment the shirts touched them, the swan skins fell off them, and her brothers stood before her in their human form and were fine and handsome—but for the youngest who had his left arm missing and instead had a swan's wing on his back. They embraced and kissed each other, and the young Queen went up to the King who was completely bewildered, began to speak and said, "Dearest husband, now I may speak and reveal to you that I am innocent and wrongly accused," and she told him about his mother's deception who had taken the three children away and hidden them. Then to the King's great joy they were fetched, and by way of punishment the wicked mother-in-law was bound to the stake and burned to ashes.

But the King and Queen and her six brothers lived for many years in happiness and peace.

KING THRUSHBEARD

A King had a daughter who was exceedingly beautiful, but so proud and haughty that none of her suitors was good enough for her. She rejected one after the other, and even made sport of them.

One day the King held a great feast and invited all men who wanted to marry her from far and near to attend. They were marshalled in a row according to their rank and dignity. First came the kings, then grand-dukes, the princes, earls and barons and last, the lesser nobility.

The King's daughter was conducted through the ranks but, with each of them, she had some fault to find. One was too fat for her. "As round as a wine-cask." The other was too tall. "Tall and thin has not much in." The third she found too short. "Short and thick is never slick." The fourth was too pale. "The pallid death!" she called him. The fifth too red. "Red as the turkey-cock!" The sixth was not straight enough. "Green log dried behind the stove!"

Thus she made sport of every one of them, but she made particular fun of a gallant king who was standing right at the head of the queue and whose chin had grown a bit crooked. "Oh," she cried laughing, "he has a chin like a thrush's beak!" and from that time he was nicknamed King Thrushbeard. However, the old King seeing that his daughter did nothing but mock the men and despised all the suitors who had gathered to woo her, was very angry and swore she should marry the very first beggar who happened to come to his door.

A few days later a wandering minstrel came and sang under the window to earn some small alms. When the King heard him he said, "Let him come up to me." Then the wandering musician in his dirty ragged clothes came in and sang before the King and his daughter and, having finished, begged for a trifle of a gift. The King said, "Your song has pleased me so much that I will give you my daughter there in marriage."

The King's daughter was horrified but the King said, "I swore an oath to give you to the first beggar who chanced to come within my gates, and I will keep my oath."

All her entreaties were of no avail, the priest was fetched and she had no choice but to be wedded to the fiddler there and then. When that was done, the King said, "Now it is not befitting that as a beggar's wife you should remain in my palace. You may just as well go away from here with your husband."

The beggarman took her by the hand and led her out of the palace and she had to follow him on foot. When they came to a big forest, she asked:
"Oh, who owns this lovely weald?"
"It belongs to King Thrushbeard.
Had you taken him it would be yours."
"Oh, woe me poor maiden, that's my meed!
Had I but taken King Thrushbeard!"

Next they were crossing a meadow, and she asked again:
"Who owns this lovely green mead?"
"It belongs to King Thrushbeard.
Had you taken him it would be yours."
"Oh, woe me poor maiden, that's my meed!
Had I but taken King Thrushbeard!"

Then they passed through a great city and she asked again:
"Who is master of this lovely city?"
"It belongs to King Thrushbeard.
Had you taken him it would have been yours."
"Oh, woe me poor maiden, that's my meed!
Had I but taken King Thrushbeard!"

"I am not at all pleased," said the fiddler, "to hear you always wishing you had married another. Am I not good enough for you?"

At length, they came to quite a tiny little hut, and she said:

"Oh good heavens! How very small the house is! To whom may this miserable hovel belong?"

The fiddler answered, "This is my house and yours, where we will live. She had to stoop to get through the low door.

"Where are the servants?" said the King's daughter.

"What servants?" answered the beggar. "Whatever you want done you will have to do yourself. Make the fire at once and put on some water, that you can cook me a meal. I am exhausted."

But the King's daughter knew nothing about fire making and cooking,

and the beggar had to lend a hand to get things done at all. When they had consumed the scanty meal they went to bed. The next morning he made her get up very early to start housekeeping for them both.

For a few days they lived in this way but they had soon eaten up all the food. Then the man said, "Wife, it can't go on like this eating and drinking and earning nothing. You must weave baskets."

He went out, cut some willows and brought them home. Then she began to weave, but the rough willows pricked her delicate hands and made them sore.

"I can see this won't do," said the man. "You had better spin. Perhaps you can manage that better." She sat down and tried to spin, but the hard thread soon cut into her soft fingers so that blood ran down them. "See," said the man, "you are really unfit for any work, a bad bargain I've made in marrying you. Now I will try and start a business in pots and earthenware and you shall sit in the market and offer them for sale."

"Alas," she thought, "if people from my father's kingdom come to the market and see me sitting there and offering things for sale, how they will laugh at me!" But complaining availed her nothing, she had to obey unless they were to die of hunger. The first time she did well, for people were glad to buy the woman's wares because of her good looks. They paid the price she asked, indeed, many gave her the money and left the pots with her into the bargain. The two lived on what she earned as long as it lasted, then the man bought a new lot of wares. With these she sat down at the corner of the market-place, displayed them all around and offered them for sale.

Then, all of a sudden, a drunken hussar came racing up, and rode into the pots so that everything was smashed to pieces. She burst into tears and, in her anguish, did not know what to do. "Alas, what will become of me," she cried. "What will my husband say to this?" She ran home and told him of her misfortune.

"What an idea to sit at the corner of the market-place with earthenware crockery!" said the man. "Just stop that weeping. I can see now that you are no good for any proper work, so I have been to the King's palace and asked if they couldn't do with a kitchen maid. They promised me to take you on. In return you shall get your food for nothing."

So the King's daughter became a kitchen maid, was at the cook's beck and call and did the dirty work. In each of her pockets she hung a little jar and in it brought home what she could get of the leftovers, and they lived on that.

It happened that the wedding of the King's eldest son was to be celebrated, so the wretched woman went upstairs and stood by the door of the hall to watch the proceedings. When the lights were lit and people were entering, each more finely dressed than the other, she thought with a sore heart of her own fate, and cursed the pride and arrogance that had brought her so low and plunged her into such abject misery. Delicious dishes were being brought in and out and from these the smell rose up to her, making her mouth water. Now and again the servants threw her a few morsels. She put them in her little jars to take home.

All of a sudden, the King's son entered clad in velvet and silk and with a gold chain about his neck. When he saw the beautiful woman standing by the door, he seized her by the hand and wanted to dance with her. But she was panic-stricken and refused, for she saw that it was King Thrushbeard who had wooed her and whom she had scornfully rejected.

Her struggling was of no avail and he drew her into the hall. Then the strings by which the jars were hanging snapped, the jars fell out, and scraps of food were scattered all over the floor. When the people saw this, they laughed and mocked her and she wished herself a thousand fathoms under the earth. She ran to the door but a man caught up with her on the stairs and brought her back. She looked at him and saw it was King Thrushbeard again.

He said to her kindly, "Be not afraid. I and the minstrel with whom you have been living in that miserable hovel are one. For love of you I had disguised myself. And I, too, was the hussar who rode through your crockery. All this was done to humble your proud spirit and punish you for the arrogance with which you made fun of me."

Then she cried bitterly, saying, "I did great wrong, and am not worthy to be your wife."

But he said, "Take comfort, the evil days are over. Now we will celebrate our wedding!"

Then the ladies-in-waiting came and dressed her in resplendent robes and her own father and his whole court came and wished her much happiness on her marriage to King Thrushbeard. Thus joy and gaiety reigned and I wish you and I had been there, too!

SNOW-WHITE AND THE SEVEN DWARFS

Once upon a time in mid-winter when snowflakes were falling like feathers from the sky, a Queen sat sewing at her window and her embroidering frame was made of fine black ebony. As she was sewing and looking out at the snow, she pricked her finger with the needle, and three drops of blood fell upon the snow. The red looked so lovely on the white snow that she thought to herself, "I wish I had a child as white as snow, as red as blood, and as black as the ebony of my embroidering frame."

Soon after she had a little daughter, who was as white as snow, her cheeks as red as blood, and her hair as black as ebony and she was called Snow-White. But when the child was born, the Queen died.

A year passed and the King took another wife. She was a handsome woman but proud and haughty, and could not bear the thought that she should be surpassed in beauty by anyone. She had a magic mirror, and she used to stand before it and look at herself and say:
"Magic mirror on the wall,
Who is the fairest of us all?"

And the mirror answered:
"Lady Queen, you are fairest of them all."

Then she was content, for she knew that the looking-glass spoke the truth.

Snow-White grew up and became ever fairer and, when she was seven years old, she was as beautiful as the clear day, and even more beautiful than the Queen herself. And once when the Queen asked her looking-glass,
"*Magic mirror on the wall,*
Who is the fairest of us all?"

It answered:
"*Lady Queen, you are fairest here, I hold,*
But Snow-White is fairer, a thousandfold."

The Queen was shocked and turned yellow and green with envy. From that very hour, whenever she set eyes on Snow-White her heart heaved in her breast, such was the hatred she bore the little girl.

And envy and pride in her heart grew ever higher like a weed, so that she knew no peace by day or night ever more. One day she called a huntsman and said, "Take the child away into the forest, I can't bear the sight of her any more. Kill her and bring me back her heart as a token."

The huntsman obeyed and took Snow-White out. When he drew his hunting-knife and was about to pierce her innocent heart, she began to cry, "Oh, dear huntsman, spare my life! I will run off into the wild woods and never come back again."

And as she was so beautiful the huntsman had pity on her and said, "Run away then, poor child." He thought, "The wild beasts will soon devour you," nevertheless he felt as if a stone had been rolled from his heart because he did not have to kill her himself. At that very moment, a young wild boar rushed out of the bushes, so he pierced it and took its heart as a token to the Queen. The cook had to boil it in salted water and the wicked Queen ate it up believing it to be Snow-White's.

Now the poor child was quite forlorn in the big forest and she was so terrified that she looked at every leaf of every tree and did not know what to do for herself. Then she began to run and ran over sharp stones and among thorns, and the wild beasts came leaping past her but did her no harm. She ran as long as her feet would carry her until evening set in. Then she saw a tiny little house and went in to have a rest. Everything in the tiny house was small and neat and clean beyond description. A little table with a white cloth stood there laid with seven little plates, and by each little plate a little spoon, and there were seven little knives and forks, and seven little cups. Against the wall stood seven little beds all in a row with snow-white counterpanes over them.

Snow-White was very hungry and thirsty, so she ate some vegetables and bread from each plate and drank a drop of wine from each little cup, for she did not wish to take everything from one. Then, being so very tired, she lay down in one of the little beds. She tried them all, but none was right for her; one was too long, another too short until at last the seventh was just right. Here she remained, said her prayers, and fell asleep.

When it got quite dark the masters of the little house came back. They were seven dwarfs who dug and delved in the mountains for gold. They lit their seven little candles, and as it was now light in the house they saw that someone had been there, for not everything was in the order they had left it.

The first said, "Who has been sitting in my chair?"

The second said, "Who has been eating off my plate?"

The third said, "Who has been taking some of my bread?"

The fourth said, "Who has been eating my vegetables?"

The fifth said, "Who has been pricking with my fork?"

The sixth said, "Who has been cutting with my knife?"

The seventh said, "Who has been drinking out of my cup?"

Then the first looked round and saw a little hollow on his bed, and he said, "Who has been treading on my bed?" The others came running up and cried, "Somebody's been lying in mine, too."

But the seventh looked into his own bed and saw Snow-White lying there asleep. At once he called the others, who came running up and cried out with great wonderment and, having fetched their seven little candles, looked at Snow-White.

"Oh my goodness, my goodness," they cried, "what a lovely child!" And they were overjoyed and took care not to wake her but let her sleep on in the little bed. And the seventh dwarf slept with his companions, an hour with each in turn, till the night was over, and thus he passed the night.

When morning came and Snow-White awoke, she saw the dwarfs and was frightened. But they were most kind and asked, "What is your name?"

"My name is Show-White," she replied.

"How do you come to be in our house?" they asked.

Then she told them how her stepmother had wanted to have her killed but the huntsman had spared her life, and she had run all day until at last she had come upon their little house.

The dwarfs said, "If you will keep house for us, cook, make the beds, do the washing, sew and knit, and keep everything tidy and clean, then you can stay with us and you shall have all you need."

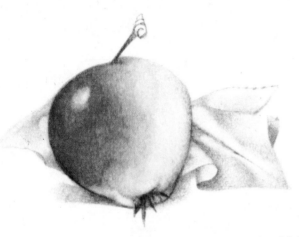

"Yes, I will with all my heart," said Snow-White.

She stayed with them and kept their house in order. In the morning they would go off into the mountains in search of gold. In the evening they came back again, and then their supper had to be ready.

Snow-White was all alone the whole day, so the good dwarfs warned her saying. "Beware of your stepmother, she will soon know that you are here, so let no one in."

The Queen, however, believing she had eaten Snow-White's heart felt certain that she was again the most beautiful of all. So she went to her looking--glass and said:

"Magic mirror on the wall,
Who is the fairest of us all?"

The glass answered:
"Queen, you are fairest here, I hold,
But Snow-White beyond the fells,
Who with the seven dwarfs dwells,
Is fairer still, a thousandfold."

Then she was very angry, for she knew that the glass told no unthruths, and she realized that the huntsman had deceived her and Snow-White was still alive. And so she pondered and pondered again how she might contrive to kill her, for as long as she herself was not the fairest in the land her envious heart knew no peace. Finally she thought of a plan. She painted her face and disguised herself as an old pedlar and was changed beyond recognition. In this disguise she went over the seven mountains to where the seven dwarfs dwelled, knocked at the door and cried, "Fine wares for sale, fine wares for sale!"

Snow-White looked out of the window and sang out, "Good-day, my good woman, what have you got to sell?"

"Good wares, fine wares," she answered, "laces of all colours." And she pulled out one which was plaited of bright-coloured silk.

"I may let the honest woman in," thought Show-White. She unbolted the door and bought the fine lace.

"Child," said the old woman, "you do look a sight! Come, I will lace your bodice properly for once."

Snow-White thought of no mischief but stood before her and let herself be laced with the new lace. But the old woman laced fast and laced so tight that Snow-White lost her breath and fell down for dead.

"Now I am the fairest," said the Queen to herself, and hurried out.

Not long after towards eventide, the seven dwarfs came home, and how horrified they were to see their dear little Snow-White lying on the ground. She neither moved nor stirred as if she were dead. They lifted her up and, seeing she was laced up too tight, they cut the lace, after which she began to breathe a little and, by and by, came to life again.

When the dwarfs heard what had happened, they said, "The old pedlar was no other but the wicked Queen. So take care and let no one come in when we are not with you."

When the vicious woman reached home, she went to the looking-glass and asked:
"Magic mirror on the wall,
Who is the fairest of us all?"

And the mirror answered as before:
"Queen, you are fairest here, I hold,
But Snow-White beyond the fells,
Who with the seven dwarfs dwells,
Is fairer still, a thousandfold."

When she heard this, the blood rushed to her heart with spite and malice to hear that Snow-White had come to life again.

"But now," she said to herself, " I will devise something that will make an end of you."

And, using her witch's skill, she made a poisoned comb. Thereupon she disguised herself again and put on the form of another old woman. She crossed the seven mountains to where the seven dwarfs dwelled, knocked at the door and cried, "Fine wares for sale, fine wares for sale!"

Snow-White looked out and said, "Just go your way, I must not let anyone in."

"But surely you are allowed to look," said the old woman, and she pulled out the poisoned comb and held it up. It pleased the maiden so well that she fell for her trickery, and opened the door.

They made a bargain and the old woman said, "Now I will comb your hair properly for once."

Poor Snow-White, suspecting no mischief, let the old woman have her way. No sooner had the woman stuck the comb into her hair than the poison in it took effect and the maiden fell down in a dead swoon.

"You paragon of beauty," said the wicked Queen, "now you are done for," and went away.

Fortunately, it was soon evening and the seven dwarfs came home. When they saw Snow-White lying as though dead on the floor, they at once suspected her stepmother, and they looked and found the poisoned comb. No sooner was it pulled out than Snow-White recovered her senses and told them what had happened. Once again they warned her to be on her guard and not to open the door to anyone.

At home the Queen stepped before the looking-glass and said:
"Magic mirror on the wall,
Who is the fairest of us all?"

It answered her as usual:
"Queen, you are fairest here, I hold,
But Snow-White beyond the fells,
Who with the seven dwarfs dwells,
Is fairer still, a thousandfold."

When she heard the looking-glass speak these words she trembled and shook with rage.

"Snow-White shall die," she cried, "even if it costs me my life." Saying this, she went into a secret room, where no one ever came, and made the most poisonous apple. Outside it looked lovely, white with rosy cheeks, so that anyone who saw it felt like eating it, but whoever ate of it was doomed to die. When the apple was ready she painted her face and, disguised as a peasant woman, crossed the seven mountains to the seven dwarfs' dwelling place.

She knocked, but Snow-White put her head out of the window and said, "I may not let anyone in, the seven dwarfs have forbidden me."

"That's all right with me," answered the peasant woman. "I will get rid of my apples anyway. Look, I will give you one."

"No," said Snow-White, I mustn't accept anything."

"Are you afraid of poisoning?" said the peasant. "Look here, I shall cut the apple into two pieces. You eat the red side, and I will eat the white."

However, the apple was so cunningly made that only the red half was poisoned. Snow-White looked at the lovely apple with longing eyes and, when she saw the peasant woman eat half of it, she could not refrain any longer, stretched out her hand, and took the poisoned red half. No sooner had she taken a single bite than she fell down dead.

The Queen looked on with a ghastly expression, laughed exceedingly loud, and cried, "White as snow, red as blood, black as ebony! This time the dwarfs cannot wake you again!"

And once home, she asked the looking-glass:
"Magic mirror on the wall,
Who is the fairest of us all?"

And it answered at last:
"Lady Queen, you are fairest of them all."

Then her jealous heart was at rest, as far as a jealous heart can know rest.

When evening came and the dwarfs returned they found Snow-White lying on the ground. No breath passed her lips and they saw that she was dead. They lifted her up and looked to see if there was anything poisonous about. They unlaced her, combed her hair, washed her with water and wine, but she looked as fresh as one alive and still had her nice rosy cheeks.

So they laid her on a bier, and sat near it, all the seven of them, and cried and bewailed her for three whole days. Then they proposed to bury her, but she looked as fresh as one alive and still had her nice rosy cheeks.

So they said, "We can never bury her in the dark earth."

And they had a glass coffin made for her so that they could see her from all sides. Then they laid her in it and wrote upon it in golden letters her name, adding that she was a King's daughter. They placed the coffin outside on a hill, and one of them always stayed by and stood guard over it. And the birds came, too, and mourned Snow-White, first an owl, then a raven, and lastly a little dove.

Now Snow-White lay for a long, long time in her coffin, but she did not change and looked as though she were asleep. She still was as white as snow, her cheeks as red as blood, and her hair as black as ebony. One day, however, a Prince appeared in the forest and came to the dwarfs' home to stay the night. He had seen the coffin on the hill and the lovely Snow-White in it and had read what was written in golden letters.

Then he said to the dwarfs, "Let me have the coffin, I will give you whatever you like for it."

But the dwarfs answered, "We will not part with it for all the gold in the world."

Then he said, "So let me have it as your gift, for without Snow-White to look on I cannot live, and I will honour and revere her as my lady love."

Since he spoke in this way, the good dwarfs took pity on him, and gave him the coffin.

The Prince had his servants carry it on their shoulders. But it happened that they stumbled over some tree-stump, and with the shock the poisoned apple piece that Snow-White had bitten off fell out of her throat. It was not long before she opened her eyes, lifted the lid of the coffin, sat up, and was alive again.

"Oh, goodness me, where am I?" she cried.

The Prince, overjoyed, said to her, "You are with me," and told her what had happened.

Then he said, "I love you better than anything in the world. Come with me to my father's palace, and you shall be my wife."

Snow-White consented and went home with him, and their wedding was celebrated with great pomp and splendour.

However, Snow-White's wicked stepmother was also invited to the wedding-feast. She decked herself out with fine clothes, stepped before the looking-glass and said:

"Magic mirror on the wall,
Who is the fairest of us all?"

The glass answered:
"Queen, you are fairest here, I hold,
But the young Queen is fairer, a thousandfold!"

The evil woman uttered a curse, and at that moment she felt angry, so angry that she did not know what to do. At first, she did not feel like going to the wedding at all, but she felt she could have no rest until she had seen the young Queen. And when she came in and saw that it was Snow-White, she was seized with rage and terror and she stood still and could not stir. But already they had put iron slippers over a coal-fire and these were brought in with tongs and placed before her. Then she was made to step into the red-hot shoes and dance till she dropped down dead.

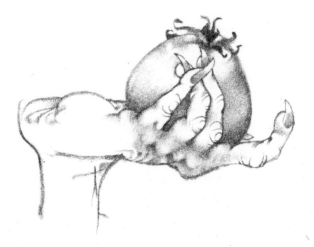

MERRY ANDREW

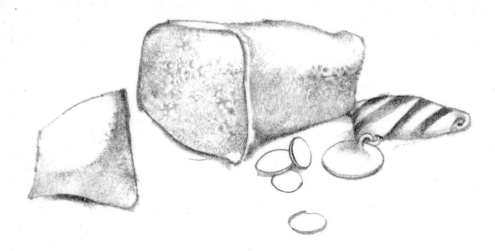

Once upon a time there was a great war, and when the war came to an end, many soldiers got their discharge. Well, Merry Andrew also got his and nothing else with it but a small loaf of army bread and four farthings in cash, and with that he went his way.

Now St. Peter had sat down by the wayside disguised as a poor beggar, and when Merry Andrew reached the spot, begged alms of him.

The soldier replied, "Dear beggarman, what am I to give you? I've been a soldier and have got my discharge, and have nothing else but this small loaf of army bread and four farthings in cash. When that is gone I'll have to go begging just like you. Even so I'll give you something." Then he divided the loaf into four parts, gave the apostle one of them and added a farthing.

St. Peter thanked him, went on, and once again crossed the soldier's way as a beggar but in a different guise. When the latter came along he begged him for a gift as before. Merry Andrew spoke the same as before, and again gave him a quarter of the loaf and a farthing.

St. Peter thanked him and went on, and for the third time, in another shape, he sat down as a beggar by the wayside, and addressed Merry Andrew. And even the third quarter of the loaf did Merry Andrew give him, and the third farthing.

St. Peter gave his thanks, and Merry Andrew went forth, and now he had no more than a quarter of the loaf and one farthing left. With that he went into an inn, ate the bread, and used the farthing to order some beer to go with it. When he was ready, he journeyed onwards, and again St. Peter, this time disguised as a discharged soldier, stopped him saying,

"Good day, comrade, can you give me a piece of bread and a farthing for a drink?"

"Where am I to get it?" answered Merry Andrew. "I've got my discharge and nothing else but a loaf of army bread and four farthings in cash. I met three beggars on the road and gave each of them a quarter of my bread and one farthing. The last quarter I ate in an inn, and with the farthing I bought myself a drink. Now it's all out, and if you haven't anything left either, we could go begging together."

"No," said St. Peter, "we needn't go quite as far as that. I know a little about healing and with that I should earn enough to provide for myself."

"Well, I know nothing about that," said Merry Andrew, "so I must go begging all by myself."

"Just come with me," said St. Peter, "and if I earn anything, you shall have half of it."

"That's fair enough," said Merry Andrew. And so they set out on their way together.

Then they came to a peasant's cottage where they heard heart-rending cries and lamentations. So they went in, and there a man was lying dangerously ill and almost dying. His wife was wailing and weeping loudly.

"Stop your wailing and weeping," said St. Peter. "I will make your husband whole again." He took an ointment out of his pocket, and cured the sick man immediately so that he could get up and was in perfect health again. With great rejoicing the man and his wife said, "How can we reward you? What shall we give you?"

St. Peter, however, would not take anything, and the more the peasant and his wife begged him to, the more he refused. But Merry Andrew nudged St. Peter, saying, "Do take something, we badly need it."

At last the peasant woman brought a lamb and told St. Peter that he really must take it but he wouldn't have it. Then Merry Andrew nudged him in the side and said, "Do take it, you silly devil, we could really do with it."

So finally St. Peter said, "All right, I will take the lamb, but I am not going to carry it. You must carry it if you want it."

"Don't worry," said Merry Andrew, "I'll carry it all right," and took it on his shoulder.

Then they set off and came into a forest. By then the lamb began to weigh Merry Andrew down, and being hungry he said to St. Peter, "Look, that's a nice place. There we might cook the lamb and eat it."

"I don't mind," answered St. Peter, "but I know nothing about cooking. If you want to do the cooking, there is a kettle for you. Meanwhile, I'll go and walk about a little till it is ready. But you mustn't start eating before I am back again. I'll make sure to be on time."

"Well, go then," said Merry Andrew, "I can cook and I'll manage all right."

Thereupon St. Peter went away, and Merry Andrew killed the lamb, made a fire, threw the meat into the kettle, and boiled it. The lamb was quite ready but still the apostle was not back yet. Merry Andrew took it out of the kettle, carved it, and found the heart. "That's supposed to be the best," said he and tasted it, but finally ate it all up.

At last St. Peter came back and said, "You may eat the whole lamb yourself. I'll just have the heart, give me that."

Then Merry Andrew took a knife and fork, and made as if he was anxiously looking about among the lamb's flesh, but could not find the heart all the same. Finally he said, "There just isn't one."

"Well, where can it be?" said the apostle.

"I don't know," replied Merry Andrew, "but look, what fools we both are looking for the lamb's heart and neither of us remembering that a lamb has no heart."

"Oh," said St. Peter, "that's a new one on me. Every animal has a heart, why shouldn't the lamb have one?"

"No, of course not, brother," said Merry Andrew. "A lamb just hasn't got a heart. Give it another thought, and you'll come to realize that it really hasn't got one."

"All right, all right," said St. Peter, "if there isn't any heart, then I needn't eat anything of the lamb, you can eat it all yourself."

"Well, what I can't eat now, I'll take along in my knapsack," said Merry Andrew, and he ate half the lamb and put the rest in his knapsack.

They went on, and then St. Peter made a stream of water flow across their path, and they had to wade through it.

St. Peter said, "You go ahead."

"No," answered Merry Andrew, "you go ahead," thinking as he did so, "If the water is too deep for him, I will stay back."

Then St. Peter strode through the water, and it only reached to his knees. Then Merry Andrew started to wade across, but the water rose and reached to his neck. Then he cried out, "Help, help, brother."

"Then will you confess that you have eaten the lamb's heart?" said St. Peter.

"No," answered Merry Andrew, "I haven't eaten it."

Then the stream swelled even higher and rose to his mouth.

"Will you now confess that you have eaten the lamb's heart?" said St. Peter.

"No, help, help, brother," cried the soldier.

So St. Peter asked once again, "Will you confess that you have eaten the lamb's heart?"

"No," answered Merry Andrew, "I haven't eaten it."

But St. Peter did not want to let him drown, so he made the water sink, and helped him across.

Then they went on and came to a kingdom where they heard that the King's daughter lay hopelessly ill. "Hey ho, brother," said the soldier to St. Peter, "This is a chance. If we cure her, we're made for life!" Suddenly, St. Peter did not walk fast enough for him. "Now swing your feet, brother," he said to him, "that we may get there in good time."

But whatever Merry Andrew tried to do to urge and drive him on, St. Peter walked slower and slower till they heard that the Princess was dead.

"That's the end," said Merry Andrew. "That comes of your sleepy kind of walk."

"You be quiet," said St. Peter. "I can do more than just cure the sick, I can bring the dead to life."

"Well," said Merry Andrew, "if that is so, then I am well pleased, but your feat should earn us at least half the kingdom."

Then they went to the royal palace where everybody was plunged into deep sorrow. However, when St. Peter told the King he would bring his daughter back to life, he was taken to her and said, "Bring me a kettle of water."

When it was brought, he ordered everybody out. Merry Andrew alone was allowed to stay with him. Then he cut off all the dead girl's limbs, threw them into the water, lit a fire under the kettle, and let them boil. When all the flesh had come off the bones, he took out the fine white bones, laid them on a table, and arranged and set them together in their natural order. When that was done, he stepped towards her and said three times, "In the name of the Most Holy Trinity, dead woman, arise!"

And at the third bidding the King's daughter arose, alive, whole and beautiful.

This made the King rejoice greatly, and he said to St. Peter "Demand your reward. Even if it is half of my kingdom, it shall be yours."

But St. Peter answered, "I desire nothing in return."

"Oh, holy simplicity!" thought Merry Andrew to himself, nudged his comrade and said, "Don't be so stupid! You may not want anything, but I need something."

St. Peter still refused to take anything but the King saw how eager the other was to have something, and ordered his treasurer to fill Merry Andrew's knapsack with gold.

Thereupon they went on their way, and when they came to a forest, St. Peter said to Merry Andrew, "Now we will divide the gold."

"Yes," he answered, "let's do that."

Then St. Peter divided the gold, and divided it into three heaps.

Merry Andrew thought to himself, "What a crazy idea he's got in his head now. He makes three lots, and there are only two of us!"

"Now I have divided it quite exactly," said St. Peter. "One share for me, one share for you, and one for the man who ate the lamb's heart."

"Oh, I ate that," answered Merry Andrew and swiftly pocketed the gold. "You can trust me when I say it."

"How can that be true?" said St. Peter. "Indeed, you said a lamb hasn't got a heart."

"Oh goodness, brother, what an idea! Of course a lamb has a heart like any other animal. Why should it be the only one to have none?"

"Well, all right, all right," said St. Peter, "keep the gold yourself, but I will not stay with you any longer. I will go my way alone."

"Please yourself, brother," answered the soldier. "Good-bye and farewell."

Then St. Peter took a different road, and Merry Andrew thought, "It's just as well that he is trotting off, he certainly is a droll fellow!"

Though he now had enough money he did not know how to manage it, and he squandered it, gave it away, and was penniless again after a short time.

Then Merry Andrew came to a country where he heard that the King's daughter had died.

"Oh, ho!" he thought, "this may come in useful. I'll bring her back to life again, and see that I get paid for it handsomely." So he went to the King, and offered to raise the dead girl to life again.

The King had heard that a discharged soldier was roaming the land bringing the dead back to life and thought that Merry Andrew was the man. Something, however, made him unsure about him, and first he consulted his councillors. They said he might as well let him try it, since his daughter was dead anyway.

Then Merry Andrew had a kettle of water brought, and bade everyone go out. He cut off all the girl's limbs, threw them into the water, and made a fire underneath, just as he had seen St. Peter do. The water began to boil, and the flesh fell off. Then he took out the bones and laid them on the table, but he did not know the order in which to lay them and placed them in all the wrong directions.

Then he stood before them and said, "In the name of the Most Holy

Trinity, dead woman, arise!" He said it three times, but the bones did not stir. Then he said it thrice more but again in vain. "You treasure of a girl, get up," he cried, "get up, or it won't go well for you."

Suddenly St. Peter appeared in the shape of a discharged soldier. He came in through the window and said, "You godless man, what are you up to there? How can the dead maiden arise when you have thrown her bones about in such confusion?"

"Dear brother, I did it all as well as I could," said Merry Andrew.

Then St. Peter said, "I will help you once more out of your predicament, but let me tell you, if you try anything like this again, you will not get away with it. Nor may you either demand or accept anything from the King for having done this."

Then St. Peter laid the bones in the right order and said three times, "In the name of the Most Holy Trinity, dead woman, arise." And the King's daughter arose, healthy and beautiful as before.

Then St. Peter went away again through the window.

Merry Andrew was glad to see that it all had turned out so well, but still he was much vexed that he was unable to take anything for it.

"I would just like to know what that fellow has in his head, for what he gives with one hand he takes away with the other. It makes no sense!"

Now the King offered Merry Andrew whatever he might wish for, but he did not dare openly to take anything. However, by means of hints and cunning he got the King to have his knapsack filled with gold, and with that he went on his way.

As he was going out, St. Peter was standing at the gate and said, "Just look what kind of a man you are! Didn't I forbid you to take anything? And here you are, with your knapsack full of gold!"

"How can I help it when they put it in?" answered Merry Andrew.

"Well, let me tell you this," said St. Peter. "Don't you ever dare to try anything of the kind again, or it will fare ill with you!"

"Well, brother, don't worry. Now I have gold, why should I bother about washing bones?"

"Yes," said St. Peter, "and a long time that gold will last! But to prevent you from treading forbidden paths again, I will endow your knapsack with the power that anything you may wish to be in it shall be there. Farewell, you will never see me again."

"Good-bye," said Merry Andrew. "It's just as well you're going away. I certainly shan't follow you!" And he gave no further thought to the magic power which had been bestowed on his knapsack.

Merry Andrew travelled about with his money and squandered and threw it away like the first time. When he had no more than four farthings left, he happened to be passing by an inn, and thought, "The money must

go," and he ordered three farthings' worth of wine and one farthing's worth of bread.

As he was sitting there drinking, the smell of a roast goose rose up to his nose. Merry Andrew looked about and peeped, and saw that the landlord had two geese roasting in the oven. Then he recalled how his comrade had told him that anything he might wish to have in his knapsack would appear there. "Oh ho! I must try that with the geese," thought Merry Andrew. So he went outside the door and said, "I wish those two roast geese out of the oven and into my knapsack." So saying, he unbuckled his knapsack, looked in, and there they were! "It works!" he said. "Now I am a made man."

Then he went away to a meadow and took out the roast geese. Just as he was enjoying his meal, two journeymen came along and stared at the goose which was still untouched with hungry eyes. "One is enough for me," thought Merry Andrew, and called the two journeymen and said, "Take the goose, and eat it to my good health."

They thanked him, went with it to the inn, ordered half a bottle of wine and a loaf of bread, and began to eat.

The landlady was looking on and said to her husband, "Those two men are eating a goose. Do go and see if it's not one of ours from the oven."

The landlord ran up and saw it. The oven was empty! "You pack of thieves," he cried. "Pay for it at once, or I'll whip you with a hazel branch!"

The two travellers said, "We are no thieves. A discharged soldier out there in the meadow made us a gift of the goose!"

"You shan't make a fool of me," said the landlord. "The soldier was here, but he went out by the door like an honest fellow. I kept an eye on him. You are the thieves and shall pay!"

But they could not pay, so he took a stick and thrashed them out of the door.

Merry Andrew went his way and came to a place with a magnificent palace and a poor inn not far from it. He went to the inn and asked for a night's lodging, but the landlord would not take him in saying, "There's no more room, the house is full of noble guests."

"How surprising," said Merry Andrew, "that they come to you and not to the splendid palace."

"Indeed," answered the landlord, "it's quite an affair to spend a night there. Those who did try it never came out alive again."

"If others have tried it," said Merry Andrew, "I'll give it a try too."

"You leave well alone," said the landlord. "It may cost you your life."

"It won't be directly a matter of life and death," said Merry Andrew, "just give me the keys and a lot of food and drink to take along."

So the host gave him the key and food and wine. With that Merry Andrew went into the palace, had a good supper, and when he at last felt sleepy, he lay down on the floor, for no beds were there.

He soon fell asleep, but in the night he was awakened by a great noise. When he roused himself, he saw nine ugly devils in the room, who had formed a circle and were dancing round him.

"Well, dance as long as you like, but none must come too close," said Merry Andrew.

But the devils pressed on ever closer, and almost stepped on his face with their dirty feet.

"Be quiet, you devil phantoms!" he said but they behaved worse and and worse. Then Merry Andrew got angry and cried, "I will soon make you quiet!" and he got hold of a leg of a chair and struck out in the very midst of them. But nine devils against one soldier were too much in the end, and when he struck out at the one before him, the others at the back seized him by the hair and pulled at it unmercifully. "You pack of devils!" cried Merry Andrew. "This is too much, but just you wait! Into my knapsack, all nine of you!"

In a trice they were in it, and he buckled it up, and threw it into a corner. All at once everything was still, and Merry Andrew lay down again and slept till it was bright day.

Then came the innkeeper and the nobleman who owned the palace to see how he had got on. When they saw him safe and sound they were amazed and said, "Didn't the ghosts harm you?"

"Certainly not," said Merry Andrew. "I've got them, all the nine of them, in my knapsack! You may now live in your palace quite at ease. No one will ever haunt it again."

The nobleman thanked him, gave him rich presents, and asked him to remain in his service, saying he would take care of him for the rest of his life.

"No," answered Merry Andrew. "I am used to wandering about, I will move on."

So he went away, and stepped into a blacksmith's yard, laid the knapsack with the nine devils in it on the anvil and asked the blacksmith and his apprentices to give it a good pounding. Then they pounded with their big hammers for all they were worth so that the devils raised a most pitiable howl.

When he opened his knapsack again, eight devils were dead, but one, who had been sitting in a crease, was still alive, slipped out, and went back to Hell.

Then Merry Andrew travelled about the world for a long time, and there would be a great deal to tell about him if only one knew. But at last he grew old and began to think about his end. So he went to a hermit who was known to be a pious man and said to him, "I am tired of roaming about and now want to strive to get into the kingdom of Heaven."

The hermit replied, "There are two roads, one wide and pleasant leading to Hell, the other, narrow and rough, leading to Heaven."

"I would be a fool," thought Merry Andrew, "to take the narrow, rough road."

So he set out and went the wide and pleasant way, and finally came to a big black gate, which was the gate of Hell. Merry Andrew knocked, and the porter looked to see who was there. But when he saw Merry Andrew he was terrified, for he happened to be the very ninth devil who had been shut up in the knapsack and had got away with a black eye. He quickly pushed the bolt in again, and ran to the chief of the devils, and said, "There is a fellow outside with a knapsack and wants to come in, but for the life of you don't let him in, or he will wish the whole of Hell into his knapsack. Once he had me pitilessly pounded in it."

So they shouted out to Merry Andrew that he should go away again.

"If they don't want me here," he thought, "I will see if I can find a lodging in Heaven, after all, I've got to stay somewhere!"

So he turned about, and went on till he got to the gate of Heaven. He knocked at it and St. Peter happened to be there. Merry Andrew recognized him at once and thought, "Here I find an old friend of mine, I should get on better."

But St. Peter said, "You would like to get into Heaven, wouldn't you?"

"Please let me in, brother," pleaded Merry Andrew. "I must get in somewhere. If they had taken me in in Hell, I shouldn't have come here."

"No," said St. Peter, "you shan't get in here."

"Then, if you won't let me in, take your knapsack back, for I won't have anything at all of yours any more," said Merry Andrew.

"Well, give it here," said St. Peter.

Then Merry Andrew gave him the knapsack through the bars, and St. Peter took it and hung it beside his seat. Then Merry Andrew said, "Now I wish myself inside my knapsack!" In a trice, he was inside it, and sitting in Heaven, and St. Peter had to let him stay there.

RUMPELSTILTSKIN

There was once a miller, who was poor but he had a beautiful daughter.

Now it happened one day that he had to speak to the King and, in order to gain in importance, the stupid miller said to him, "I have a daughter who can spin straw into gold."

The King said to the miller, "That is skill after my heart. If your daughter is as clever as you say she is, bring her tomorrow to my palace, I will put her to the test."

So there was the poor miller's daughter, and for the life of her she did not know what to do. She had no idea how straw could be spun into gold.

Nevertheless the girl was brought to the King the next day and he led her into a roomful of straw. He gave her a spinning wheel and said, "Now get down to work at once. And if you have not spun this straw into gold by the morning, you shall die!" Whereupon he locked the room, and left the girl there all alone.

The miller's daughter thought only of her fate. She was sure to die since she could not spin the straw into gold. Then she began to cry. Suddenly the door flew open, a tiny wee little man came in and said, "Good evening, Mistress Miller. Why are you crying so bitterly?"

"Alas," answered the girl, "I am to spin gold out of straw, and don't know how to do it."

Said the dwarf, "What will you give me if I spin it for you?"

"My necklace," said the girl.

The dwarf took the necklace, sat down at the wheel and whirr, whirr,

whirr, three turns, and the spool was full of gold. Then he put on another and, whirr, whirr, whirr, three turns, and the second spool was full of gold, too. And so he went on until the morning when all the straw was spun and all the spools were full of gold.

At sunrise the King came, and when he saw the gold, he was amazed and overjoyed but his heart only grew more greedy for gold. He took the miller's daughter into a larger room full of straw, and ordered her to spin it into gold by the next morning if she valued her life.

The girl wept again but, as before, the door opened again and the little man appeared and said, "What will you give me, if I spin the straw into gold for you?"

"The ring on my finger," answered the girl.

The dwarf took the ring and began to turn the wheel again. By morning he had spun all the straw into glittering gold.

The King was delighted beyond measure, but he still was not satisfied with the gold he had. So he took the miller's daughter to another, much larger room full of straw and said, "You must spin all this into gold during the night. If you succeed you shall become my wife."

"Even if she is a miller's daughter," thought the King, "I shall not find a richer wife in the whole world."

When the girl was alone, the dwarf came again for the third time and said, "What will you give me if I spin the straw for you this time?"

"I have nothing left to give," answered the girl.

Then the dwarf said, "You must promise me your first child when you become Queen."

"Who knows how it will all end," thought the miller's daughter. And, since there was no other way to help her out of her trouble, she promised the dwarf what he asked for. In return, he once more spun the straw into gold.

When the King came in the morning and found everything done according to his wishes, he married her and so the miller's fair daughter became Queen.

A year later, she brought a fine child into the world. She had forgotten all about the man, when, all of a sudden, he entered her chamber and said, "Now give me the child you promised."

The Queen was frightened and offered the little man all the treasures of the kingdom if he would let her keep the baby. But the dwarf said, "No, a living thing is dearer to me than all the treasures of the world."

Then the Queen began to lament and cry so much that the little man took pity on her. "I will give you three days," he said. "If by that time you have discovered my name, you shall keep your child."

Now the Queen thought all night long of all the names she had ever heard, and sent out messengers all over the country to inquire far and wide for any other names there still might be.

When the little man appeared the following day, she began with Caspar, Melchior, Balthazar, and gave all the names she knew one after the other. But to every one of them the little man said, "That's not my name."

On the second day she had inquiries made in the neighbourhood to find out what names people had, and she recited to the little man the most uncommon and the queerest names she had heard. "Is your name Ripbeast or Muttonchop or Spiderlegs?" But to each of these he said, "That's not my name."

On the third day one messenger returned and said to her, "I could not find a single new name but, as I was walking round the edge of the forest, at the foot of a high mountain which is very remote, I saw a little house. There was a fire burning in front of it and quite a ridiculous little man was jumping around the fire, hopping on one leg and singing:
"Today I bake, tomorrow I brew,
The next I'll fetch the child from the Queen:
Oh, how glad I am that no one knew
That my name is Rumpelstiltskin."

You can imagine how overjoyed the Queen was to hear the name. Then, only a moment later, the dwarf came in and asked, "Now, Lady Queen, what is my name?"

At first she asked, "Is your name Conrad?"

"No,"

"Is it Harry?"

"No."

"Can it be that you are called Rumpelstiltskin?"

"The devil told you! The devil told you!" screamed the dwarf, and in his anger plunged his right leg so deep into the ground that he went down to his waist. Then in his rage he seized his left leg with both hands and tore himself in two.

THE TWO BROTHERS

Once upon a time there were two brothers, one rich and the other poor. The rich brother was a goldsmith, an evil-hearted man; the poor brother earned his living by making brooms, and was good and honest. The poor brother had two children, twin-brothers, who were as alike as two peas. Now and then the two boys would go to their rich uncle's house and, once in a while, they got something to eat from the leftovers.

One day, as the poor man went into the forest to fetch brushwood, he happened to see a bird that was of solid gold and more beautiful than any he had ever set eyes upon. He picked up a pebble, threw it at the bird, and was lucky enough to hit it. But only one golden feather fell, and the bird flew away.

The man picked up the feather and brought it to his brother, who looked at it and said, "This is pure gold," and gave him a lot of money for it.

On another day, the poor brother climbed a birch-tree to cut off a few branches. Then the same bird flew out of it and, having searched further, the man found a nest with an egg in it that was made of gold. He took the egg home with him and brought it to his brother, who said again, "It's pure gold," and gave him what it was worth.

At last the goldsmith said, "I should like to have the bird itself."

The man went to the forest for the third time, and again he saw the golden bird sitting in the tree. So he picked up a stone and threw it at the bird and brought it down and took it to his brother, who gave him a huge pile of money for it. "Now I have something to go on with," he thought and went home well content.

The goldsmith was crafty and cunning, and knew only too well what kind of a bird it was. He called his wife and said to her, "Roast me the bird, and take care that none of it gets lost. I wish to eat it all myself." It was no ordinary bird, but so wonderful that whoever ate its heart and liver would find a gold piece under his pillow every morning. The wife got the bird ready, stuck it on a spit, and roasted it.

However, it so happened that just as the wife had to leave the kitchen to do some other work, the children of the poor broom-maker came running in, saw the spit and turned it round a few times. When two small pieces fell off the bird into the pan, the one said, "We can eat those few bits, no one will notice." Then, as they were eating, the goldsmith's wife appeared and seeing they were eating something she said, "What is it you are eating?"

"A few bits that have dropped off the bird," they answered.

"That was the heart and the liver," said the woman terrified. So that her husband should not miss anything and get angry, she quickly killed a cockerel, took out the heart and liver, and put them into the golden bird.

When it was ready, she served it to the goldsmith who ate it all himself and left nothing. The next morning, however, when he looked under his pillow hoping to find the gold piece, there was no more there than at any other time.

The two boys didn't know what good fortune had been theirs. The next morning, when they got up, something dropped with a tinkling noise on to the floor, and when they picked it up, there were two gold pieces. These they brought to their father, who was astonished and wondered how it could have come about. But when next morning they found another two, and so on every day, he went to his brother and told him the strange story.

The goldsmith knew at once what had happened. The boys had eaten the golden bird's heart and liver. In order to have his revenge, the envious and wicked man said to his brother, "Your children are in league with the Evil One. Don't accept the gold, and don't tolerate them any more in your house, for he has them in his power and will bring ruin to you."

The boys' father was afraid of the Evil One and, hard as he found it, he led the twins out into the forest and with a sad heart left them there.

The two children ran about the forest trying to find their way home, but they couldn't, and in the end got completely lost. At last, they came upon a huntsman who asked, "Whose children are you?"

"We are the poor broom-maker's boys," they answered, and told him that their father didn't want to keep them in his house because there was a gold coin lying under their pillow every morning.

"Well," said the huntsman, "that in itself is nothing bad as long as you stay honest and do not start idling about and become lazy-bones."

The good man liked the children and, as he had none of his own, he took them into his house and said, "I will take the place of your father and bring you up." He taught them the craft of the huntsman, and the gold coins which each of them found every morning, he kept for them for the future.

When they grew up, their foster-father took them into the forest one day and said, "You shall do your shooting test today and, if you are successful, you will become hunters."

They went with him to lie in wait and stayed a long time but no game appeared. The huntsman looked up above him and seeing a flock of snow-geese flying in a triangle said to one of the boys, "Now bring down one from each corner." He did so and thus passed his test.

Soon afterwards yet another formation of geese came flying past in the form of a figure two. Now the foster-father bade the other boy bring down one from each corner, and his trial-shot was also successful. The foster-father said, "I now release you from your apprenticeship. You are accomplished huntsmen."

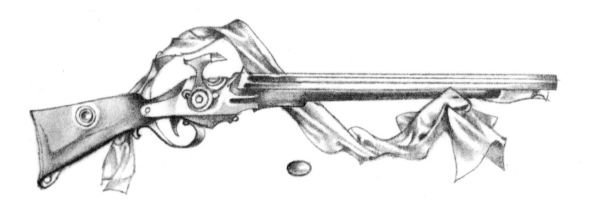

Afterwards, the two brothers went further into the forest together, took counsel and came to an agreement. In the evening as they sat down to supper, they said to their foster-father, "We will not touch the wine, nor take a single morsel of food until you have granted us a favour."

"What is your request then?" he asked.

They answered, "We have now learnt our craft, and must try our luck in the world. Give us leave to go on our way."

Then the huntsman said with pleasure, "You talk like honest huntsman. That which you yearn for has also been my wish. Go on your way, you will prosper." Then they ate and drank merrily together.

When the day came for the boys to leave, the foster-father presented both of them with a good rifle and a dog, and let them take as many saved gold coins as they wanted. Then he accompanied them part of the way and, during the leave-taking, gave them a bright and shiny knife and said, "If you ever part, thrust this knife into a tree at the cross-roads. The one that comes back will see by this knife how his absent brother has prospered, for the blade will go rusty if he dies, but as long as he is alive, it will stay bright."

The two brothers went further and further away, and came into a forest which was so large that they found it impossible to come out of it in one day. So they stayed there overnight and ate what they had in their hunting pouches. But on the second day they didn't reach the end of the forest either. As they had nothing to eat one of them said, "We'll have to shoot something, or go hungry." He loaded his gun and looked around. As an old hare came running past he raised the gun, but the hare cried:

"Dear huntsman, let me live,
Two of my young to you I'll give."

And indeed, it at once sprang into the underwood and brought out two

young hares. But the little animals played so merrily and were so well-behaved that the huntsmen didn't have the heart to kill them. So they kept them, and the little hares followed close on their heels wherever they went.

Soon afterwards a fox came sneaking by, which they wanted to shoot, but the fox cried:

"Dear huntsmen, let me live,
Two of my young to you I'll give."

And indeed, he did bring two fox cubs, but the huntsmen could not kill these either. They put them with the hares for company, and they all followed on one behind the other.

Before long a wolf came out of the brushwood, the huntsmen levelled their guns at him, but the wolf cried:

"Dear huntsmen, let me live,
Two of my young to you I'll give."

The huntsmen added the two young wolves to the other animals, and they went along with them, too.

Then came a bear, who wanted to trot about alive a little longer, and cried:

"Dear huntsmen, let me live,
Two of my young to you I'll give."

The two young bears were added to the others, and now there were eight animals in the company.

Then, who should come but a lion, shaking his mane. The huntsmen weren't scared and aimed at him, but the lion also said:

"Dear huntsmen, let me live,
Two of my young to you I'll give."

He, too, brought two of his cubs along, and so the huntsmen had two lions, two bears, two wolves, two foxes and two hares which followed them.

However, this was not the way to ease their hunger, and they said to the foxes, "Listen you prowlers, get us something to eat, for you are crafty and cunning."

They answered, "Not far from here is a village from which we have stolen many a chicken. We will show you the way there."

They went into the village, bought themselves something to eat and also fed their animals. Then they went on. The foxes knew their way about the district very well, particularly where the chicken yards were, and so were able to show the huntsmen exactly where to go.

They wandered about awhile, but could find no place where they could stay together whereupon the huntsmen said, "There's no other way. We must separate." So they divided the animals between them and each got one lion, one bear, one wolf, one fox, and one hare. Then they took leave of each other, pledged each other brotherly love unto death and stuck the knife which their foster-father had given them into a tree. Then one went east and the other west.

The brother who had walked to the west with his animals came to a city where everything was covered in black crape. He went to an inn, and asked the innkeeper if he could give shelter to his animals. The innkeeper gave him a stable with a hole in the wall. The hare crept out and brought himself a cabbage; the fox brought himself a chicken and, when he had eaten it, a cock also. But the wolf, the bear and the lion being too big could not get out. The innkeeper led them to a place where a dead cow was lying on the grass so that they could eat their fill. And not until the huntsman had taken care of his animals did he ask the innkeeper why the city was draped with mourning crape.

"Because tomorrow our King's only daughter is going to die," said the innkeeper.

"Is she dangerously ill?" asked the huntsman.

"No," answered the innkeeper, "she is hale and hearty but even so she's got to die."

"But why?" asked the huntsman.

"There is a high mountain outside the city, where a dragon lives, and it must have a pure maiden every year, or it would lay waste the whole country. Now all the pure young maidens have been given up to it except one, and she is the King's daughter. However, there is no escape, she must be given up to it, and tomorrow is the day of the sacrifice."

The huntsman said, "Why don't they go and kill the dragon?"

"Alas," said the landlord, "so many knights have tried it but all have lost their lives. The King has promised his daughter in marriage to the man who conquers the dragon, and after his death the victor shall inherit the kingdom."

The huntsman said no more, but the following morning, he took his animals and climbed up Dragon's Hill with them. At the top was a small church, and inside on the altar stood three filled cups. An inscription lay beside them: "Whoever drinks from these cups shall become the strongest man on earth, and shall wield the sword that lies buried before the threshold."

The huntsman did not drink, instead he went out and sought the sword buried in the earth, but found it impossible to move it from its place. So he went in and drained the cups, and then he was strong enough to lift up the sword, and his hand was able to wield it with ease.

When the hour approached that the King's daughter was to be sacrificed to the dragon, she came accompanied by the King, the marshal, and the courtiers. She saw from afar the huntsman high above on Dragon's Hill and thought it was the dragon waiting for her. She hung back at first but since she knew the whole city would be destroyed if she didn't go on, she forced herself to continue her awesome journey. The King and the courtiers returned home full of grief, but the King's marshal waited behind to watch everything from a distance.

When the Princess got to the top of the mountain it was not the dragon but the young huntsman standing there. He tried to comfort her, and assured her he was going to save her. Then he led her into the church, and locked her in.

Before long the seven-headed dragon came with a loud roar. When he saw the huntsman, he was astonished and said, "What business brings you up here on the mountain?"

The huntsman said, "I have come to fight you."

The dragon replied, "So many knights have lost their lives here, and

I shall soon be rid of you, too." And the dragon breathed fire from its seven mouths. The fire should have set fire to the dry grass and the huntsman was expected to suffocate in the vapour, but the animals came at a run and trampled the fire out. Then the dragon rushed upon the huntsman, but he swung his sword so that it sang in the air and sliced off three of its heads. Then the dragon became really furious, reared itself up in the air, spat out flames of fire at the huntsman, and intended to rush at him, but the huntsman once more drew his sword and cut off three more of its heads. Then the monster lost most of its strength, and sank down intending to hurl itself at the huntsman yet again, but the huntsman, with the last of his strength, cut off its tail. Then

unable to fight any more, he called up his animals who tore the dragon to pieces.

Now that the fight was over, the huntsman unlocked the church door, went in and found the Princess lying on the floor unconscious. During the struggle she had been overcome by fear and terror. He carried her out and, when she came to again and opened her eyes, he showed her the dragon torn to pieces and assured her she was now free of it for ever.

She was overjoyed and said, "Now you shall become my dearest husband, for my father has promised me to the man who would slay the dragon." Then she took off her coral necklace and divided it among the animals as a reward, and the lion got the little golden clasp. Then she gave her handkerchief with her name on it to the huntsman, who went and cut the tongues out of the seven dragon's heads, and wrapped them in the handkerchief to keep them safe.

After this, as he felt so weak and tired from the fight and the fire, he said to the Princess, "We are both so faint and weary, we ought to sleep a little now." She agreed, and they lay down on the ground.

The huntsman said to the lion, "You shall keep watch, that no one attacks us in our sleep."

The lion lay by their side, but he, too, was tired from the fight, so he called to the bear and said, "Lie down beside me, I must sleep a little, but if anyone comes, wake me."

Then the bear lay down beside him, and he called to the wolf and said, "Lie down beside me, I must sleep a little, but wake me if anyone comes."

Then the wolf lay down beside him but he, too, was tired, so he called the fox and said, "Lie down beside me, I must have a little sleep, but wake me if anyone comes."

Then the fox lay down beside him but he, too, was tired, and so he called the hare and said, "Lie down beside me, I must have a little sleep, but wake me if anyone comes."

So the hare sat down beside him, but the poor hare was also tired, and fell asleep. Now the King's daughter, the huntsman, the lion, the bear, the wolf, the fox, and the hare, were all fast asleep.

However, the marshal whose duty it had been to watch, waited until all was quiet on the mountain. Then he plucked up courage, and climbed to the top and found the dragon dead on the ground, torn to pieces. Not far from it he found the King's daughter, the huntsman and all his animals in a deep sleep. And, because he was a bad and a wicked man, he took his sword and cut off the huntsman's head and seized the Princess in his arms and carried her down the hill.

When she woke up, she was frightened to find herself being carried by the marshal. The marshal said, "You are in my hands and you shall say it was I who killed the dragon."

"That I cannot do," she answered, "for it was the huntsman with his animals who did it."

He drew his sword and threatened to kill her, if she didn't obey him. So she was forced to promise she would say anything he wanted her to. Then the marshal brought her before the King who was beside himself with joy when he saw his child whom he believed to have been torn to pieces by the monster.

The marshal said to him, "I have slain the dragon and delivered the Princess. The entire kingdom, therefore I demand, and her hand in marriage, as was promised."

The King asked his daughter if what the marshal said was true.

"Yes," she answered, "it is true. But I shall make it a condition that the wedding shall not take place before a year and a day is out." For she hoped to hear from her beloved huntsman during that time.

On Dragon's Hill, the animals were still lying asleep by the side of their dead master. A big bumble-bee came and sat on the hare's nose, but the hare knocked it off with his paw, and slept on. The bumble-bee came a second time, but again the hare knocked it off and went on sleeping. Then it came for the third time and stung him on the nose, and that woke him up! As soon as the hare was awake, he woke the fox, the fox woke the wolf, the wolf woke the bear, and the bear woke the lion. And when the lion awoke and saw that the Princess was gone and his master dead, he started roaring terribly and cried, "Bear, why didn't you wake me?" The bear asked the wolf, "Why didn't you wake me?" and the wolf asked the fox, 'Why didn't you wake me?" and the fox asked the hare, "Why didn't you wake me?" The poor hare all alone did not know what to say in reply, and the blame remained with him.

They were about to set upon him, but he begged them saying, "Don't kill me. I will bring our master back to life again. I know of a mountain on which a root grows, and whoever has it placed in his mouth will be cured of any illness and healed of any wound. But the mountain is two hundred hours distant."

"You must run there and back in twenty-four hours," said the lion, "and bring the root back with you."

The hare galloped away, and in twenty-four hours he was back again bringing the root with him. The lion put the huntsman's head on again and put the root in his mouth. Immediately the heart started beating and life was restored. The huntsman was horror-struck when he did not see the maiden beside him, and thought, "She must have gone away while I was sleeping in order to get away from me."

The huntsman was sad and wandered about the world and let the animals dance before people. It so happened that after exactly one year had passed, he came back again to the very same city where he had saved the King's daughter from the dragon, and this time he found the city draped in crimson cloth. He asked the innkeeper, "What does this mean? A year ago, the city was draped in black crape. What does the crimson cloth signify?"

The innkeeper answered, "A year ago, our King's daughter should have been sacrificed to the dragon, but the marshal fought it and killed it and tomorrow their wedding is to be celebrated. That's why the city is draped in crimson for rejoicing."

The next day when the wedding was to have taken place the huntsman said to the innkeeper, "Would you believe it if I told you that I shall eat bread from the King's table today?" "Nay, I wouldn't," said the innkeeper. "I would rather bet you a hundred gold pieces that you won't."

The huntsman accepted the wager, and laid down a pouch with a hundred gold pieces in it. Then he called the hare and said, "Go to the palace and fetch me some of the bread that the King is eating."

Now the hare was the smallest and could not pass the order on to anyone else, but had to go himself. "Alas," he thought, "when I leap along the streets all alone, the butcher's dogs will chase me." As he had guessed, so it happened. The dogs chased him and wanted to tear his fur for him. But he sprang away and found shelter in a sentry-box without the soldier noticing. Then the dogs came and wanted to chase him out, but the soldier struck them with his rifle-butt so that they ran off barking and howling.

When the hare saw that the coast was clear, he sprang towards the royal palace, and straight to the King's daughter, sat down under her chair, and scratched her foot. Then she said, "Off with you!" thinking it was her dog. The hare scratched her foot for the second time, and she said again, "Off with you!" thinking it was her own dog. But the hare would not be put off, and scratched for the third time. Then she looked down and recognized the hare by his collar. She took him on her lap, carried him into her chamber, and said, "Dear hare, what do you want?"

He answered, "My master, who killed the dragon, is here and has sent me to ask for bread from the King's table."

Then the Princess was full of joy, and she had the baker come and ordered him to bring the bread from the King's table.

The little hare said, "But the baker must also carry it there for me, so that the butcher's dogs may do me no harm."

So the baker carried it for the hare as far as the door of the inn, then the hare got up on his hind legs, took the bread into his forepaws and brought the loaves to his master.

Then the huntsman said to the innkeeper, "See, the hundred gold pieces are mine." The innkeeper was astonished but the huntsman went on, "The King's bread I have, but I will also eat from the King's roast."

The innkeeper said, "Indeed, I would like to see that." But he was no longer keen on betting. The huntsman called the fox and said, "My little fox, go to the palace and fetch me the roast such as the King eats."

The red fox knew how to slink along the sides of the streets and round corners without being seen by a single dog. Soon he had sat down under the Princess's chair and was scratching her foot. She looked down and recognized the fox by his collar, took him into her chamber with her, and said, "Dear fox, what do you want?"

The fox answered, "My master, who killed the dragon, is here and sent me to ask for a roast such as the King eats." Then she bade the cook come, and he had to prepare the joint the way the King ate it, and carry it for the fox as far as the door of the inn. Then the fox took the roast, and brought it to his master.

"You see," said the huntsman to the innkeeper, "bread and meat are here, but I will also have vegetables such as the King eats."

Then he called the wolf and said, "Dear wolf, go to the palace and fetch me vegetables such as the King eats."

Then the wolf went directly to the palace, because he was afraid of no one, and when he got to the Princess's chair he pulled at her dress from behind so that she had to look round. She recognized him by his collar and took him with her into her room, and said, "Dear wolf, what do you want?"

He answered, "My master, who killed the dragon, is here, and I am to ask for some vegetables such as the King eats."

She bade the cook come again and had him prepare some vegetables just as the King ate them, and he had to carry them for the wolf as far as the door. There the wolf took the dish from him and brought it to his master.

"You see," said the huntsman, "now I have bread, meat and vegetables, but I will have a pudding as well, one that the King likes to eat."

Then he summoned the bear and said, "Dear bear, you are fond of licking something sweet. Go to the palace and fetch me a pudding that the King likes to eat."

The bear ambled to the palace, and everyone got out of his way. But when he came to the sentries, they held their rifles at the ready, and would not let him pass into the royal palace. So the bear raised himself up on his hind legs, slapped the sentries with his paws with such a force that the whole guard ran away. Then he went straight to the King's daughter, placed himself behind her and growled a little. When she looked round she recognized the bear, bade him follow her into her chamber and asked, "Dear bear, what do you want?"

He answered, "My master, who killed the dragon, is here, and I am to ask for a sweet pudding such as the King eats."

Then she had the pastry cook come, told him to bake a sweet pudding that the King liked and to carry it for the bear as far as the door of the inn. There the bear first licked up the sugar plums which had fallen off, then took the bowl and brought it to his master.

"Behold," said the huntsman to the innkeeper, "now I have bread, meat, vegetables, and a pudding, but I will also drink wine, the same wine as the King."

He called the lion and said, "Dear lion, you also like a good drop of wine. Go and fetch me wine such as the King drinks."

So the lion tramped through the streets and the people ran away from him, and when he came to the sentries they wanted to bar his way, but he roared once, and everyone sprang aside. The lion went to the royal chamber, and knocked on the door with his tail. Then the King's daughter came out and got a fright when she first saw the lion, but she recognized him by the golden clasp from her necklace and bade him come with her into her chamber. She said, "Dear lion, what do you want?"

He answered, "My master, who killed the dragon, is here, and I am to ask for wine such as the King drinks."

Then she bade the cupbearer to give the lion the same wine that the King drank.

The lion said, "I will go along and see that I get the right wine." He went down with the cupbearer, and when they came to the cellar, the cupbearer drew him the rough wine that the King's servants drank.

But the lion said, "Wait! I want to taste the wine first." He drew himself half a measure and swallowed it down. "No," he said, "that's not the right kind."

The cupbearer looked at him, and was about to give him wine from another cask, which was for the King's marshal when the lion said, "Wait! I will try the wine first." So he drew himself half a measure and drank it. "This is better, but still not right."

Then the cupbearer got angry and said, "What does such a stupid beast understand about wine?" But the lion gave him a blow behind the ears that felled him roughly to the ground and when the cupbearer had picked himself up again, he led the lion in silence to a special, small cellar where the King's wine lay and from which no ordinary man had yet drunk.

The lion drew himself half a measure, and tasted it. Then he said. "This is very likely the right kind," and bade the cupbearer fill six bottles. Then they went upstairs but when the lion got out of the cellar into the open, he staggered from one side to the other, and was a little bit drunk. The cupbearer had to carry the wine for him as far as the door of the inn. There the lion took the basket in his mouth and brought the wine to his master.

The huntsman said, "Now I have bread, meat, vegetables, a pudding and wine such as the King has. Now I will have a banquet with my animals." And he sat down, ate and drank, and gave the hare, the fox, the wolf, the bear and the lion something to eat and drink from it and they all made merry, for he saw that the King's daughter still loved him. And when the feast was over, he said to the innkeeper, "I have eaten and drunk as the King eats and drinks, and now I will go to the King's court and marry the King's daughter."

The innkeeper asked, "How can you do that, when she already has a bridegroom, and the marriage is being celebrated today?"

Then the huntsman pulled out the handkerchief which the King's daughter had given him on Dragon's Hill, and in which the monster's seven tongues were tied, and said, "What I hold in my hand will help me to accomplish that."

Then the innkeeper inspected the contents of the handkerchief, and said, "I may believe anything, but I won't believe this. I am willing to wager my house and home on it."

Then the huntsman took a pouch with a thousand gold pieces in it, placed it on the table, and said, "This I wager against you."

The King at the royal table asked his daughter, "What did all the wild animals want which came to see you, and went in and out of my palace?"

She answered, "I may not tell you, but send a messenger down and let him fetch the master of those animals. You will be doing what is right."

So the King sent a servant to the inn to invite the stranger to the palace, and the servant came just as the huntsman had made the bet with the innkeeper. "See," said he, "the King has sent a servant and has given me an invitation to go to the palace. But I am not going just yet," and to the servant he said, "I beg His Majesty to send me royal clothes, a carriage and six, and servants to wait on me."

When the King received this reply, he said to his daughter, "What should I do?"

She said, "Let him come in the way he asks, and you'll be doing what is right."

So the King sent the huntsman royal clothes, a carriage and six, and servants to wait on him. When the huntsman saw the carriage and horses and servants coming, he said to the innkeeper, "See, now I am being fetched in the way I asked." And he put on the royal garments, took the handkerchief with the dragon's tongues in it with him, and drove to the King's palace.

When the King saw him coming, he said to his daughter, "How am I to receive him?"

She answered, "Go and meet him, and you will be doing what is right."

So the King went to meet him and led him upstairs, and the huntsman's animals followed him. The King seated him near himself and his daughter. The marshal, as bridegroom, sat on the other side, but he no longer recognized the huntsman.

Just then, the seven dragon's heads were brought in for display, and the King said, "The dragon's seven heads were cut off by the marshal, therefore I am giving him my daughter in marriage today."

Then the huntsman stood up, opened the seven mouths, and said, "Where are the dragon's seven tongues?"

The marshal was panic-stricken, turned pale and did not know what answer he should make. Finally, in his confusion he said, "Dragons have no tongues."

"Liars should have none either," said the huntsman, "but the dragon's tongues shall be the victor's tokens." He unfolded the handkerchief and there they lay, all the seven of them. And then he put each tongue back in the mouth to which it belonged, and it fitted exactly. Then he took the handkerchief on which the name of the Princess was embroidered, showed it to the maiden, and asked her to whom she had given it.

"To him who killed the dragon," she replied.

And then he called his animals, took the collar off each and the golden clasp from the lion, showed them to the Princess and asked to whom they belonged.

She answered, "The necklace and the golden clasp were mine. I divided them among the animals who helped overcome the dragon."

Then the huntsman said, "When I, exhausted from the fight, was resting and sleeping, the marshal came and cut off my head. Then he carried off the King's daughter and pretended that it was he who killed the dragon. That he is a liar I have proved with the tongues, the handkerchief, and the necklace."

Then he recounted how the animals had healed him by means of a magic root, and that he had wandered about with them for a year, and at last had come back here and had learnt about the marshal's treachery from the innkeeper.

The King then asked his daughter, "Is it true that this man killed the dragon?" And she replied, "Yes, it is true; now I can reveal the marshal's infamous deed, since the truth has come to light through someone else, for under threat of force I had to promise to keep silence. This was the reason why I made the condition that the marriage should not be celebrated till after a year and a day."

Then the King summoned twelve councillors to pronounce judgement on the marshal, and their verdict was that he should be torn to pieces by four oxen. So the marshal was executed, and the King gave his daughter to the huntsman and appointed him his viceroy.

The wedding was celebrated with much joy, and the young King sent for his father and his foster-father, and bestowed a great many treasures on them. Nor did he forget the innkeeper. He sent for him and said, "See, I have married the King's daughter, and your hearth and home are mine."

"Yes," said the innkeeper, "so it is only fair."

But the young King said, "I am merciful. You shall keep your hearth and home, and as to the thousand gold pieces, I'll make a present of them to you as well." Now the young King and Queen were of very good cheer and lived happily together. He often went out hunting, since it was his favourite pastime, and his faithful animals always went with him. Yet there was a forest nearby that was supposed to be haunted. Once in it, it was no easy

matter to get out again. The young King felt a great desire to hunt there, and begged the old King for his permission to go there.

He rode out with a large hunting party and, when he came to the forest, he saw a snow-white deer and said to his men, "Wait here till I return. I wish to give chase to that beautiful creature." And he rode into the forest after it, followed only by his animals.

The attendants waited till evening, but the young King did not come back. So they rode home and related to the young Queen what had happened.

The young King had ridden on and on after the beautiful animal, but was never able to overtake it. When he thought it was near enough to be shot at, it bounded away, and finally vanished altogether.

Suddenly he realized that he had ridden deep into forest. So he took his horn and blew it but received no answer, for his men could not hear it. Moreover, night was falling, and he saw that he couldn't get home that night. So he got off his horse, made a fire near a tree and resolved to spend the night there.

As he was sitting by the fire with his animals, he thought he heard a human voice. He looked round, but could see nothing. Soon afterwards he heard a groan as if from above and, looking up, he saw an old woman sitting in the tree who kept wailing, "Oh, oh, oh, how cold I am!"

He said, "Come down and warm yourself if you are cold."

But she answered, "No, your animals would bite me."

"They will do you no harm, granny," said the young King. "Just come down."

But the old woman was a witch, and she said to him, "I will throw down a wand from the tree. If you strike them on the back with it, they won't harm me." Then she threw down a small wand, and he struck them with it.

At once they lay still and were turned into stone. When the witch was safe from the animals, she touched the young King with a wand, too, and turned him to stone. Then she laughed, and dragged him and the animals into a ditch, where a number of similar stones already lay.

When the young King did not come back, the Queen's anguish and sorrow grew from day to day.

And then it so happened that the other brother, who had gone east when the two separated, came to the kingdom. He had been looking for work and had found none, so he had wandered around from place to place and had taught his animals to dance. Then, one day, it occurred to him that he should go and look for the knife which they had thrust into the tree trunk when they parted, that he might learn how his brother was faring.

When he got there, his brother's side was half rusty and half bright. He was alarmed and thought, "My brother must have met with some great misfortune, but perhaps I can still save him, for half the knife is still shiny."

Then he and his animals travelled westward, and when he came to the city, the sentries came to meet him, and asked if they were to announce him to his consort. They told him that the young Queen had been in great anxiety about his staying away so long, and was afraid he had perished in the haunted forest. To be sure, the sentries were convinced that he was the young King himself, so much did he look like him with his wild animals running after him.

Then he realized that they were talking about his brother and thought, "I had better pretend to be him, then I can rescue him more easily." So he let himself be escorted by the sentry into the palace and was received with great joy. The young Queen thought no other but that he was her husband, and asked him why he had stayed away so long.

"I lost my way in the forest," he answered, "and couldn't find my way out any sooner."

That night he was taken to the royal bed, but he laid a double-edged sword between himself and the young Queen. She didn't know what it was supposed to mean, but did not dare to ask.

He stayed at the palace for a few days, and meanwhile learnt everything concerning the haunted forest. At last he said, "I must hunt there once more."

The old King and the young Queen tried to dissuade him, but he insisted on going, and set out with a large hunting party. When he reached the forest, he fared just as his brother had done before him. He saw a white deer and said to his men, "Stay here, till I come back. I wish to chase that fine creature."

Then he rode into the forest, and his animals ran after him. He could not overtake the deer either and got so deep into the forest that he was forced to spend the night there. When he had made a fire, he heard somebody wailing overhead. "Oh, ho, ho, ho! I am so cold!" He looked up, and there was the same witch sitting in the tree.

"If you're cold," he said, "then come down, granny, and warm yourself."

"No," she answered, "your animals will bite me."

But he said, "No, they won't hurt you."

Then she cried out, "I am going to throw down a wand. Just hit them with it, and they won't harm me."

Hearing this, the huntsman no longer trusted the old woman, and said, "I won't hit my animals, you come down, or I'll come up and fetch you."

Then she cried, "What exactly are you going to do? You can do me no harm."

But he replied, "If you don't come, I'll shoot you down."

"Shoot away," she said, "I am not afraid of your bullets."

So the huntsman took aim and fired at her, but the witch was proof against lead bullets and gave a shrill laugh, and cried, "You shall not hit me yet!"

The huntsman knew how to trick her and he tore three silver buttons off his coat and loaded his gun with them. The witch was powerless against them and, the moment he pulled the trigger, she came hurtling down with a shriek. Then he placed his foot upon her and said, "Old witch, if you don't tell me this instant where my brother is, I'll seize you with both my hands, and throw you into the fire!"

Then the witch was really frightened, and begged for mercy, saying, "He's in a ditch with his animals turned to stone."

Then he forced her to go there and threatened her saying, "Old monkey, now you shall bring my brother and all his creatures lying there back to life again, or you end in the fire."

So she took a wand and touched the stones. Then his brother and his animals came to life again, and many others with them, merchants, woodcutters and shepherds. They got up, thanked him for their deliverance, and set out for home.

When the twin brothers saw each other again, they kissed each other, and rejoiced heartily. Then they seized the witch and put her in the fire, and when she was dead the forest opened up and became light and clear, so that the royal palace could be seen about three hours away.

The two brothers then went home together, and on the way told each other about their adventures. And when the one said that he was the King's viceroy over the whole country, the other said, "I know that, of course, for when I came to the city I was taken for you. I was shown all royal honours and the young Queen took me for her husband. I had to eat by her side and sleep in your bed."

When the other heard that, he got so jealous and angry that he drew his sword and struck off his brother's head. But when he saw him lying there dead with his red blood flowing, he was overwhelmed with regret. "My brother delivered me," he cried, "and in return I have killed him!" and loud were his lamentations.

Then his hare came and offered to fetch some of the special root that had once saved him, raced off and brought some back. The dead brother was brought back to life, and didn't even notice his wound.

Then they went on, and the young King said, "You look like me, wearing royal garments like myself, with the same animals following you. Let's go into the palace through opposite gates and thus appear before the old King from two sides at the same time."

So they separated, and the sentries came to the old King at the same time from both gates announcing that the young King with his animals had returned from the hunt.

"It is not possible," said the King, "the gates are an hour's distance apart."

Meanwhile, however, the two brothers entered the courtyard from both sides and mounted the steps. Then the King said to his daughter, "Well, can you say which is your husband? The two look exactly alike. I can't tell which is which."

Then she was in great distress and couldn't tell. At last she remembered the necklace she had given the animals, looked and found her little golden clasp on one of the lions. Then, in her joy, she cried, "The man who is followed by this lion is my true husband!"

The young King laughed and said, "Yes, that's the right one," and they sat down together, ate and drank and were merry.

That night when the young King went to bed he found the two-edged sword his brother had placed there. Then he realized how true to him his brother had been.

CLEVER GRETHEL

Once upon a time there was a cook whose name was Grethel. She wore shoes with red heels, and when she went out in them she would sway and turn, and think to herself, "You really are a pretty girl!" And when she came home, she would drink some wine for sheer joy. Then, since wine awakens the appetite, she would taste the best food that she had cooked until she had eaten her fill. She said to herself, "The cook must know what the food tastes like."

One day, her master said to her, "Grethel, I have a guest coming tonight. Get two fine chickens ready."

"Very good, sir," answered Grethel.

She killed the chickens, plucked them, scalded them in boiling water and stuck them on the spit. Then as evening approached, she put them on the fire to broil. The chickens began to sizzle and turn brown, but still the guest hadn't arrived.

Grethel called out to her master, "If the guest doesn't come soon I must take the chickens off the fire. It will be a frightful shame if they are not eaten when they are at their juiciest."

So the master said, "I will go myself and fetch my guest."

As soon as the master had turned his back, Grethel went to the spit and moved the chickens to one side and thought, "Standing so long near the fire makes one hot and thirsty. Who knows when those two will come! Meanwhile I'll run along to the cellar and have a drink of wine." She ran downstairs, held a jug to the tap of a cask and pulled herself a drink. "One good drop of wine asks for another," said Grethel and took another drink.

Then she went upstairs and put the chickens on to the fire again, spread some butter on them, and turned the spit around. The roasted chickens smelled so good, that Grethel thought to herself, "I should just make sure these chickens are quite alright. I think they should be tasted." She passed her finger over the fowls, licked her finger, and said, "Oh, my! The chickens are so good! Indeed, a wicked shame for them not to be eaten at once!"

She ran to the window to see if her master and his guest were coming yet, but saw nobody. She went to the chickens again, and thought, "One wing is going to get burnt, so it's better I cut it off and eat it." So she cut it off and found it very tasty.

When she had eaten it she thought, "The other wing must come off as well, or the master will notice there's something missing." When the two wings had been consumed, she went again to look for her master, but could not see him. "Who knows," she thought, "they may not come at all. Perhaps they have found somewhere else to eat." Then she said to herself, "Grethel, cheer up! Once a thing is started, it should be seen through to the end. Go and have another drink and eat up the chicken. When it's all gone you'll be at peace. A gift from God must not be wasted."

So she ran once more down to the cellar for some wine and ate up one chicken quite merrily.

When one chicken was inside her and her master still had not come, Grethel looked at the other one and said, "Where the one is, there should be the other. The two go together. What is right for one is right for the other." So she took the second chicken and it went the way of the first.

But as she was in the middle of her feasting, her master came back and called, "Hurry up, Grethel. My guest will be here directly."

"Very good, sir," answered Grethel, "I'll get it ready."

Meanwhile, the master looked to see if the table was properly laid, took the big knife with which he was going to carve the fowls, to sharpen it on a stone outside.

The guest in the meantime had come, and knocked politely and courteously at the door. Grethel ran to see who was there and, when she saw the guest, put her finger to her lips and said, "Keep quiet and make haste to get out of here. If my master catches you, you will be the worse for it. It's true he has invited you for supper, but only to cut off both your ears. Just listen, he is sharpening the knife now."

The guest heard the noise of a knife being sharpened and ran out of the house as fast as he could. Grethel was not idle either but ran screaming to her master, "Indeed, it's a fine guest you have invited!"

"Why, Grethel? What do you mean?"

"He has just taken both the chickens. I was about to serve them from the platter when he snatched them away and ran off with them."

"That's just like him," said the master feeling sorry about the loss of his fine fowls.

"If only he had left me one, at least there would be something for me to eat!"

He shouted after the guest to stop but the latter pretended not to hear. Then he ran after him with the carving knife still in his hand, crying, "Only one, only one!" meaning that the guest should leave him one chicken and not take both.

However, the guest thought he meant he should give up only one of his ears, and rushed headlong through the streets as if the devil were after him, intending to get both his ears safely home.

THE GOLDEN GOOSE

There was once a man who had three sons. The youngest was called Dumm-ling, which means Dunce or Simpleton. He was despised, made fun of and ignored at every opportunity.

It so happened that the eldest brother decided to go into the forest to cut wood and, before he left, his mother gave him a nice fine sponge cake and a bottle of wine so that he wouldn't suffer from hunger and thirst.

When he got into the forest he met a little wizened, grey-faced old dwarf who bade him good day and said, "Please give me a piece of the cake you have in your pouch and a drop of your wine. I am so hungry and thirsty."

But the clever son answered, "If I give you my cake and my wine, I shall have nothing left for myself. Go on your way." And he left the little man standing there and walked on.

Soon after, when chopping the tree he miscalculated, missed, and the axe cut into his arm so that he had to go home and have it bandaged. And this had been the little grey man's doing.

Thereupon the second son went into the forest and, like the eldest, his mother gave him a sponge cake and a bottle of wine. He, too, met the old grey dwarf who stopped him to ask for a piece of the cake and a drop of wine. But the second son also spoke quite brusquely and said, "Whatever you get, I shall lose. Go on your way!" and he left the dwarf standing there.

It was not long before he was punished. After dealing the tree a few blows he cut his leg and had to be carried home.

Then Dummling said, "Father, now let me go out and cut wood."

The father replied, "Your brothers have been injured doing it. Don't meddle with it. You know nothing about cutting trees."

But Dummling begged and begged till the father gave in at last and said, "Go there then, you'll be wiser from your mistakes."

His mother gave Dummling a cake, one that had been cooked with water and in ashes, and a bottle of sour beer. He came into the forest and also met the old grey dwarf.

The dwarf greeted him and said, "Give me a piece of your cake and a drink out of your bottle. I am so hungry and thirsty."

"I have only a plain cake baked in the ashes and sour beer," said Dummling. "But if you find it to your taste, we will sit down and eat together."

Then they sat down, and when Dummling unwrapped his plain cake, it had turned into a fine sponge cake and the beer into good wine. They ate and drank and the dwarf said, "You have a kind heart and are willing to share what you have with others, so I will bring good fortune to you. See that old tree there, go and cut it down, and you'll find something in the roots." Then the little man said good-bye.

Dummling went over to the tree, cut it down and, when it fell, a goose was sitting among its roots with feathers of pure gold. He lifted it out, took it with him and went to an inn to spend the night. Now the innkeeper had three daughters and when they saw the goose, they wondered what a miraculous bird it was, and positively yearned to possess one of its golden feathers.

The eldest thought to herself, "I am sure I'll find an opportunity to pull out just one feather," and when Dummling left the room for a while, she seized the goose by the wing but her fingers and hand stuck fast to it.

Soon after that the second daughter came with no other idea than to take a golden feather for herself. But as soon as she touched her sister she got stuck, too.

Finally, the third sister came with the same intention. Her two sisters shouted, "Keep away for heaven's sake, keep away!" But she didn't understand why she should not come in, and thought to herself, "Why shouldn't I be there, when they are there!" And she leapt forward, but scarcely had she touched her sister than she stuck to her. So they had to keep company with the goose all night.

The next morning, Dummling put the goose under his arm, and set out without as much as a thought for the three girls who were hanging on to it. They just had to follow him at a trot, now right, now left, as the fancy took him.

Out in the fields they met the parson and, on seeing Dummling's procession, he said, "Shame on you, you disgraceful girls! Why are you chasing this lad through the fields? It's indecent!"

With these words, he seized the youngest by the hand to pull her back. But the moment he touched her, he, too, got stuck, and had to run on behind.

Before long, the sexton came along and, seeing his master, the parson, following on the heels of three girls, was astounded and cried out, "Hey parson! What's the big hurry? Don't forget we have a christening today!" And he ran up to him and caught him by the sleeve but he too stuck fast.

As they were thus trudging along one behind the other, two peasants with their mattocks came across the field. The parson calling out to them, begged them to cut him and the sexton free. However, the moment they

touched the sexton, they stuck to him, and now there were seven of them running behind Dummling and his goose.

Next they came to a city where a King ruled who had a daughter, so sad that nobody could make her laugh. He had proclaimed that whosoever could make her laugh should marry her. When Dummling heard about this, he appeared before the Princess with his goose and its train of people. When she saw the seven people running one behind the other after him and his goose, she burst out into loud laughter, and laughed and laughed and couldn't stop.

Then Dummling asked for her to become his wife, but the King didn't like his would-be son-in-law, and made all kinds of excuses saying that he would first have to produce a man who could drink dry a cellar full of wine.

Dummling thought the grey dwarf might help him, so he went into the forest, and at the place where he had cut down the tree, he saw a man looking very miserable. Dummling asked him what was the matter.

The man answered, "I am terribly thirsty and cannot quench my thirst at all. Cold water doesn't agree with me. I did empty a cask of wine, but what's a drop like that on a dry stone?"

"Well, I can help you," said Dummling, "just come along with me, and you shall have your fill."

Then he took him into the King's cellar and the man fell upon the big casks and drank and drank until his hips ached, and before the day had passed had drunk the cellar dry.

Again, Dummling demanded his bride, but the King was annoyed to think that a low-born fellow, whom everyone called a simpleton, should walk off with his daughter. So he laid down new conditions. First he would have to produce a man who could eat up a mountain of bread. Without delay Dummling went straight into the forest. There, on the same spot as before, sat a man who was tightening his belt and looking the picture of misery.

He said to Dummling, "I've eaten a whole ovenful of grated bread but what good is that when one is as hungry as I am? My stomach remains empty, and I am tightening my belt to help stop the pangs of hunger, but I fear I shall starve to death."

Dummling was overjoyed to hear this and said, "Get up and come with me. You shall eat your fill."

He took him to the King's court. The King had all the flour in the whole kingdom brought to the palace, and a monstrous mountain of bread baked from it. Then the man from the forest stood before it and began to eat and, in a day, the whole mountain had disappeared.

For the third time Dummling asked for his bride, but the King again found an excuse and demanded a ship that could sail both on land and on water. "The moment you come sailing along in it, you shall have my daughter for your wife."

Dummling went straight into the forest and there he found the grey old dwarf. The dwarf said, "I've drunk and I've eaten for you, and I'll also give you the ship you need. I am doing all this because you once took pity on Then he gave Dummling the ship that could sail on both land and water, and when the King saw it, he could no longer refuse to give him his daughter.

The wedding was celebrated, and after the King's death Dummling inherited the kingdom and he and his wife lived happily ever after.

THE PEASANT'S WISE DAUGHTER

There was once a poor peasant who had no land, but merely a small hovel and an only daughter. One day the daughter said, "We should beg our lord the King for a little piece of newly-cleared land." When the King heard about their misery he even made them a gift of a little plot of grass land. She and her father dug it up and were going to sow a little rye and corn. They had almost dug and turned the field, when they suddenly found in the earth a mortar made of pure gold.

"Listen," said the father to the girl, "since His Majesty was so gracious and presented the field to us as a gift, we should give him the piece of gold in return."

The daughter would not agree to this, saying, "Father, we have the mortar but not the pestle. We must look for the pestle, too, so until then keep silent about it."

But he would not listen to her, took the mortar, carried it to the King and said he had found it on the heath. Then he offered it to His Majesty as a token of respect.

The King accepted the mortar and asked if he had found anything else. And the peasant said that he hadn't.

Then the King said he must produce the pestle, and try as the peasant would to convince the King that he did not have it, it availed him no more than if he had spoken to the winds. He was flung into jail and was to stay there until he produced the pestle.

The servants brought him bread and water every day, and then they heard the man cry out continually, "Alas, had I but listened to my daughter! Alas, had I but listened to my daughter!"

Then the servants went to the King and told him how the prisoner kept crying, and wouldn't eat or drink. The King ordered the servants to bring the prisoner before him and asked him, "What did your daughter say?"

"She said I shouldn't bring the mortar, or I should have to find the pestle as well."

"If you have such a clever daughter, let her come here."

So she had to come before the King, and he said that if she really was so clever, he would ask her a riddle. If she could solve it, he would marry her.

At once the daughter agreed to try and solve it. Then the King said to her, "Come to me not clothed, not naked, not riding, not driving, not in the road, and not off the road, and if you can do that, I will marry you!"

Then she went away and took everything off till she was naked, so she was not clothed; then she took a big fishing net and stepped inside it, and wrapped it all around her, so she was not naked. She hired a donkey, and tied the fishing-net on to its tail so that it had to drag her along in the net, and so she was not riding, and neither was she driving. Moreover, the donkey had to drag her in the rut, so that she only touched the ground with her toe, and thus she was neither in the road nor off the road. And when she came to him in that way, the King said that she had solved the riddle, and everything had been duly fulfilled. Then he released her father from prison, and took her as his wife, and put her in charge of all the royal possessions.

Several years passed, and one day it so happened that some peasants halted with their wagons in front of the castle, having sold all their wood. Some had oxen and others horses yoked to their wagons. There was one farmer who had three horses, and one of these gave birth to a young foal, which ran away and lay down between two oxen hitched to another wagon. When the peasants saw this they began to quarrel. The owner of the oxen wanted to keep the foal claiming it was the oxen who had given birth to it. And the other said no, his horse had had the foal and so it was his.

The quarrel came before the King, and his verdict was that the foal should stay where it had lain and so it was that the owner of the oxen got it, though he really had no right to it.

Then the other went away weeping and lamenting over his little foal. He had heard that the Queen was very gracious as she had also come of poor peasant stock. He went to her and begged her to help him to get his young foal back again.

She said, "If you promise me that you won't give me away, I will tell you what to do. Tomorrow morning, when the King is reviewing the guards, place yourself there in the middle of the road where he must pass by. Take a big fishing-net, and pretend you're fishing, and fish on in this way and shake out the net as if you had it full of fish." And she also told him what answer to give should the King ask him what he was doing.

The next day the peasant stood there and fished on dry ground. When the King passed by and saw the man, he sent his messenger to ask the foolish man what he was supposed to be doing.

"I am fishing," he answered.

The messenger asked how he could be fishing where there was no water. The peasant said, "It is just as easy for me to fish on dry ground as for two oxen to give birth to a foal."

The messenger went back and took the answer to the King. He ordered the peasant to be brought before him and said that this idea was not his, it had come from someone else. But the peasant would not confess. So they laid him on a heap of straw and beat him till he confessed that he had had the idea from the Queen.

When the King came home, he said to his wife, "Why have you been false to me? I don't want you as my wife any longer. Go back again to where you belong, to your peasant hut."

Yet he granted her one grace, that she should take with her the one thing that was most precious and dearest to her in the world.

"Yes, dear husband," she said, "if it is your order, I will do as you say," and she fell into his arms and kissed him and said she wanted to take him.

Then she had a strong sleeping potion made in order to drink a farewell to him. The King took a deep draught but she drank very little. Soon he fell into a deep sleep, and when the Queen saw it, she called a servant, took a fine white linen cloth and wrapped the King in it. Then the servants had to carry him to a coach and she drove him home to her little house. Then she laid him in her little bed, and he slept all through the day and night.

When he awoke, he looked round and said, "Dear heaven, where am I?" He called for his servants, but no servant was there.

Finally, his wife came to his bedside and said, "My dear Lord and King, you ordered me to take with me from the palace what I held best and most dear. I have nothing better and dearer than you, so I took you with me."

Tears rose to the King's eyes and he said, "Dear wife, you shall be mine and I yours," and he took her back with him to the royal palace, and they are probably still living there to this very day.

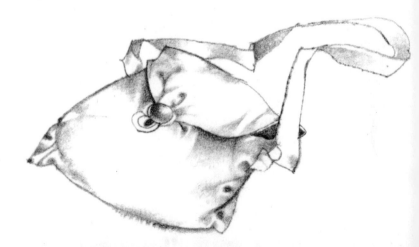

THE POOR MILLER'S BOY AND THE CAT

In a certain mill lived an old miller who had neither wife nor children. There were three boys who worked for him and once, when they had served him for many years, he called them and said, "I am old now and only fit to sit behind the stove. Set out for far countries and whichever of you brings me back the best horse, to him I will give the mill. In return he shall take care of me until my death."

The third of the lads, however, was the stable-boy, Hans, whom the others took for a simpleton. They grudged him even the chance of getting the mill, and thought anyway that he wouldn't really want it.

Then all the three set out together and, when they reached the edge of the village, the two said to simple Hans, "You may as well stay here, you will never in your life get even a nag."

All the same, Hans did go with them and, when it was night, they came to a cavern and there they lay down to sleep. The two clever lads waited till Hans was asleep, then they climbed out and left little Hans lying there. They thought what a fine clever thing they had done. But mind, even so, they shall not prosper!

When the sun rose, Hans woke up to find himself lying in a deep cavern. He looked around on every side and cried, "Oh dear, where am I?" Then he got up and clambered up out of the cavern, went into the forest, and thought, "Here I am all alone and deserted, how can I ever find a horse now?"

As the thought this, he met a small tabby cat which said in quite a friendly way, "Hans, where are you going?"

"Oh, you cannot help me," said Hans.

"I know very well what your wish is," said the little cat. "You want to find a handsome horse. Come with me and be a faithful servant to me for seven years, and I will give you one, such a beauty you have never seen in your life."

"Well, isn't this a strange cat," thought Hans. "But I will chance it and see if what she says is true."

She took him with her into her enchanted little house, and there she had none but kittens serving her. They leapt nimbly up and down the stairs, and were merry and cheerful. In the evenings, when they sat down to dinner, three of them made music; one played the bass-viol, the other the fiddle and the third put a trumpet to her mouth and blew up her cheeks for all she was worth.

When they had risen from the dining table, it was carried away and the cat said, "Now, Hans, come and dance with me."

"No," he replied. "I couldn't dance with a pussy-cat. I have never done such a thing in my life."

"So, take him to bed," she said to the cats.

Thus one of them lighted him on his way to the bed-chamber, one took off his shoes, another his stockings and, finally, one blew out the candle.

Next morning, they came again and helped him get out of bed. One put on his stockings, one tied his garters, one fetched his shoes, one washed him and another dried his face with her tail.

"That feels very soft," said Hans.

He, too, had to serve the cat, however, and chop wood into fine sticks every day. To do that, he was given an axe of silver, some wedges and a saw, also of silver, and a mallet of copper.

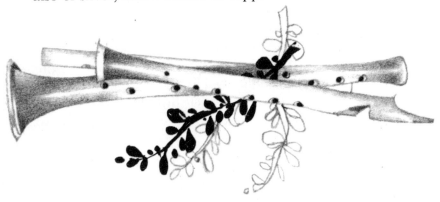

Well, he chopped the wood fine, stayed in the house, had his good meat and drink, but never saw anyone but the tortoiseshell cat and her servants. One day she said to him, "Go out and mow my meadow, and dry the grass." She gave him a scythe of silver and a whetstone of gold, but bade him return everything in good order again.

So Hans went and did as he had been bidden. This accomplished, he carried the scythe, the whetstone and the hay to the house, and asked if she was not yet ready to give him his reward.

"No," said the cat, "you must first do some more things for me. Here are planks of silver, a carpenter's axe, a square, and everything that is needed, all made of silver. With these you must build me a little house."

So Hans built the little house, and said that he had done everything now, and still had no horse. Even so, the seven years were gone like six months. Then the cat asked if he would like to see her horses, and Hans said he would. Thereupon she opened the little house for him and the moment she opened the door, there were twelve horses standing there. Oh, so proud, shiny and glistening that the heart in him rejoiced to see them.

The cat gave Hans something to eat and to drink and said, "Go home, I will not give you your horse now, but in three days time I will comme and bring it."

So Hans got ready to depart and she showed him the way to the mill. But in all the seven years Hans had been with her, the cat had not given him any new clothes, so he had to keep on the ragged old smock which he had worn when he first came and which had become much too small for him everywhere.

When he got home, he found the other two miller's boys there. They certainly had brought with them a horse each, only the one that belonged to the first was blind, and the other's was lame.

They asked him, "Where is your horse, Hans?"

"It will come in three days' time," said Hans.

They laughed, saying, "Well, Hans, where do you expect to get a horse from? That will be a beauty, for sure."

Hans went into the dining-room, but the miller said he should not sit down to eat with them, as his smock was so worn at the elbows and in rags that they would be ashamed should anyone call.

So they gave him a little food to eat outside and, when they went to rest in the evening, the other two did not allow him to lie in a bed. So in the end, Hans had to creep into the goose-house and lie down on some hard straw.

When he awoke, the three days had passed and there came a coach with six horses. Oh, how they shone! They were a delight to behold. A servant brought a seventh horse which was for the poor miller's boy.

Then a resplendent Princess stepped out of the carriage and went into the mill. This Princess was the little tortoiseshell cat whom poor Hans had served for the seven years.

She asked the miller where his lowliest servant was.

"He's in such rags and tatters that we cannot have him in the mill," said the miller. "He lies in the goose-house."

Then the King's daughter, for such she was, said that they should go at once and fetch him. So they fetched Hans out of the goose-house and he came holding his old smock together to cover himself.

Then the servant unpacked some magnificent garments, washed him and dressed him and, when he was ready, no king could have looked more handsome.

Then the Princess asked to see the horses brought by the other miller's boys and they brought the one horse which was blind and the other which was lame. Then she bade the servant bring the seventh horse, and the miller said that such a magnificent horse had never yet come into his courtyard.

"This is for the third miller's boy," the Princess said.

"Then it is he who must have the mill," said the miller.

But the Princess said to the miller that he was to have the horse and keep his mill as well. Then she took her faithful Hans, bade him sit in the coach, and drove off with him.

First, they drove to the little house which he had built with the silver tools but now it had become a great castle, and everything inside was of silver and gold. Then she married Hans and he was rich, so rich that he had enough money to last for as long as he lived.

No one should say that he who is foolish will never make good.

ALLERLEIRAUH

Once upon a time there was a King who had a wife with golden hair, and she was so beautiful that her equal was not to be found on earth.

Now it happened that she fell ill, and when she felt she was about to die she called the King and said, "If you wish to marry again after I am dead, do not take anyone to wife who is not just as beautiful as I am and who has not such golden hair as I have. This you must promise me." The King gave her his promise, and she closed her eyes and died.

For a long time the King was inconsolable and had no thought of marrying again. At length, however, his councillors said, "There is no other way, the King must get married again that we may have a Queen."

So messengers were sent out far and wide to seek a bride who would equal the late Queen in beauty. But there was none to be found in the whole world, and even if one had been found, there was none who had such golden hair. So the messengers returned home empty-handed.

The King had a daughter who was just as beautiful as her mother before she died, and she also had her mother's golden hair. When she had grown up, the King looked at her one day and saw that she was like his late wife in every way and suddenly he fell passionately in love with her. So he said to his councillors, "I will marry my daughter, for she is the living image of my late wife and anyway, I can find no bride to equal her."

The councillors were shocked when they heard this, and said, "God has forbidden that a father should marry his daughter. No good can come from such a sin, and the kingdom itself shall go to rack and ruin."

Even more shocked was the daughter when she learnt of her father's resolution, but she hoped to turn him away from his intention. So she said to him, "Before I grant your wish, first I must have three dresses. One as golden as the sun, one as silvery as the moon and one as radiant as the stars. Also, I demand a mantle, made from a thousand different pieces of fur sewn together, and every animal in your kingdom must give a piece of its skin for this purpose." What she really thought was, "It is quite impossible to procure all that fur, and thus I shall turn my father from his evil design."

The King, however, did not give up, and had the cleverest maidens in the kingdom weave the three dresses, one as golden as the sun, one as silvery as the moon and one as radiant as the stars. His huntsmen were ordered to catch every single animal in the whole of his kingdom and to take a piece of its skin. Thus a mantle was made of a thousand different kinds of fur.

At last, when everything was ready, the King had the mantle brought in, spread it out before her, and said, "Tomorrow is the wedding day."

The King's daughter now saw there was no longer any hope of turning her father's heart, so she made up her mind to run away. That night, when everyone was asleep, she got up and took three of her most precious things; a golden ring, a golden spinning-wheel and a golden reel. She pressed the three dresses—one like the sun, the other like the moon and the third like the stars—into a nutshell, put on the mantle made of all kinds of fur, and blackened her face and hands with soot. Then she commended herself to God and went away and walked the whole night until she came to a great forest. As she was tired, she sat down in a hollow tree, and fell asleep.

The sun rose and she slept on, and she was still asleep when it was broad daylight.

Then it so happened that the King whose forest it was came there hunting. When his dogs came to the tree, they sniffed and ran about barking. The King said to the huntsmen, "Well, go and see what kind of wild animal is hiding there."

The huntsmen obeyed his order and when they came back they reported, "There is a strange animal lying in the hollow tree, such as we have never seen before. There are a thousand furs on its skin, and it is lying asleep."

The King said, "See if you can catch it alive, then fasten it to the carriage and take it back to the palace."

When the huntsmen laid hold of the maiden, she woke up full of fright and cried out to them, "I am a poor child forsaken by father and mother, please have pity on me and take me with you."

Then they said, "Allerleirauh—which means furs-of-all-kinds—you will be useful in the kitchen. Just come along, you can sweep up the ashes."

So they put her in the carriage and drove home to the royal palace. There they showed her a small cupboard under the stairs where no light of day ever came, and said, "Hairy animal, here you can live and sleep." Then they sent her into the kitchen, where she carried wood and water, stirred the fire, plucked the poultry, picked the vegetables, swept up the ashes, and did all the hard work.

Thus for a long time Allerleirauh led a truly wretched life. Alas, fair princess, what is to become of you next!

However, it happened that a feast was to be held in the palace, and she said to the cook, "May I run upstairs for a while and look on? I will only stand outside the door."

The cook answered, "Yes, go on up there, but mind you are back here again in half an hour and sweep the hearth."

Then Allerleirauh took her little oil lamp, went into her cupboard, took off her dress of fur and washed the soot off her face and hands, so that her full beauty stood revealed again.

Then she opened the nut, and took out her dress which shone like the sun. Then, when she was ready, she went upstairs to the festival and everyone stepped aside for her to pass, for they did not know her and all of them thought she was no less than a king's daughter.

The King came to meet her, gave her his hand and danced with her and thought in his heart, "Never have my eyes seen anyone so beautiful!"

When the dance came to an end she curtsied and, as the King turned his head, she vanished and no one knew whither. The guards standing in front of the palace were called in and questioned, but none had seen her.

Meanwhile, Allerleirauh had run back to her cupboard, quickly taken off her dress, blackened her face and hands and put on her fur-mantle. When she came back to the kitchen, she was about to start her work sweeping the hearth, when the cook said, "Leave that alone till tomorrow, and make bread soup for the King. I, too, want to have a look upstairs; but don't let any hairs fall in, or you shall get nothing more to eat."

Then the cook went away and Allerleirauh made bread soup for the King as best she could. When it was ready, she went to her closet to fetch her golden ring, and put it in the bowl in which the soup was to be served.

When the dance was over, the King had the soup brought to him and ate it. It tasted so good that it seemed to him he had never eaten better soup in his life. When he came to the bottom, he found the golden ring lying there, and could not understand how it had got there. Then he ordered the cook to appear before him.

The cook was terror-stricken and said to Allerleirauh, "You must have let a hair fall into the soup. If that is so you shall get a beating."

When he appeared before the King, the King asked who had made the soup.

"I made it," answered the cook.

But the King said, "That is not true, for the soup was made in another way, and much better than usual."

So he answered, "I must confess I did not make it, it was made by the wild, hairy animal."

Said the King, "Go and send it up to me."

When Allerleirauh came the King asked, "Who are you?"

"I am a poor child who has no father and no mother."

Then the King asked, "What do you do in my palace?"

She answered, "I am only good enough to have boots thrown at my head."

He asked again, "How did you come by the ring which was in the soup?"
She answered, "The ring? I know nothing about it."

So the King learnt nothing, and had to send her away again.

Some time later, there was another festival and, as before, Allerleirauh begged the cook for permission to go and look on.

He answered, "Yes, but come back again in half an hour and make the King the bread soup he is so fond of."

So she ran into her cupboard and washed quickly. Out of the nut she took the dress that was as silvery as the moon, and put it on. Then she went upstairs looking like a king's daughter. The King came forward to meet her and was overjoyed to see her again and, as the dance was just beginning, they danced together. However, when the dance was over, she again disappeared so quickly that the King could not see where she had gone.

She hurried to her cupboard, made herself the hairy animal again and went into the kitchen to make the bread soup. When the cook had gone upstairs, she fetched the little golden spinning-wheel, put it in the bowl and the soup was poured over it.

Then the soup was taken to the King, who ate it and enjoyed it just as much as the time before. He sent for the cook and again he had to confess that it was Allerleirauh who had made it. Allerleirauh appeared before the King, but she answered that she was only good enough to have boots thrown at her head, and she knew nothing at all about the little golden spinning-wheel.

When the King held a feast for the third time, everything happened in just the same way as on the previous occasions.

But the cook said, "You are a witch, Fur-Skin. You always put something into the soup that makes it so good that the King likes it better than mine."

Yet, as Allerleirauh begged him so much, he let her off for half an hour as before.

This time she put on the dress which shone like the stars, and entered the hall. Again the King danced with the beautiful maiden and thought that she was more beautiful than ever before. And, while they were dancing, he slipped a golden ring on her finger without her noticing it. He had also given orders that the dance should go on for a very long time.

When it was over, the King would have held her fast by the hand but she tore herself loose, and sprang away so quickly among the guests that she vanished from his sight. She ran as fast as she could to her little cupboard under the stairs. But, as she had long overstayed her half hour, she had no time to take off her lovely dress and, instead, threw the fur-mantle over it. Nor did she, in her haste, make herself completely black, and one of her fingers remained white.

Then Allerleirauh ran into the kitchen, made the bread soup for the

King and, as soon as the cook was away, dropped the golden reel into it.

When the King found the reel at the bottom, he sent for Allerleirauh whereupon he noticed the white finger and saw the ring he had slipped on it while they were dancing. He grasped her by the hand and held her fast and, as she was trying to break loose and run away, the mantle of fur parted a little, and the star-dress shone forth. The King caught hold of the mantle and tore it off. Then her golden hair fell around her shoulders and she stood there in full splendour no longer able to hide herself. When she had washed the soot and ashes from her face she was more beautiful than anyone had ever seen on earth.

The King said, "You are my dear bride, and we will never part again!"

Whereupon their wedding was celebrated, and they lived happily ever afterwards.

THREE FORTUNE'S FAVOURITES

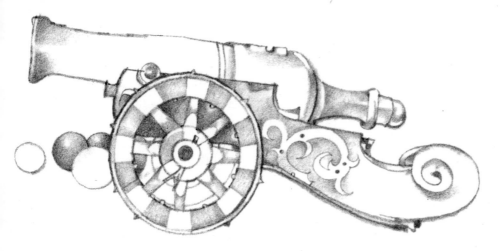

Once upon a time a father called his three sons to him and gave the eldest a cockerel, the second a scythe, and the third a cat. "I am old now," he said, "and my end is near, so I would like to provide for you before I die. Money I have none, and what I give you now seems of little worth, but it's up to you to make a sensible use of it. You only have to find a country where such things are still unknown, and your fortune is made."

After their father's death, the eldest set out with his cockerel, but wherever he went the cockerel was already well known. In every town he saw it from afar sitting on church steeples and turning with the wind. In the villages he could hear more than one crowing, and there was no one to be surprised at seeing the bird. Its reputation was not rare enough to make a fortune out of it.

At last, however, it did happen that he came to an island where the inhabitants had never heard of a cockerel and didn't even know how to divide the time. They knew, indeed, when it was morning or evening, but at night, unless they slept right through, no one knew how to tell the time.

"Look," said the eldest son, "What a gorgeous bird it is. It has a crown as red as a ruby on its head and wears spurs like a knight. In the night he will call you three times at certain intervals and, when it calls for the third time, the sun will be about to rise. When he crows in broad daylight, take warning and prepare for a change in the weather."

The people were highly pleased with this, they kept awake one whole night to listen, and were delighted to hear the cockerel calling the time, loudly and distinctly, at two, four and six o'clock. They asked the young man if the bird was for sale and what price he demanded for it.

"About as much gold as a donkey can carry," he answered.

"A mere pittance for such a precious creature," they called out with one voice, and gave him what he asked.

When he returned home a rich man, his brothers were astonished, and the second said, "Now, I will set out and see if I can sell my scythe and make such a bargain." At first this seemed impossible, for everywhere he went he met peasants with scythes as good as his over their shoulders. Yet at last, as luck would have it he, too, came to an island where the people had never heard of a scythe. When the corn was ripe, they placed cannons near the edge of the fields and shot it down. But it was a hazardous affair, many shots went far beyond, others hit the ears instead of the straw and shot them off. There was a great deal of waste and besides the noise was abominable.

Then the young man came and mowed it down so quietly and so quickly that the people gaped open-mouthed in sheer amazement. They were willing to give him whatever he demanded, and he took away a horse laden with as much gold as it could carry.

Now the third brother also wanted to find the right buyer for his cat. He fared just as the others. As long as he remained on the mainland he met with no success. There were cats all over the place and in such profusion that the newly born kittens were usually drowned.

Finally, he crossed over to an island in a ship, and there his luck was in.

It so happened that nobody there had ever seen a cat, though they were overrun with mice. The vermin danced on the tables and chairs regardless of whether the master of the house was at home or not. The people groaned in despair about the pests, even the King himself was at a loss to know what to do. In all corners of the palace mice squeaked and gnawed through everything they could get their teeth in.

The cat started hunting immediately and before long had cleared several halls. Then the people begged the King to buy the wondrous animal for the kingdom. The King was only too glad to give what the third brother demanded, which was a mule laden with gold. Thus he came home with the greatest treasure of all.

THE OLD GRANDFATHER
AND THE GRANDSON

There was once a very very old man. His eyes had turned dim, his ears had gone deaf, and his knees were shaking. Now when he was sitting at the table he could hardly hold the spoon. So he spilt the soup on the table-cloth, and some of it even flowed back out of his mouth.

His son and the latter's wife, his daughter-in-law, loathed this nauseating sight, and so in the end the old grandfather was made to sit in the chimney-corner and was given his food in a little earthen bowl, not even enough to eat his fill. Then he cast a melancholy look towards the table, and his eyes became wet with tears.

On one occasion his shaky hands could not even hold the little bowl fast, so it dropped to the ground and broke to pieces. The young woman chided him, but he sat there saying nothing, and only sighed. Thereupon she bought him a small wooden bowl for a few farthings, and out of this he now had to eat.

One day as they were thus sitting, the little four-year-old grandson started putting some little boards together on the ground.

"Now what is it you're doing there?" asked the father.

"I am making a little trough," answered the child. "Father and Mother shall eat from it when I grow big."

For a while the man and his wife looked at each other. In the end, they began to cry. At once they fetched the old grandfather back to the table, and henceforth they always let him eat with them even when he spilt a little.

THE TOMTIT AND THE BEAR

One summer's day a bear and a wolf were walking in the forest, when the bear heard a bird sing so beautifully that he said, "Brother wolf, what kind of a bird is it that can sing so sweetly?"

"It is the King of birds," said the wolf. "To him we must bend our knees and pay homage."

But in fact, it was a tomtit, or a "hedge-king" as some people know it.

"If that is so," said the bear, "then I should like to see the royal palace. Come, take me there."

"That's not as easy as you imagine," said the wolf. "You must wait till the Queen comes."

Soon afterwards the Queen came, with some food in her bill. Then came the King as well to feed their young. The bear would have liked to go straight in, but the wolf held him back by the sleeve and said, "No, you must wait till their Majesties have gone again."

So they took good note of the hole where the nest was, and trudged off again. But the bear knew no peace until he could see the royal palace and, after a short while went back to it. This time the King and Queen had both flown off for more tit-bits. The bear peeped in and saw five or six young lying in the nest.

"Is this the royal palace?" cried the bear. "It's a pitiable place! And you are no royal children. You must be changelings!"

When the young tomtits heard this, they were terribly angry, and cried, "No, that we are not. Our parents are respectable people. Bear, you shall answer for this!"

The bear and the wolf got frightened, turned tail, and took refuge in their dens.

The young tom its cried and made a dreadful noise, and when next the parents came with their bills full of food they said, "We won't touch a single fly's leg, even if we starve, until you tell us whether or not we are really your children. The bear has been here and called us changelings!"

"Just calm down," said their parents. "The matter shall be settled."

Then the King and the Queen flew to the bear's den and called in, "Old Growly Bear, why did you insult our children? It will cost you dear, for it can only be settled by a bloody war."

Thus war was declared on the bear. Every four-footed animal was called together — oxen, donkeys, steers, stags, deer and every other animal on earth.

The tomtits in turn called to arms every creature that could fly in the air. Not only birds both big and small, but also midges, hornets, bees and flies had to come along.

When the time came for the war to begin, the King sent out scouts to find out who was going to command the enemy troops. The midges were the most cunning of all, and they flew about in the forest where the enemy were gathered, and hid under leaves of the trees where the orders were to be given.

The bear stood up, called the fox to appear before him and said, "Fox, you are the slyest of all animals. You shall be our general and lead us."

"Good," said the fox, "but what signal shall we agree upon?" Nobody knew. Then the fox said, "I have a fine, long and bushy tail that looks like a red plume. When I raise my tail high, then things are going well and you must march into battle. But, if I let it hang down, then run as fast as you can."

When the midges heard this they flew home and revealed everything in full detail to the tomtits.

When the day dawned on which the battle was to be fought, the four-footed animals came running with a din that made the heart tremble. The tomtits also came flying through the air with their army. They buzzed, shrieked and swarmed enough to fill everyone with dread and fear.

And then the attack started and they charged on both sides.

The tomtits sent in the hornet with orders to settle underneath the fox's tail and sting with all its might.

When the fox felt the first sting, he squirmed, lifted one leg but bore it bravely and still held his tail up.

At the second sting he had to let it drop for a moment.

After the third, however, he could no longer bear the pain, shrieked, and tucked his tail between his legs. When the animals saw that, they thought everything was lost and fled, head over heels, each to his lair.

The birds had won the battle.

Then the King and Queen flew home to their children, crying, "Children, rejoice! Eat and drink to your heart's content, we have won the war!"

But the young tomtits said, "We won't eat yet. The bear must first come to our nest, beg our pardon and say that we are your own children."

So the tomtits flew to the bear's den and cried, "Growling Bear, come and stand before our children's nest, apologize and say that they are our children. Otherwise we'll break every bone in your body!"

Then the bear in the greatest alarm crawled to the nest and begged their pardon. Now at last the young tomtits were satisfied, sat down together, ate and drank, and made merry until late into the night.

THE WATER OF LIFE

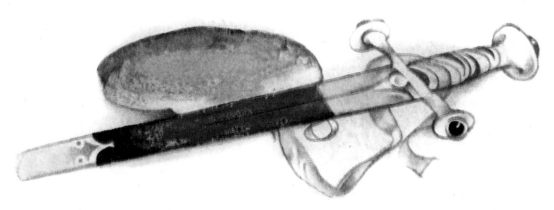

Once upon a time there was a King who was so ill that no one believed he could still escape with his life. The King had three sons and they were very much grieved at their father's sickness. They went down into the palace garden and wept. There they met an old man who asked them the cause of their sorrow. They told him that their father was so ill that he would certainly die, for nothing seemed to help him. Then the old man said, "There is yet one means I know of; that is the Water of Life. If he drinks it he will get well again. The only thing is it's difficult to find."

Then the eldest son said, "I will make sure to find it," went to the sick King and begged him to let him go abroad to seek the Water of Life, for it alone could cure him.

"No," said the King, "the danger is too great, I'd rather die than expose you to it."

However, so long did the young man entreat him that the King at last agreed.

The Prince thought, "If I bring the water, then my father will love me best, and I shall inherit the kingdom."

So the Prince set out and when he had ridden a certain time, a dwarf was standing in his way, who called to him, saying, "Whither away so fast?"

"Stupid dwarf," said the Prince, "that's none of your business."

But the little dwarf got angry and cast a bad spell on the young man.

Before long the Prince came to a gorge in the mountains, and as he rode on it seemed to become narrower and narrower till at last he could not go a step further; it was impossible to turn the horse, or even to dismount, so he sat there stuck fast. The sick King waited for him a long time, but he never came.

Then the second son said, "Father, let me go forth into the world and seek the Water of Life," and he thought in his heart, "If my brother is dead, the kingdom will fall to me."

At first the King would not let him go either, but at last he gave in. So the Prince set out on the same road as his brother had taken, and he, too, met the dwarf who stopped him and asked where he was off to in such a hurry.

"Little busybody," said the Prince, "it's none of your business," and rode on without looking back again.

However, the dwarf bewitched him, and just like his brother he found himself in a mountain gorge, and could go neither forwards nor backwards. But that is how the haughty fare.

When even the second son failed to return, the youngest begged permission to leave the country and fetch the water, and the King had to let him go in the end.

When the dwarf met him and asked where he was off to in such a hurry, he stopped and talked to him and answered saying, "I am going in search of the Water of Life, for my father is very sick."

"And do you know where it is to be found?"

"No, that I don't," said the Prince.

"Well, as you have been friendly to me and not haughtily like your false brothers, I will help you and tell you how to find the Water of Life. It springs from a well in the courtyard of an enchanted castle, but you shall never get in unless I give you an iron rod and two loaves of bread. With the rod strike three times on the iron castle gate, and it will spring open. Inside two hungry lions will be lying with their jaws open, but throw each a loaf, and they will be quiet. Then make haste and take some of the Water of Life before it strikes twelve, otherwise the gate will shut again and you will be imprisoned."

The Prince thanked him, took the rod and the bread, and set out on his way again. And when he reached his destination, everything was as the dwarf had said. The gate sprang open at the third stroke of the rod, and when he had fed the lions with the bread, he entered the castle and came into a great and beautiful hall.

There he found a number of enchanted princes. He took the rings off their fingers and also a sword and a loaf of bread lying there. In the next chamber he found a beautiful maiden. She was very happy to see him, kissed him and said he had broken the spell she was under, and should have the whole of her kingdom, and that if he came again in a year, their wedding would be celebrated. She also told him where the well with the Water of Life was to be found, but added he must hurry and draw the water before it struck twelve.

Then he went on, and finally came to a chamber with a fine, freshly made bed in it. As he was tired, he decided to take a little rest. So he lay down and fell asleep. When he awoke, the clock was striking a quarter to twelve. Thereupon he sprang up full of fear, ran to the well, drew some water out of it with a cup that was standing nearby, and hurried to get out in time. Just as he was going through the iron gate, the clock struck twelve, and the gate closed with such a force that it sliced off a piece of his heel.

He was happy to have the Water of Life, and set off for home. On his way he encountered the dwarf again. When the dwarf saw the sword and the loaf, he said, "There you have won something of great value. With that sword you will be able to strike down whole armies, and the bread will never run out."

The Prince did not want to come home to his father without his brothers, and said, "Good dwarf, can you tell me where my two brothers are? They set out earlier than I in search of the Water of Life and didn't come back."

"They are shut fast between two mountain-sides," said the dwarf, "I imprisoned them there by my spell, because they were exceedingly haughty."

The Prince entreated him so long to free his brothers that the dwarf finally let them go, but he warned him against them saying, "Be on your guard, they have bad hearts."

The Prince was overjoyed to see them when they came back, and told them how he had fared.

Then they rode on together, and found themselves in a country pestered with famine and war, and the King already believed that he must perish, so dire was the need.

The Prince went to him and gave him the bread, and he fed the whole kingdom with it. The Prince also let him have his sword, with which he defeated the armies of his enemies, and henceforth could live in peace and quiet. Then the Prince took his sword and his loaf back, and the three brothers rode on. But they were to pass through two more lands where hunger and war raged, and each time the Prince gave the Kings his bread and sword, and now he had saved three countries.

And then they embarked on a ship and sailed across the sea. During the voyage the two elder brothers spoke together.

"The youngest has found the Water of Life, and we have not, for this Father will give him the kingdom which by rights belongs to us, and thus he will deprive us of our fortune."

This made them revengeful, and they came to an agreement that they would cheat him. They waited till he was fast asleep, then poured out the Water of Life from his cup into their own, and filled their brother's cup with salty sea-water.

When they came home, the youngest brought the sick King his cup for him to drink the water that was to make him well again. Scarcely, however, had he drunk a drop of the salty sea-water than he became even more ill than before. And while he was lamenting over this, the two elder sons came and accused the youngest of wanting to poison their father, saying it was they who brought the true Water of Life, and handed it to him. No sooner had he drunk of it than he felt his illness disappear and became hale and hearty as in his young days.

After this the two went to the youngest brother, and said, "True, you found the Water of Life. But we had all the trouble and now we have the reward. You should have kept your eyes open for we took it away from you while you were asleep upon the sea. And when the year is up, one of us will go and bring the fair Princess here. But take care not to betray any of this. Our father does not trust you, and if you say a single word you shall lose your life. If you keep silent, however, you will be spared."

But the old King was angry with his youngest son, and believed he had sought to take his life. So he summoned the court to assemble and pronounce the sentence on him that he should be secretly killed.

One day when the Prince was riding to the hunt, the King's huntsman had been ordered to go with him. When they were all alone away in the forest, the huntsman looked so sad that the Prince said, "My good man, what is the matter with you?"

The huntsman answered, "I dare not tell you, but I must."

Then the Prince said, "Just speak out, I will forgive you."

"Alas," said the huntsman. "I am to shoot you dead, the King has ordered it so." This frightened the Prince who said, "My dear man, spare my life. I will give you my royal clothes, give me yours in return."

The huntsman said, "With all my heart. For I could never have shot you anyway."

Then they changed clothes, and the huntsman went home, but the Prince went away through the wood.

Some time after, three carriages full of gold and precious stones came to the old King for his youngest son. These had been sent by the Kings who had beaten their enemies with the Prince's sword and fed their countries with his bread, and now wanted to show their gratitude.

Then the old King thought, "Is it possible that my son really was innocent?" And he said to his men, "If only he were still alive! How it grieves me that I had him killed!"

"He is still alive," said the huntsman. "I didn't have the heart to execute your command," and told the King what had taken place.

Then the King let it be proclaimed throughout all kingdoms that his son was to be allowed to come home again where he would be graciously received.

Meanwhile, the Princess in the enchanted castle had a road built of glittering gold and told her courtiers that whoever came riding on horseback straight over it would be the right man and should be let in. But whoever came on one side of the road would not be the right one, and was not to be admitted.

Soon the time had passed, and the eldest son thought he should go to see the Princess, say that he had been her deliverer, and receive her hand in marriage and her kingdom into the bargain. So he rode forth, and when he came to the castle and saw the beautiful golden road, he thought, "It would be a terrible pity to ride on it," and he turned aside and rode to the right of it. However, when he came riding to the gate, the servants told him he was not the true bridegroom, and should turn back.

Soon after that the second Prince set out, and when he came to the golden road, the moment his horse set foot on it he thought it would be a shame to ride on it as it might get damaged. So he turned away and rode to the left of it. But when he came to the gate, the guards said he was not the true bridegroom either and he too should turn back.

Now that the full year had passed, the third Prince wanted to come out of the forest and go to his beloved to forget his sorrows in her dear company. So he set out thinking of her all the time and longing to be with her, and did not notice the golden road at all. So his horse rode over it right in the middle, and when he came to the gate, it was opened to him and the Princess welcomed him with great joy. The marriage was celebrated and, when it was over, she told him that his father had summoned him to his presence and had forgiven him.

So he went on horseback to him and told him how his brothers had deceived him. The old King wanted to punish them, but they had gone to sea and never came back to the end of their days.

THE WORN OUT DANCING SHOES

Once upon a time, there was a King who had twelve daughters, each one fairer than the other. They all slept together in one great chamber where their beds stood side by side, and at night when they were in bed, the King would come, lock the door and bolt it. But when he opened the door every morning, he would see that their shoes were worn out with dancing, and no one could tell how it happened.

Then the King issued a proclamation that, whosoever could find out where they had been dancing at night, might choose one of them for his wife and become King after his death. But anyone who came forward and did not find out the truth within three days and three nights would forfeit his life.

Not long afterwards a Prince came forward and volunteered to undertake the risk. He was well received and, in the evening, they led him into a room adjoining the bedchamber of the Princesses. The servants made up a bed for him there, and he prepared himself to watch where they went and danced. So that the Princesses might not do anything in secret, the door of their bedroom was left open.

However, the Prince's eyes began to feel like lead and he fell asleep. When he woke up in the morning, all twelve Princesses had been out dancing, for their shoes were standing there with holes in the soles.

Nor did things go any differently on the second and the third nights, so his head was cut off without mercy. And after him came many more brave men who volunteered for the risky venture, but all of them had to leave their heads behind.

Now it so happened that a poor soldier who had been wounded and could serve no longer, found himself on the road to the city where the King lived. While walking along he met an old woman who asked him where he was going. "I really don't know myself," he answered and added jokingly, "I should like to find out where the King's daughters dance their shoes to shreds, and then become King."

"That's not so very difficult," said the old woman. "You just mustn't drink the wine that is brought to you in the evening, and only pretend to be fast asleep."

Then she gave him a little cloak and said, "When you put this round you, you will become invisible, and can creep after the twelve maidens."

With all this good advice, the soldier started to take the matter seriously. He took heart, went before the King and offered himself as a suitor. Like the others, he too was well received and dressed in royal clothing.

In the evening towards bedtime, he was conducted to the chamber near the Princesses' room and, when he was about to go to bed, the eldest Princess came and brought him a cup of wine. But he had tied a sponge under his chin, let the wine run into the sponge, and did not drink a single drop. Then he lay down, and after lying there for a few moments, began to snore like one in the deepest sleep.

The King's twelve daughters heard this and laughed. The eldest said, "He, too, might have done better to save his life." Then they got up, opened wardrobes, chests and boxes, and took out magnificent dresses. Then they dressed themselves before their mirrors, skipped about, and looked forward to the dancing.

Only the youngest said, "You are all full of joy but I have a strange feeling that misfortune is about to befall us."

"You are a silly little snow-goose," said the eldest, "You are always scared. Have you forgotten how many Princes have already been here without success? As for the soldier, I needn't even have given him the sleeping-wine. The fool wouldn't have woken up anyway."

When they were all ready, they first cast a glance at the soldier, but he had his eyes closed, did not move or stir, and so they believed they were now quite safe. Then the eldest went to her bed and knocked on it. At once it sank into the earth, and they stepped down through the opening, one after the other.

The soldier, who had seen everything, did not hesitate, hung his little cloak about him, and stepped down after the youngest. In the middle of

the staircase he suddenly trod on the edge of her dress. She was so frightened that she cried, "What's happening? Who is treading on my dress?"

"Don't be so silly," said the eldest, "You only got caught on a hook."

Then they went all the way down, and when they were down, they were standing in a magnificent avenue of trees, where all the leaves were of silver and shimmered and glittered. The soldier thought, "I'd better take a token with me," and broke off a branch. The tree made a tremendous crackling noise, and again the youngest cried, "Something is wrong! Did you hear that noise?"

But the eldest said, "Those are shouts of joy because we have freed our Princes so early."

Thereupon they came into an avenue of trees where all the leaves were of gold, and finally into a third where there were leaves of diamonds. From both avenues of trees the soldier broke off a twig, and each time the tree made such a noise that the youngest started with fright. But the eldest insisted that it was festive shouting.

They went on and came to a big lake on which stood twelve little boats, and in each boat sat a handsome young Prince. They had been waiting for the twelve Princesses, and each took one into his boat, while the soldier seated himself in the boat with the youngest.

Then the Prince said, "I don't know why, but the boat seems much heavier today. I must row with all my strength to push it forward at all."

"Perhaps it is the warm weather?" said the youngest. "I feel very warm, too."

On the other side of the lake there stood a fine castle from which came the jolly music of trumpets and kettle-drums. They rowed there, entered, and each Prince danced with his beloved.

The soldier, being invisible, danced along too, and when one of the Princesses held a cup of wine, he drank it up, so that it was empty before she lifted it to her lips. The youngest was alarmed at this, but the eldest always silenced her. They danced there till three the next morning when all their shoes were in shreds, and they had to stop.

The Princes ferried them back again across the water, and this time the soldier sat in front with the eldest. On the shore they took leave of their Princes, and promised to come again the following night.

When they got to the stairs, the soldier ran ahead, and lay down in his bed, and when the twelve came tripping up slowly and wearily, he was snoring so loudly that they could all hear it and said, "We are safe with this one."

Then they took off their fine robes, put them away, placed the worn out dancing shoes under their beds, and lay down.

The next morning the soldier resolved not to say anything yet but to observe the strange goings-on still more. So he went again with them the second and the third night. Everything was just the same as the first time, and each time they danced till their shoes were worn out. The third time, however, he took with him a cup of wine as a token.

When the hour came for him to give his answer, the soldier took the three twigs and the cup of wine with him and went to the King. The twelve Princesses were standing behind the door, listening to what he had to say.

The King asked, "Where did my twelve daughters dance their shoes to shreds in the night?"

The soldier answered, "With twelve Princes in an underground castle," and he described everything that had happened, and produced the tokens.

Then the King bade his daughters appear before him, and asked them if the soldier had told the truth. Seeing that they had been discovered, they confessed everything. Thereupon the King asked the soldier which one he would like to have in marriage.

He answered, "I am no longer young, so please give me the eldest."

The marriage was celebrated on the very same day, and he was promised the kingdom on the King's death.

BEARSKIN

There was once a young fellow who joined the army as a volunteer. He was brave and was always in the foremost ranks where the fight was thickest. As long as the war lasted, his life was good but, when peace was restored, he was discharged from the army and the captain told him he might go where he pleased.

His parents were dead and he no longer had any home to return to. So he went to his brothers and begged them to take him in until the war broke out again. But the brothers were hard-hearted.

"What can we do with you?" they said. "You are no use to us. Go and see how you can look after yourself."

The soldier had nothing left but his rifle. He put it on his shoulder and made ready to go out into the world. He got to a wide moor on which there was nothing to see but a clump of trees. With a heavy heart he sat down underneath them, and contemplated his fate.

"I have no money," he thought. "I have learnt nothing but the profession of arms and, now because there is peace in the land, they don't need me any more. I foresee that I am bound to starve."

All of a sudden, he heard a roar and, as he looked round, a stranger stood before him, wearing a green coat, and though he looked quite stately, he had an ugly cloven foot.

"I know what you are in need of," said the man. "You shall have gold and goods as much as you can squander but first, I must find out if you are fearless, so that my money doesn't go up in smoke."

"A soldier and fear? How can they go together?" he answered. "You can put me to the test."

"Very well," answered the man, "just look behind you."

The soldier turned round and saw a huge bear growling and coming towards him at a canter. "Oh ho!" cried the soldier. "I will tickle your nose till you won't feel like growling any more." He took aim and shot the bear through the muzzle so that it did not stir again.

"It is clear that you're not lacking in courage," said the man. "But there is still another condition which you must fulfil."

"If it doesn't spoil my chance of salvation," answered the soldier, seeing only too well that it was the devil who stood before him.

"That you shall see for yourself," answered the devil. "For the next seven years you may neither wash, nor comb your beard and hair, cut your nails, neither say the Lord's Prayer. I will give you a jacket and a cloak which you shall wear all that time. If you die within those seven years, you are mine. On the other hand, if you live, you will be free and rich as long as you live."

The soldier's thoughts turned to the great need he was in and, as he had faced death so many times before, he resolved to risk it again.

The devil took off his green coat, gave it to the soldier, and said, "Put this coat on and whenever you put your hand in the pocket, you'll always find it full of money." Then he skinned the bear, and said, "This shall be your cloak and your bed, for you must sleep on it, and never get into any other bed. And because of this apparel you shall be called Bearskin."

Thereupon the devil vanished.

The soldier put the coat on, felt at once in the pocket, and found that it was full of money. Then he threw the bearskin round his shoulders and went forth into the world. He was of good cheer, refraining from nothing that did him good and the money harm.

The first year things went passably well, but by the second he already looked like a monster. His hair covered nearly the whole of his face; his beard resembled a piece of coarse matting; his fingers had claws and his face was so covered with filth that had one sown cress there, it would have grown. Everyone who saw him ran away, but since he always gave money to the poor to pray for him that he might not die within the seven years, and paid well for everything, he always managed to find shelter.

In the fourth year, he came to an inn but the landlord would not take him in. He was not even willing to let him have a place in the stable, for fear that his horses would run away. However, when Bearskin thrust his hand into his pocket and brought out a handful of ducats, the innkeeper relented, and gave him a room in an outhouse. However, Bearskin had to promise not to let anyone see him so that the inn wouldn't get a bad name.

One evening, Bearskin was sitting alone, wishing with all his heart that the seven years were past, when he suddenly heard a loud lamenting in an adjoining room. He had a compassionate heart, so he opened the door and saw an old man crying bitterly and wringing his hands in despair. Bearskin

went nearer but the man sprang to his feet and made to run away. But when he heard a human voice, he grew less afraid and, by kind and comforting words, Bearskin got him to reveal the cause of his sorrow.

He said his fortune had gradually dwindled away, that he and his daughters had to go hungry and, he was so poor, that he couldn't even pay the innkeeper and was about to be put in prison.

"If you have no further troubles," said Bearskin, "I have money enough."

He called for the innkeeper, paid him and put a purse full of gold into the poor man's pocket.

When the old man saw he had been delivered from his troubles, he didn't know how to show his gratitude.

"Come with me," he said to Bearskin. "My daughters are wonders of beauty, choose one of them for your wife. When the one you choose hears what you have done for me she won't refuse. You certainly look a bit odd but she'll know how to put you straight again."

The suggestion appealed to Bearskin and he went with the old man. But when the eldest saw him, she was so horrified by his looks that she screamed and ran away.

The second stood still and studied him from head to foot but then she said, "How can I take as a husband one who no longer looks human? Indeed, the shaved bear that was once shown here and paraded as a man pleased me much better, for it at least had on the fur coat and white gloves of a hussar."

But the youngest daughter said, "Dear father, he must be a good man to have helped you out of your distress. If you promised him a bride in return, your word must be kept."

It was a pity that Bearskin's face was covered with dirt and hair, otherwise they might have seen how delighted he was on hearing these words. He took a ring off his finger, broke it in two and gave one half to her, keeping the other for himself. He wrote his name on her half and her name on his, and begged her to take good care of it.

Then he took his leave and said, "I must wander about for three more years. If I come back we'll celebrate our wedding. But if I don't, you are free, for then I am dead. But pray to God to preserve my life."

The poor bride dressed herself all in black, and tears came into her eyes whenever she thought of her husband.

Her sisters, however, had nothing for her but scorn and they made fun of her. "Take care," said the eldest, "When you give him your hand, he'll hit it with his paw." "Beware," said the other. "Bears are fond of sweets, and if you please him he'll eat you up." Again the eldest sneered, "You must always do his will, or he'll start growling." And the second said, "But it will be a merry wedding. Bears dance well."

The young bride, however, said nothing and did not allow her sisters to put her off waiting for her husband to return.

All this time Bearskin was wandering about in the world. He went from place to place, doing good deeds wherever he could, and gave generously to the poor so that they would pray for him.

At length, the last day of the seven years dawned. Again he went out on to the moor, and sat down under the clump of trees. Before long, the wind whistled and the devil stood before him. He looked very annoyed. Then he threw Bearskin his old coat and demanded his green coat back.

"Oh no," said Bearskin. "First you shall make me clean."

Then the devil had to fetch some water, wash Bearskin, comb his hair and cut his nails. Bearskin looked like a gallant warrior again and was more handsome than ever.

Then the devil disappeared and Bearskin felt much relieved and light of heart. He went into town, bought a magnificent velvet coat and a coach drawn by four white horses. Then he drove to his bride's house.

No one recognized him. The father took him for a noble military gentleman and led him into the room where his daughters were sitting. He was made to sit down between the two eldest ones. They poured him wine, placed the choicest food before him, and thought that in all the world they hadn't seen a handsomer man.

But the youngest daughter sat opposite him in her black clothes and did not raise her eyes or speak a word.

When Bearskin finally asked the father if he would give him one of his daughters in marriage, the two eldest jumped up, ran into their rooms to put on their best dresses, for each fancied she was the chosen one.

The moment the "stranger" was alone with his bride, he brought out the half-ring and placed it in a glass of wine which he handed her across the table. She took the wine but when she had drunk it and found the half-ring lying at the bottom, her heart began to pound. She took the other half which she was wearing on a ribbon round her neck, put the two together, and the two parts fitted perfectly.

Then he said, "I am your betrothed bridegroom whom you knew as Bearskin. But by the grace of God, I had my human shape restored to me and have once more become myself." Then he went up to her, embraced and kissed her.

Meanwhile, the two sisters had come into the room dressed in their finest clothes. When they saw that the handsome man had fallen for their younger sister, and heard that he was really Bearskin, they ran out of the room in rage and fury. Such was their anger that one drowned herself in a well and the other hanged herself on a tree.

That evening, there was a knock at the door. When the bridegroom opened it, he found the devil standing there in his green coat.

"You see," said the devil, "I now have two souls for your one!"

THE SPIRIT IN THE BOTTLE

There was once a poor woodcutter who toiled from morn till late at night. At last, when he had managed to save some money, he said to his son, "You are my only child. I will now spend the money that I have earned from the sweat of my brow on your education. If you learn something honest, you will be able to support me in my old age, when my limbs have grown stiff and I must sit at home all day."

So the boy went to college and worked hard, so much so that he earned his masters' praise and stayed there for some time. When he had studied at several schools, but was not yet perfect in all things, the little pittance that his father had earned ran out, and the young man was forced to return home.

"Ah," said the father sorrowfully, "there's nothing more I can give you, and in this time of dearth, I can't earn a farthing more than our daily bread."

"Dear father," answered the son. "Please don't trouble your mind about it. If it is God's will, it will all turn out for the best. I will soon adjust to it somehow."

When the father was about to go out into the forest to earn some money by chopping wood and selling it in bundles for firewood, the son said, "I'll come along and help you."

"Oh, but my son," said the father. "You will find it rough going. You're not used to heavy work, you won't stand it for long. Besides, I have only one axe and no money to buy another with."

"Go to our neighbour," suggested the son. "He will lend you an axe till I have earned enough to buy one for myself."

So the father borrowed an axe from his neighbour and, next morning at daybreak, they went out into the forest together. The son helped his father and was quite nimble and energetic doing the work. Soon the sun was right overhead, and the father said, "We will have a rest and take our midday meal. After that we will get on as well as ever."

The son took his bread in his hand, and said, "You have a rest, father, I am not tired. I will wander about and look for birds' nests."

"Oh, you foolish boy," said the father. "Why do you want to move about? You will be tired, and will no longer be able to even raise your arm. Stay here, and sit down beside me."

However, the son did go into the forest. He ate his bread there, was very cheerful and peered among the green branches to see if he might discover a nest. He went here and there till at last he came upon an awesome oak, which certainly was many hundreds of years old. Not even five men could have spanned it with their arms outstretched. He stood looking at it and thinking, "Many a bird must have built its nest here."

All of a sudden, he thought he heard a voice. He listened and heard someone calling with a truly muffled sound, "Let me out, let me out!"

He looked all round but discovered nothing, yet the voice seemed to be coming from underground.

Then he called back, "Where are you?"

The voice answered, "I am held below near the roots of the oak. Let me out, let me out!"

The student started clearing the space under the tree and looking about among the roots till at last he found a glass bottle in a small hollow. He lifted it up and held it to the light. Then he saw a thing shaped like a frog leaping up and down inside it.

"Let me out, let me out!" it cried again, and the student, with no thought of evil, took the plug out of the bottle. At once a spirit rose out of it, and started to grow, and grew so fast that in a few moments he stood before the student half as tall as the tree by which he was standing.

"Do you know," it cried in a truly terrible voice, "what your reward is for letting me out?"

"No," answered the student fearlessly, "how should I know?"

"I will tell you," cried the giant. "I shall have to break your neck for freeing me."

"You ought to have told me before," answered the student, "then I should have left you shut inside. But my head shall stand firm for all you can do. This is an affair of more people than one."

"More people here, more people there," cried the spirit, "You shall have your due reward. Do you imagine that I was shut up in there for such a long time for a favour? No, it was my punishment. I am the high and mighty Mercurius. Whosoever lets me out must have his neck broken."

"Go easy, not so fast," answered the young man. "I can hardly believe that it was you who was shut in that small bottle, and that you are a real spirit. If you really can get back into the bottle, I will believe you and then you can have your way and do with me as you like."

"That's but a trifling trick for me," said the spirit haughtily. He drew himself up and made himself as thin and small as he had been before, then he

crept in through the neck of the bottle. Scarcely was he in than the young man pressed in the cork he had drawn out, and threw the bottle under the roots of the oak back to where it had been before. So doing, he got the better of the spirit.

The student wanted to go back to his father, but the spirit cried so plaintively, "Oh, do let me out! Do let me out!"

"No," answered the scholar, "not a second time! Once caught again, I would not let out anybody who has sought to deprive me of my life."

"Set me free," cried the spirit, "and I will give you such riches that you will have enough for the rest of your life."

"No," answered the scholar. "You will cheat me the same as you did the first time."

"You are throwing away your good fortune," said the spirit. "I wont' harm you in any way but will give you a rich reward."

The scholar thought, "I will risk it. Perhaps he will keep his word, and I am always a match for him."

Thereupon he took out the stopper, and the spirit ascended as he did the previous time, blew himself up in all directions, and became as big as a giant.

"Now you shall have your reward," he said and handed the student a small piece of rag, just like a plaster, and said, "If you rub a wound with the one end, the wound heals. And if you pass over steel or iron with the other end it will turn them into silver."

"I must try it first," said the student and he went up to a tree, tore off a piece of bark with his axe and smeared it with one end of the plaster. At once it closed together and was healed.

"Well, you have spoken the truth," he said to the spirit, "and now we can part." The spirit thanked him for his deliverance, and he in turn thanked the spirit for his gift, and returned to his father.

"Where have you been roaming?" his father scolded him. "How did you come to forget your work? I knew from the first you would be a good-for-nothing."

"Don't worry, father, I will make up for it. Look, I am going to chop that tree down."

He took the plaster, smeared the axe with it and dealt the tree a powerful blow. But the iron axe head had turned into silver, and the edge was too soft.

"Look here, father, what a bad axe you've given me, it is no good at all."

The father got a fright and said, "Oh, what have you done now? I'll have to pay for the axe and I don't know how I can. That's all the good I have got from your work."

"Don't get angry," answered the son. "Anyhow I will pay for the axe."

"Oh, you silly ass," cried the father. "Where will you get the money to pay for it? You have nothing beyond what I give you. These are students' pranks sticking in your head, but of wood-cutting you have no idea."

A moment later, the son said, "Father, you see I can work no more. We'd better call it a day."

"What!" he replied, "Do you mean to say I should sit with my hands in my lap like you? I must go on working, you can pack up and go home."

"Father," pleaded the student. "I am in the wood for the first time and I don't know my way alone. Please come along with me."

His anger abated, the father finally allowed himself to be persuaded, and went home with his son. Then he said to the boy, "Go and sell the wretched axe, and mind you get something for it. The rest I must earn and pay my neighbour."

The son took the axe into the town to a silversmith. He tested it, laid it on the scales, and said, "It is worth four hundred thalers but I haven't got as much in cash."

The son said, "Give me what you've got. I will wait for the rest."

The silversmith gave him three hundred thalers, and remained a hundred in his debt. Then the son went home and said, "Father, I have got the money. Go and ask the neighbour what he wants for the axe."

"That I know already," answered the old man. "One thaler and six groschen."

"Well give him two thalers and twelve groschen, that is double and should be enough. See, I have money galore." And he gave his father a hundred thalers, saying, "You shall never go short again. Live in comfort and ease."

"My goodness! How have you come by such riches?" said the father.

Then his son related how it had all come about, and how, trusting in his luck, he had come to make such a good bargain. With the rest of the gold he went to college again and continued his studies. And, because he was able to heal all wounds with his plaster, he became the most famous doctor in the world.

THE TWO TRAVELLERS

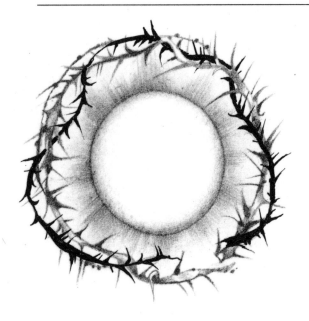

Hill and dale meet not together, but the children of man do, both good and bad.

Thus, too, a shoemaker and a tailor once met on their travels. The tailor was a handsome little fellow, always merry and of good cheer. He saw the shoemaker coming and as he guessed from his carpet bag what trade the other was in, he sang out a little mocking song to him:

"Sew me the seam,
Draw me the thread,
Spread it right and left with pitch
Knock the peg firm on the head."

The shoemaker, however, was not one to take a joke. So he pulled a face as if he had drunk vinegar, and looked as if he were going to seize the tailor by the collar. But the little fellow broke into a smile and handed him a bottle saying, "It was not ill meant, have a drink, and wash the gall down."

The shoemaker took a powerful draught, and the stormy look on his face began to subside. He gave the bottle back to the tailor and said, "I have taken a hearty draught, maybe because I drink a lot but not that I am very thirsty. Shall we go wandering together?"

"Suits me," answered the tailor, "only if you have a mind to go to a big town where there is plenty of work."

"That's just where I wanted to go," said the shoemaker. "There is nothing to earn in a small nest and in the country, people prefer to go barefoot."

So they travelled on together always putting one foot before the other like the weasel in the snow.

They both had plenty of time, but not much to eat. When they came to a town, they went about and paid their respects to the traders. Since the little tailor looked so sprightly and gay, and had such red cheeks, everyone was glad to give him work to do and, when his luck was in, the master's daughter gave him a parting kiss as well. Whenever he fell in with his fellow-traveller again, he always had more in his bundle than the shoemaker.

The sullen shoemaker made a wry face and quoted, "The greater the rogue the greater the luck."

But the tailor only laughed and sang, and shared all he got with his comrade. When a few groats tinkled in his pocket, he made a proper spread and struck the table joyfully with his fist. His motto was "Easy come, easy go."

They had travelled for some time when they came to a great forest through which the road passed to the royal city. There were two paths leading through it, one of which took seven days to go and the other only two, but neither of the travellers knew which was the shorter. The two travellers sat down under an oak-tree and took counsel about how they should provide for themselves and for how many days they should take bread with them.

The shoemaker said, "One must look ahead of where one goes. I will take bread for seven days."

"What!" said the tailor, "to carry bread for seven days on your back like a beast of burden, and not be able to look around? I shall trust in God and not overburden myself. The money I have in my pocket is as good in summer as in winter, but bread gets dry and even mouldy in the hot weather. Neither does my coat reach farther than down to my ankles. Why should we not find the right way? Bread for two days for me, and that's all."

So each bought his bread, and they went into the forest to try their luck.

It was as quiet in the forest as in a church. No wind blew, no brook gurgled, no bird sang, and no sunshine shone through the leafy branches. The shoe-maker did not say a word. The heavy load of bread was pressing against his back so that perspiration streamed down his dark gloomy face. But the tailor was quite lively, skipped about, or sang a catch of a song, and thought to himself, "God in heaven must feel pleased to see me so merry."

Thus it went for two days but, on the third day, the forest did not come to an end and the tailor had consumed all his bread. His heart sank a little lower. Even so, he did not lose courage and put his trust in God and his luck. On the third day, when evening came, he lay down hungry under a tree and the next morning he rose hungry again. The fourth day was the same and, when the shoemaker sat down on an uprooted tree and ate his meal, the tailor could do nothing but look on.

When he begged for a piece of bread, the other just laughed and said mockingly, "You have always been so jolly, so you can try for once to see what it feels like to lack joy. The birds that sing too early in the morning are pounced upon by the hawk in the evening."

In short, he showed no pity.

But on the fifth day, the poor tailor could no longer stand up and was so weak that he could hardly utter a word. His cheeks had turned white and his eyes were red. Then the shoemaker said to him, "Today I'll give you a piece of bread, but I will take out your right eye in return."

Of course, the unhappy tailor still wished to save his life and had no other choice. Once more he wept with both eyes and then he opened them

wide. The shoemaker, who had a heart of stone, took a sharp knife and took out his right eye.

Then the tailor recalled what his mother had once told him when he had been pilfering in the pantry. "Eat what you can, suffer what you must."

When he had eaten his dearly-bought bread, he got upon his feet again, forgot his misfortune, and consoled himself with the thought that he could still see fairly well with one eye. But the sixth day came and hunger made itself felt again, and nearly ate up his heart. In the evening he fell down near a tree, and on the seventh morning he was so faint he could not get up. He was at death's door. Then the shoemaker said, "I will be merciful to you, and once more give you bread. But you shall not have it for nothing. I shall put out your other eye in return."

The tailor saw what light-hearted life he had led, begged the Lord to forgive him, and said, "Do what you will. I will bear what I must but remember, our Lord God does not hold judgement every moment, and the hour shall come when the evil which you do to me, and which I have not deserved, shall be paid for. When times were good, I shared with you all I had. My trade is such that one stitch must be just the same as the other. When I no longer have my eyes and can do no sewing, I shall have to go begging. At least do not leave me here alone when I am blind, otherwise I shall perish."

But the shoemaker, who had long driven God out of his heart, took the knife and took out his left eye. Then he gave him a piece of bread to eat, handed him a staff, and led the tailor behind him.

When the sun set, they came out of the forest, and nearby in the field stood a gallows. The shoemaker led the blind tailor under it, left him alone and went on his way.

Tired, in pain and hungry, the unfortunate man fell asleep and slept the whole night. When dawn was breaking he woke up but did not know where he was. Two condemned criminals were hanging on the gallows, and a crow sat on the head of each of them. Then one crow began to speak, "Brother, are you awake?"

"Yes, I am awake," answered the other.

"Then I will tell you something," resumed the first. "The dew that falls over us this night from the gallows, gives to everyone who washed in it his eyes back again. If blind people only but knew it, think how many could get their eyesight back."

When the tailor heard this, he took his handkerchief, pressed it to the grass and, when it was moist with dew, he washed his eye-sockets with it. At once, what the crow had said came true, and the sockets were filled with two fresh and healthy eyes.

It was not long before the tailor saw the sun rise behind the mountains. Across the plain before him lay the great royal city with its splendid gates and a hundred towers, and the golden balls and crosses that stood on the spires began to glow. He could see every leaf on the trees, and could watch the birds flying past, and the gnats dancing in the air. He took a needle out of his pocket and, as he could thread it as well as he had ever done before, his heart jumped for joy. He threw himself on his knees, thanked God for the mercy he had shown him, and said his morning prayer. Nor did he forget to offer prayers for the men on the gallows, who hung there like the heart in a bell, and which the wind struck against each other. Then he took his bundle on his back, forgot the heartache he had suffered, and went along singing and whistling.

The first thing he met was a brown foal skipping about free in the field.

He seized it by the mane, intending to swing himself on to its back and ride into the town. But the foal pleaded for its freedom. "I am still too young," it said. "Even a light tailor like you would be sure to break my back in two. Let me run about till I am strong. There may come a time when I can repay you this kindness."

"Run along," said the tailor. "I can see you are a giddy young fellow like myself."

He gave it a smack on the rump with a switch, and the foal kicked out its hind legs for joy, set its course over hedge and ditch, and ran away into the open fields.

However, the little tailor had had nothing to eat since the day before. "True enough, the sun fills my eyes, but there is no bread to fill my mouth. The first thing I meet which is even half palatable will pay for it." A moment later a stork came striding gravely over the meadow towards him.

"Halt, halt," cried the tailor, and seized him by the leg. "I don't know if you are fit to eat, but my hunger does not give me much time to be choosy. I must cut off your head and roast you."

"Don't do that," answered the stork. "I am a sacred bird to whom no one ever does any harm, and I am very useful to men. If you spare my life, I may repay your kind deed some other time."

"Run off then, Cousin Longlegs," said the tailor.

Then the stork rose up, let his long legs hang down, and flew off in a leisurely way.

"How will it all end?" said the tailor to himself. "I am getting hungrier and hungrier and my stomach more and more empty. Whatever gets in my way now is lost." Whereupon he saw on the pond a couple of young ducks swimming towards him.

"You have come just in time," he said and grabbed one of them and was about to wring its neck. But that moment, an old duck hidden among the reeds screeched and swam to him with her bill open, and begged him entreatingly to take pity on her dear children.

"Just think," she said, "how your mother would grieve if someone wanted to take you away and put an end to you."

"Don't worry," said the good-natured tailor, "you shall keep your children," and he set the captive duck upon the water again.

When he turned, he found himself standing in front of a hollow tree and saw wild bees flying in and out. "Here I shall at once find a reward for my good deed," said the tailor. "The honey will refresh me."

But the Queen-bee came out and said in a threatening and warning voice, "If you touch my people, and destroy my nest, then you shall feel the sting of ten thousand red-hot needles. Leave us in peace and go on your way, and we will do you a service in return some other time."

The good tailor saw that here, too, there was nothing to be done. "Three dishes empty and nothing on the fourth, that is a bad feast."

So with his empty rumbling stomach he dragged himself on into the city. There he found an inn and arrived just as the bell was ringing for dinner. He had some food prepared for him at once and sat down to enjoy a good meal. When he was satisfied, he said, "Now I can do some work again."

He went round the city, sought out a master, and soon found good accomodation, too. As he had learnt his trade well, down to the last detail, it was not long before he became famous and everyone wanted to have a new coat made by the little tailor. His reputation grew daily.

"I cannot improve my skill," he said, "and yet, I am better off from day to day."

Finally, the King ordered him to attend his court as the court tailor.

However, such is the way of the world that on the same day, his former fellow-traveller the shoemaker also became the court-shoemaker. When the latter caught sight of the tailor and saw that he again had two good eyes, his conscience struck him.

"Before he takes revenge on me," he thought to himself, "I must dig a pit for him."

But he who digs a pit for others falls in himself.

In the evening, when he had finished work and dusk began to fall, he sneaked along to the King and said, "Your Majesty, the tailor is a braggart, and has made a boast he will restore to you the old crown that was lost many years ago."

"That would only please me," said the King, and he summoned the tailor to appear before him the next morning, and ordered him either to bring the crown back, or to leave the city for ever.

"Oho!" thought the tailor, "only a fool or a rogue gives more than he has got. The peevish King demands from me what no man can accomplish, so I will not wait till tomorrow but clear out of the town this very day."

So he tied up his bundle with a string, but when he was past the city gate he felt sorry to be giving up his good fortune and turning his back on the city where he had fared so well.

He came to the pond where he had met the ducks. Just at that moment, the old mother duck whose children he had left unscathed, was pluming herself with her bill. She knew him at once, and asked him why he was so downcast.

"You will not wonder when you hear what has befallen me." And the tailor told her of his fate.

"If it's nothing more than that," said the mother duck, "then we can deal with the situation. The crown fell into the water and lies below at the bottom of the pond. Before long we shall have it brought up again. In the meantime, just spread your handkerchief on the bank."

Then the mother duck dived with her twelve young ones under the water and, five minutes later, she was up again, sitting in the middle of the crown which was resting on her wings. The twelve ducklings swam around and helped to carry it by putting their bills under it. They swam towards the bank and laid the crown on the handkerchief. You wouldn't believe how magnificent the crown was when the sun shone on it. It glittered like a hundred thousand diamonds.

The tailor tied his handkerchief together by the four corners and took it to the King, who was overjoyed and put a golden chain round the tailor's neck.

When the shoemaker saw that his trick had miscarried, he thought of another and stepped before the King saying, "Your Majesty, the tailor has become boastful again. He has boasted that he will copy in wax the entire royal palace with everything in it, fast or loose, inside and out."

The King ordered the tailor to appear and ordered him to carry out his boast, to copy in wax the entire royal palace with everything in it, fast or loose, inside and out, but warned him that if he should not succeed, or if so much as a single nail on the wall were missing, he should spend all his life underground in a dungeon.

The tailor thought, "This is getting worse and worse. No man can endure it!" So he threw his bundle on his back and started his wanderings again.

When he came to the hollow tree, he sat down and hung his head. Then the bees came flying out, and the Queen-bee asked him if he had a stiff neck as his head hung so much away.

"Oh no," answered the tailor. "It is something else that saddens me." And he told her what the King had demanded of him.

The bees started buzzing and humming among themselves, and the Queen-bee said, "Go home, but come again at about this time tomorrow, and bring a large handkerchief with you and all will be well."

So the tailor turned back again, but the bees flew on ahead to the King's palace, straight into the open windows and crawled about in all the corners, and took in everything as precisely as possible. Then they hurried back and built the castle in wax with such speed that you would think it was growing under your very eyes.

By evening everything was ready, and when the tailor came next morning, the whole of the magnificent building stood there, and not a single nail on the wall or a single tile of the roof was missing. At the same time it was soft, snow-white and sweet-smelling like honey.

The tailor packed it carefully in his handkerchief and brought it to the King, who was overcome at the marvel and had it placed in the largest hall. In return he made the tailor a present of a large house built of stone.

But the shoemaker did not relent and went to the King for the third time, and said, "Your Majesty, it has come to the tailor's knowledge that no water comes from the spring in the middle of the palace courtyard. He has boasted that he will make it spout up to the height of a man and be as clear as crystal."

The King had the tailor summoned to his presence, and said, "If tomorrow a jet of water does not spring up in my courtyard as you have promised, the executioner shall cut off your head in that very yard."

The poor tailor did not hesitate, and hurried out to the city gate. This time it was a matter of life and death, and tears were rolling down his face.

While he was walking thus full of grief, the foal whom he had once given his liberty and who had by then grown into a handsome bay horse came leaping towards him. "Now the time has come," he said to the tailor, "for me to repay your good deed. I know exactly what you need, but help is coming. Get on my back. I can now carry two of your size."

The tailor took heart again, sprang with one leap onto the horse's back and it went full speed to the city, straight to the palace courtyard. Then it galloped as quick as lightning three times round it, and the third time it plunged down violently.

Instantly, there was a terrific clap of thunder. A piece of earth, the size of a cannon-ball, shot into the air and over the castle, followed directly by a jet of water as high as a man on horseback. The water was crystal-clear, and there were sunbeams dancing on it. When the King saw this, he stood up in astonishment, then went and embraced the tailor in view of all the people.

But his good fortune did not last long. The King had many daughters, one more beautiful than the other, but he had no son. Thereupon the malicious shoemaker took himself to the King for the fourth time, and said, "Your Majesty, the tailor persists in his bragging. Now he has boasted that if he wanted to, he could have a son brought to Your Majesty through the air."

The King bade the tailor to be summoned, and said, "If within nine days you produce a son flown to me through the air, you shall have my eldest daughter in marriage."

"The reward is high, of course," thought the tailor. "In such a case one would do everything possible. But the cherries hang too high for me. If I climb up after them, the bough will break under me, and I shall fall."

He went home, sat down cross-legged on his work-bench and pondered what could be done. "It can't be done," he cried at last, "I will go away since I can't live here in peace."

So he tied up his bundle and hurried out through the gate. When he got to the meadows, he saw his old friend the stork. He was stalking up and down like a philosopher. He halted at times, contemplated a frog from a closer distance and, at last swallowed it up.

The stork drew nearer and greeted the tailor. "I can see," he began, "you have your knapsack on your back. Why are you leaving the city?"

The tailor told him what the King had demanded of him and that he found it impossible to fulfil.

"Don't let your hair turn grey on account of that," said the stork. "I will help you out of your trouble. I have now been bringing children in swaddling-clothes into the city for a long time, so for once I can also fetch a little Prince out of the well. Go home and don't worry. Nine days from today take yourself to the royal palace, and I will come, too."

The good tailor went home and was in the palace at the appointed time. Not long after, the stork came flying there, and knocked at the window. The tailor opened it, and Cousin Longlegs came in carefully and stepped with solemn steps over the smooth marble floor. In his beak he had a child who was as lovely as an angel, and stretched out its little hands towards the Queen. The stork laid it on her lap, and she fondled and kissed it, and was beside herself with joy. Before flying away again, the stork took his travelling bag off his back and handed it over to the Queen. Inside were paper bags full of bright coloured drops, and these were divided among the little Princesses. But the eldest got none of these, instead she got the merry tailor for her husband.

"I feel," said the tailor, "as if I have won the greatest prize on earth.

My mother was right after all, she always said that whoever trusts in God and also has good luck, can never want for anything."

The shoemaker had to make the shoes in which the merry tailor danced at his wedding-feast and afterwards was ordered to leave the town for ever.

The road to the forest took him past the gallows. Worn out with anger, rage and the heat of the day he threw himself down. When he closed his eyes to sleep, the two crows swooped down from the heads of the hanged men with a loud cry, and pecked his eyes out. In his madness he ran into the forest and must have perished there, for he was never seen or heard of since.

ONE-EYE, TWO-EYES, AND THREE-EYES

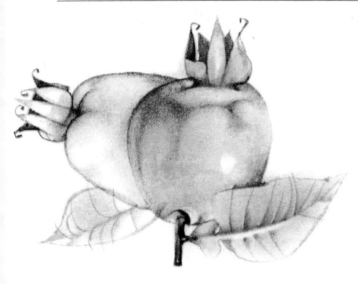

Once upon a time there was a woman who had three daughters. Of these the eldest was called One-Eye, because she had only a single eye in the middle of her forehead; the second was called Two-Eyes because she had two eyes like everyone else, and the youngest Three-Eyes because she had three eyes. The third eye was in the middle of her forehead.

However, as Two-Eyes looked no different from other people, her sisters and her mother hated the very sight of her. They said to her, "You with your two eyes are no better than common people. You are not one of us." They pushed her around, handed down their old clothes to her, and gave her left-overs to eat. And, whenever they could, they wounded her sensitive heart.

One day, when Two-Eyes had to go out into the field to tend the goat, she was still very hungry because her sisters had given her so little to eat. So she sat down on a ridge and started crying so much that two streams of tears ran down her face. Raising her eyes in her distress, she saw a woman standing beside her who asked, "Why are you weeping, Two-Eyes?"

Two-Eyes answered, "Why shouldn't I weep? Since I have two eyes like other people, my sisters and my mother can't abide me. They push me from one corner to another, throw old clothes at me, and give me nothing to eat but left-overs from their meals. Today they gave me so little that I am still terribly hungry."

The wise woman said, "Two-Eyes, dry your tears. I will tell you something so that you shall never go hungry any more. Just say to your goat,
"Goat, goat bleat!
Little table, set!"

and a freshly laid table will be standing before you with the choicest food on it, and you can eat to your heart's content. When you have had enough and don't need the table any longer, just say,
"Goat, goat, bleat!
Little table, go!"

and it will vanish again before your very eyes."

Then the wise woman went away, and Two-Eyes thought, "I must try it at once if what she said is true, for I am absolutely famished. So she said,
"Goat, goat, bleat!
Little table, set!"

And no sooner had she spoken the words than a little table stood there covered with a little white cloth, and on it a plate and a knife and fork and a silver spoon, and the choicest dishes stood on it still steaming and warm as if they had just come from the kitchen.

Then Two-Eyes said the shortest grace she knew, helped herself, and ate heartily. And when she was satisfied, she said what the wise lady had taught her,
"Goat, goat, bleat!
Little table, go!"

At once the little table and everything that stood on it vanished again.

In the evening, when she came home with her goat, she found an earthenware bowl that the sisters had placed there for her, but she did not touch it. The next day she went out again with her goat, and left the few scraps that she had been offered untouched. The first time and the second time the sisters did not notice it, but when it happened a third time they did question it and said, "There's something wrong with Two-Eyes. She leaves the food untouched every day now, whereas before she ate everything that was offered to her. She must have found other ways and means of finding food."

In order to discover the truth, One-Eye decided to go with Two-Eyes when she took the nanny-goat to pasture, to watch what she did there, and to see whether anyone brought food and drink to her.

Now when Two-Eyes set out again, One-Eye came up to her and said, "I will come along to the field and see that the goat is properly tended and taken to a good piece of pasture." However, Two-Eyes realized what One-Eye was after, and drove the goat into high grass, and said, "Come, One-Eye, we will sit down and I'll sing something for you." One-Eye sat down, tired from the unaccustomed walking and the heat of the sun, and Two-Eyes started singing,

"One-Eye, are you awake?
One-Eye, are you asleep?"

Then One-Eye shut her one eye and fell asleep. And when Two-Eyes saw that One-Eye was fast asleep and could not discover anything, she said,
"Goat, goat, bleat!
Little table, set!"

and sat down at the little table and ate and drank her fill. Then she called again,
"Goat, goat, bleat!
Little table, go!"

and everything at once disappeared. Two-Eyes woke One-Eye saying, "One-Eye, you want to tend the goat, but you fall asleep over it. In the meantime, the goat could have run away into the wide world. Let's go home now."

So they went home, and Two-Eyes once again left her little bowl untouched, and One-Eye was unable to tell her mother why Two-Eyes didn't want to eat.

The next day the mother said to Three-Eyes, "This time you shall go along and observe whether Two-Eyes eats anything out there, for she must be eating and drinking in secret."

Three-Eyes came up to Two-Eyes and said, "I will come along with you and see whether the goat is properly tended and taken where it can feed." However, Two-Eyes knew what Three-Eyes had in mind, and drove the goat where the grass was high, and said, "We will sit down here, and I will sing something for you."

Three-Eyes sat down, tired after the walk and from the heat of the sun, and Two-Eyes started again the same song and sang,
"Three-Eyes, are you awake?"

But instead of singing
"Three-Eyes, are you asleep?"

as she should have done, she thoughtlessly sang,
"Two-Eyes, are you asleep?"

and sang all the time,
"Three-Eyes, are you awake?
Two-Eyes, are you asleep?"

Then the two eyes of Three-Eyes dropped and slept but the third did not fall asleep. To be sure, Three-Eyes shut it, but only out of cunning as though it were asleep as well. Yet she blinked and could see everything very well indeed. And when Two-Eyes thought Three-Eyes was fast asleep so she sang,
"Goat, goat, bleat!
Little table, set!"

and ate and drank to her heart's content, and then bade the little table to go away again,
"Goat, goat, bleat!
Little table, go!"

and Three-Eyes had seen everything. Then Two-Eyes came up to her, woke her up and said, "Oh, Three-Eyes you have been asleep? What a fine goatherd you are! Come, we must go home now!"

And when they came home, Two-Eyes again did not eat, and Three-Eyes said to the mother, "Now I know why Two-Eyes does not eat. When she is out there, she says to the goat,
"Goat, goat, bleat!
Little table, set!"

and then a little table appears before her laid with the best food, much better than we have here. And when she has eaten her fill, she says,
"Goat, goat, bleat!
Little table, go!"

and everything vanishes again."

Then the envious mother screamed at Two-Eyes, "You want to live better than we do? You shall soon lose your fancy for it!" She fetched a butcher's knife and stuck it in the goat's heart and it dropped dead.

When Two-Eyes saw that, she went out full of sorrow, sat down in a field and shed bitter tears. Then, all of a sudden, the wise lady stood again beside her and said, "Little Two-Eyes, why are you weeping?"

"I have a good reason to weep," answered Two-Eyes. "The goat that laid the table so finely every day has been stabbed by my mother. Now I must once again suffer from hunger and misery."

Then the wise lady said, "Two-Eyes, I'll give you a good piece of advice. Ask your sisters to give you the innards of the slaughtered animal, bury them in the ground in front of the door, and it will bring you good luck." Then she vanished.

Two-Eyes went home and said to her sisters, "Dear sisters, please give

me something from my goat. I don't ask for anything good, just give me the innards."

Then they laughed and said, "As long as that's all you want, you can have them."

So Two-Eyes took the innards and quietly buried them in the earth outside the front door as the wise lady had advised her.

The next morning when they woke up and went to the door, they saw a magnificent tree standing there, which had leaves of silver with fruit of gold hanging in between, and there was nothing more beautiful and more precious in the wide world. They did not know how the tree had got there in the night, only Two-Eyes realized that it had grown out of the goat's innards, for it stood just on the spot where she had buried them in the ground.

Then the mother said to One-Eye, "Climb up, my child, and pick the fruit of the tree." So One-Eye climbed up, but when she wanted to get hold of one of the golden apples, the branch slipped out of her hand. This happened every time, so she could not break off a single apple no matter how she placed herself.

Then the mother said, "You climb up, Three-Eyes. With your three eyes you can see better than One-Eye." One-Eye slipped down, and Three-Eyes climbed up. But she was no more skilful, and no matter how she tried the golden apples always slipped out of her reach.

Finally, their mother lost patience and climbed up herself, but could not grasp the fruit any better than One-Eye and Three-Eyes could before her, and groped in the empty air.

Then Two-Eyes said, "I will climb up myself, perhaps I shall have better luck." Nor did the sisters forget to cry out, "You with your two eyes! What do you think you can do?" But Two-Eyes climbed up the tree and the golden apples didn't draw back from her but dropped down into her hand themselves, so that she could pluck them one after the other, and brought a whole apronful down with her. The mother took them away, and instead of treating poor Two-Eyes any better, as they should have done, the mother, One-Eye and Three-Eyes only became envious that she alone was able to bring down the fruit, and treated her even harder than before.

It so happened that one day as they were standing together near the tree, a young knight was riding by.

"Quick, Two-Eyes, hide somewhere so that we needn't be ashamed of you," cried the two sisters and hurriedly covered poor Two-Eyes with an empty cask which was standing just by the tree, and they also pushed underneath the cask the golden apples which Two-Eyes had picked.

Now when the knight came nearer he turned out to be a handsome gentleman. He halted, admired the magnificent tree of gold anb silver, and said to the two sisters, "Who does this fine tree belong to? Whoever gives me one branch from it can demand anything he likes in return." One-Eye and Three-Eyes answered that the tree belonged to them, and they would be glad to break off a branch for him. They both tried very hard indeed, but could never do it, for the branches and the fruit always slid away from them.

Then the knight said, "It's certainly strange that the tree belongs to you, and yet you have not the power to break anything off it."

Just then Two-Eyes managed to roll out a few golden apples from under the cask so that they rolled towards the knight's feet, for Two-Eyes was angry to hear her sisters not telling the truth. On seeing the apples, the knight was astonished and asked where they came from. One-Eye and Three-Eyes answered they had still another sister, who was not allowed to show herself, as she had only two eyes like other common people. But the knight demanded to see her and cried, "Come out, Two-Eyes."

Then Two-Eyes came quite happily from under the cask, and the knight marvelled at her great beauty and said, "Surely you can break off a branch of the tree for me, Two-Eyes."

"Yes, of course," answered Two-Eyes, "I can easily do that, for the tree is mine." And she climbed up and with little effort broke off a branch with fine silver leaves and golden fruit and handed it to the knight.

Then the knight said, "Two-Eyes, what should I give you in return?"

"Alas," said Two-Eyes, "from early morning till late at night I suffer from hunger and thirst, and have to endure sorrow and misery. If you would take me with you and save me from this life, I would be happy."

So the knight lifted Two-Eyes on to his horse, and took her home to his father's palace. There he gave her beautiful clothes, food and drink to her

heart's content, and because he loved her so much, he became betrothed to her, and the wedding was celebrated with great joy.

At first the two sisters envied her greatly her luck. "However, the marvellous tree remains with us," they thought, "and even if we can't break any fruit off it, everybody will come to our house to admire it. Who knows what luck may still be in store for us!"

But the next morning the tree had vanished, and their hopes were gone, too. And when Two-Eyes looked out of her palace chamber, to her great pleasure there it stood, in front of her window.

Two-Eyes lived happily for a long time. One day, two poor women came to the palace begging for alms. When Two-Eyes looked into their faces, she recognized in them her own sisters One-Eye and Three-Eyes. They had sunk to such poverty that they had to beg their bread at people's doors. However, Two-Eyes bade them welcome, helped them and took care of them, so that they were both mightily sorry for the wrong they had done to their sister in their young days.

THE SEVEN FRIENDS

There were once seven friends. The first was Master Schulz; the second Jackli; the third Jarli; the fourth Jergli; the fifth Michael; the sixth Hans; the seventh Veitli. All resolved to go out into the world, to seek adventure and perform great deeds. But so that they might go weapon in hand and secure, they thought it a good thing to have only a single spear made, but a very long and strong one. All seven took hold of this spear together. In front went the boldest and manliest, which was Master Schulz, and then followed the others, all in their correct order, and Veitli was the last.

Now it happened one day in July when they had covered a long distance, and still had a good way to go to reach the village where they were to put up for the night, that a big beetle or hornet flew past them behind a bush, humming in a very hostile way.

Master Schulz was so frightened that he nearly dropped the spear, and broke out in a cold sweat all over his body. "Hark, hark," he cried to his friends. "I hear a drum."

Jackli, who was holding the spear behind him and whose nose was affronted with I don't know what kind of smell, said, "Surely there is something afoot, for I taste powder and matches."

Hearing that, Master Schulz took to his heels and, in a trice, jumped over a hedge. But he jumped straight on to the prongs of a rake which had been left there by the haymakers. The handle struck him in the face and dealt him a savage blow.

"Oh me, oh my!" yelled Master Schulz. "Take me prisoner, I surrender, I surrender!"

The other six friends leapt over, one over the other in a heap, crying, "If you surrender, I surrender too! If you surrender, I surrender too!"

At last, as there was no enemy wanting to bind and take them away, it dawned on them that they had been deceived. For fear the story might get abroad and they be taken for fools and laughed at, they swore an oath to each other to keep silent until one of them should unwittingly give the story away.

Then they wandered on. The second dangerous thing that happened to them can hardly be compared with the first. Several days later, their journeyings took them through a fallow field where a hare sat sleeping in the sun, his ears standing up in the air and his big glassy eyes bulging out of their sockets. They all took fright at the sight of this terrible, wild beast, and considered amongst themselves what would be the least dangerous thing to do. If they resolved to flee, the danger was that the monster might pursue and devour them to the last morsel. So they said, "We must fight out a great and dangerous struggle, a good beginning is half the battle!"

Then all the seven seized the spear, Master Schulz in front and Veitli behind. Master Schulz was forever trying to hold the spear back, but Veitli at the back had become quite bold, and wanted to rush forward crying,
"Heave to in every comrade's name,
Or I wish you may go lame."

But Hans knew how to parry this, and said,
"By heavens, you can gabble fast,
But at a dragon-hunt, you're ever last."

Michael cried,
"It's no mistake, not by a hair,
But that the Devil himself is there."

Then it was Jergli's turn and he said,
"If it's not him, it's his mother,
Or the Devil's own step-brother."

Now Jarli had a bright idea, and said to Veitli,
"Advance, Veitli, advance, advance,
I will behind you take a stance."

But Veitli chose not to listen, and Jackli said,
"It's Schultz's place the first to be,
No one deserves the honour but he."

Thereupon Master Schulz took heart, and said pompously,
"Well, march forward bravely to the fray,
And show our valour as we may."

Then they all struck out at the "dragon" as one man. Master Schulz blessed himself, and called upon God for help, but all this was of no avail and as he was thrusting nearer and nearer to the foe, he cried out in the greatest alarm, "Oho! Oho! ho! ho! ho!"

This alerted the hare, which took fright and swiftly took to his heels.

When Master Schulz saw him so ready to clear the battlefield, he shouted for joy,·
"Oh Veitli, onwards, look there,
The monster is nothing but a hare."

Then the seven friends went on, seeking further adventures till they came

to the Moselle, a mossy, still and deep river, spanned by few bridges, which could only be crossed in many places in boats. The friends, not being acquainted with this, shouted to a man who was working on the other side of the water and asked how one might get across.

Now because of the distance and their way of speaking, the man did not understand, and asked in his own dialect, "What? What?"

Master Schulz thought that he was saying, "Wade, wade!" And being the foremost, he got ready to wade across the Moselle. Before long he sank in the mud and was drowned in the oncoming deep waves.

His hat, however, was blown across to the other bank, and a frog sat down beside it and croaked, "Wat, wat, wat!"

The six friends on the opposite side heard that and said, "Listen, comrades, it's Master Schulz calling us. If he can wade across, why cannot we?"

So they all hurriedly jumped into the water, and were drowned. Thus one frog took the lives of seven men, and not one of the seven friends ever reached home again.

SWEET PORRIDGE

Once upon a time there was a poor, good little maiden who lived alone with her mother, and they no longer had anything to eat. So the child went out into the forest, and there she met an old woman who knew all about her poverty. She made her a gift of a little pot. It was enough for her to say, "Cook, little pot, cook," and the pot would cook good, sweet millet-gruel, and when she said, "Stop, little pot," it stopped cooking.

The girl brought the pot home to her mother, and now they were rid of poverty and hunger, and ate sweet porridge as often they wanted to.

One day the girl had gone out for a time and the mother said, "Cook, little pot, cook." And it did cook and she ate her fill. Then she wanted the pot to stop cooking but did not know the word.

So it cooked on and on, and the porridge boiled over the edge. Still it went on cooking, till the kitchen and the house were full, and then the next house, and then the street, as though it were about to feed the whole world. There fell in that little town the greatest calamity, and no one knew what to do.

At last when only one single house remained, the child came home and just said, "Stop, little pot." Then it stood still and stopped cooking.

From that day onwards, anyone who wanted to come back to the town had to eat his way through the porridge!

SNOW-WHITE AND ROSE-RED

There was a poor widow who lived alone with her two daughters. In the garden in front of their cottage there were two rose trees. One bore white roses and the other red ones. The two girls so resembled the two trees — one so ivory-complexioned and one so rosy — that they were named Snow-white and Rose-red after the trees.

They were pious and good, and more hardworking and cheerful than any other two children in the world. Only Snow-white was quieter and more gentle than Rose-red. Rose-red preferred to skip about in the fields and meadows, pick flowers and catch butterflies, while Snow-white sat at home with her mother, helped her with the household chores, or read aloud to her when there was nothing else to do.

The two children were so devoted to each other that whenever they went out together they always walked hand in hand. And when Snow-white would say, "We will never be parted," Rose-red would answer, "Not as long as we live," and their mother would add, "What the one has she must share with the other."

Often they ran about alone in the forest and picked red berries, but no animal ever did them any harm. On the contrary, they loved and trusted them; the little hare would eat cabbage-leaves out of their hands, the roe would graze by their side, the deer spring quite merrily past and the birds would stay perched on the branches and sing for all they were worth. No misfortune ever befell them. When they stayed in the forest very late, when night descended upon them, they would lie down side by side on the moss and sleep till morning. Their mother knew where they were and was not worried.

Once when they had stayed in the forest overnight, and the dawn had roused them, they saw a beautiful child in a shining white robe sitting near their resting-place. He got up and looked at them most kindly, but said nothing and walked off into the forest. They looked about and saw then that they had been sleeping on the very edge of a gorge, and would certainly have fallen into it in the dark had they gone but a few steps further. Their mother told them that they must have seen a guardian angel who watches over good children.

Snow-white and Rose-red kept their mother's little cottage spick and span and it was a delight to look into it. Rose-red looked after the house, and every morning made a posy of one red and one white rose for her mother before she woke up. In winter Snow-white would make the fire and hang the kettle on the hook, and the kettle was of brass and glittered like gold, so clean was it scoured and polished.

In the evening, when the snowflakes were falling, the mother would say, "Go, Snow-white, and bolt the door," and then they would sit down near the hearth, and the mother would take her glasses and read aloud from a big book, and the two girls would listen sitting and spinning. And by their side a little lamb lay on the ground, and behind them on a perch sat a white dove with its head tucked under its wing.

One evening, when they were sitting peacefully together, there was an urgent knock at the door.

The mother said, "Quick, Rose-red, open the door, it will be a traveller seeking shelter."

Rose-red went and unbolted the door thinking it was some poor wanderer, but it wasn't. It was a bear that stuck its huge black head in the door. Rose-red cried out in alarm and sprang back. The lamb bleated, the dove fluttered its wings, and Snow-white hid behind her mother's bed.

But the bear began to speak and said, "Don't be afraid, I'll do you no harm. I am half frozen, and would like only to warm myself in your house."

"You poor bear," said the mother. "Lie down by the fire, only be careful that your fur doesn't catch fire." Then she cried, "Snow-white, Rose-red, come out, the bear will do you no harm, he means well."

Then the two girls came out of hiding, and little by little the lamb and the dove, too, approached the bear and were not at all afraid of him.

The bear said, "Brush the snow out of my fur for me," and they fetched the broom and brushed the bear's fur free of snow. He stretched out comfortably near the fire growling contentedly. It was not long before they became quite familiar with their guest and treated the clumsy beast as a playmate. They tousled his fur, laid their feet on his back, and rolled him to and fro, or they would take a hazel rod and tickle him with it, and laugh when he growled. The bear was glad to put up with all that, only when they became too rough, he cried,

"Snow-white and Rose-red,
You will beat your suitor dead!"

When bedtime came and the others were going to bed, the mother said to the bear, "You can lie here near the fire so you will be sheltered from the cold and the bad weather."

As soon as dawn broke, the two children let him out and he trotted off over the snow into the forest.

From then on the bear came every evening at the same time, would lie

down by the hearth, and let the children play with him as much as they liked. And they got so used to him that the door was never bolted till after their companion had come.

When spring drew near, and outside all was green, the bear said to Snow-white one morning, "I must go away now and may not come back all summer."

"Where are you going then, dear bear?" asked Snow-white.

"I must go into the forest and guard my treasures from the bad dwarfs. In winter when the earth is frozen hard, they stay below ground and can't work their way through, but now that the sun has thawed and warmed the earth, they come up and look for things to steal. And whatever is once in their hands and lies buried in their caves does not easily see the light of day again."

Snow-white was sad about the parting, and when she had unbolted the door for him, and the bear was pushing his way out, he caught his fur on the door-handle and a piece of his coat was torn. Then Snow-white thought she caught sight of gold gleaming through his fur, but she was not sure of it. The bear made off and soon disappeared among the trees.

After some time, the mother sent the children into the forest to gather brushwood. They came across a big tree which lay felled to the ground, and beside it there was something leaping up and down in the grass, but they could not see what it was. They came nearer and saw a dwarf with a wizened old face and a white beard, almost four feet long. The end of the beard was caught in a crack of the tree, and the little man was jumping up and down like a puppy on a leash with no hope of getting loose. He glared at the girls with his fiery red eyes shrieking, "What are you standing there for? Can't you come here and help me?"

"How did you get yourself into such a predicament, little man?" inquired Rose-red.

"You stupid prying goose," retorted the dwarf. "I was going to split the trunk to get some small pieces of wood for the kitchen. With thick logs it is easy to burn the little amount of food a fellow like me needs. We don't gobble down as much as you big greedy people. I had the wedge driven in, and everything would have been all right, only the confounded wedge was too slippery and sprang out unexpectedly, and the tree fell together again and trapped my lovely white beard. Now it's held fast, and I can't get it out. You laugh, you silly pasty-faced creatures! Fie! You are abominable!"

The children tried very hard, but pull as they might it was stuck fast.

"I will run and fetch some help," volunteered Rose-red.

"Crazy blockheads!" snarled the dwarf. "Fetching some help, my foot! You are two, too many for me as it is. Can't you think of something better?"

"Don't be so impatient," said Snow-white, "I'll manage somehow." And she pulled a little pair of scissors out of her pocket, and cut the end of his beard off.

No sooner was the dwarf cut free than he grasped a sack filled with gold that was hidden among the roots of the tree and lifted it up muttering to himself, "Stupid wretches! Fancy cutting off a piece of my fine beard!" With these words he swung the sack onto his back, and went off without giving the children as much as another look.

Sometime later, Snow-white and Rose-red went out to catch some fish for a meal. When they got near the brook they saw something like a big grasshopper hopping about by the water as if it were about to jump in. They ran towards it and recognized the dwarf.

"Where are you off to?" asked Rose-red. "Don't tell me you want to get into the water."

"I am not such a fool as that," cried the dwarf, "can't you see that the confounded fish wants to pull me in?"

The little man had been sitting there fishing and, by bad luck, the wind had tangled his beard up with the fishing-line. Soon afterwards, a big fish had taken the bait and the feeble dwarf was not strong enough to pull it out. The fish was powerful and was dragging the dwarf towards the river. Though he held on to the tufts of grass and reeds, it was of no avail. He had to follow the fish's movements and was now in great danger of being dragged into the water.

The girls had come just in time, held him firmly and tried to disentangle the beard from the line. But in vain. The line and the beard were entwined fast together. There was nothing for it but to use the scissors again, and a little piece of beard was lost in the process.

When the dwarf saw what had happened he screamed at them, "Is it good manners, you toads, to disfigure a person's face? Not enough that you cropped the tip of my beard, the last time. Now you have cut off the best part of it for me! I can't show myself among my people now! I wish you had to run and had lost the soles of your shoes!" Then he picked up a sack of pearls, and without saying another word, dragged it along behind him and disappeared behind a stone.

It so happened that not long after this the mother sent the two girls into town to buy thread, needles, laces and ribbons. The journey took them across a heath on which mighty pieces of rock lay scattered here and there. Then they saw a big bird hovering in the air, circling slowly above them, dropping lower and lower and finally it pounced upon something near a rock not far off. Soon after they heard a piercing, piteous cry. They ran to the spot, and were horrified to see that an eagle had seized their old friend the dwarf and was about to carry him off. Full of pity, the children at once held on to the dwarf and struggled with the eagle until it released its prey.

Scarcely had the dwarf recovered from his fright than he shrieked in his shrill voice, "Couldn't you have handled me with more care? You have torn my thin little coat and it is now in tatters and full of holes. Clumsy awkward riff-raff that you are!" Then he took up his sack of precious stones, and slipped back again under the rocks into his cave.

By now the girls were used to his being ungrateful, so they went on their way and attended to their business in town.

On their way home they had to cross the heath again, and this time they took the dwarf by surprise. He had emptied out his sack of precious stones onto a clean piece of ground thinking that no one would be going that way at such a late hour. The setting sun shone upon the sparkling stones. They glittered and gleamed so magnificently in all colours of the rainbow that the children stopped to look at them.

"Why are you standing there gaping?" cried the dwarf, his ashen face turned purple with rage.

He was about to call them some more bad names, when suddenly a loud growling could be heard and a black bear came ambling towards them out of the forest. Terror-stricken, the dwarf sprang up but he could not get to his cave in time, the bear was already too close.

Then in anguish he cried, "Dear Mister Bear, spare me, I will give you all my treasures. Look at all these lovely jewels lying here. Spare my life, what good is a feeble little fellow like me to you? You would not feel me between your teeth. There, take the two bad girls, they will be a tender morsel for you, as young quails. Eat those instead and be blessed!"

The bear did not heed his words, but dealt the malicious creature a single blow with his paw, and the dwarf lay motionless on the ground.

The girls had run away, but the bear called after them, "Snow-white and Rose-red, don't be afraid. Wait, I will come with you."

Then they recognized his voice, and stopped. When the bear came up to them, his bear's skin suddenly dropped off him, and there he stood, a handsome young man, clad all in gold.

"I am a King's son," he said, and was bewitched by that wicked dwarf, who had stolen my treasures, to run about in the woods as a wild bear until I was freed by his death. Now he has got his well-deserved punishment."

In time Snow-white married the prince and Rose-red married his brother, and they divided the treasures the dwarf had gathered in his cave between them. Their old mother lived many long years peacefully and happily with her children. However, she took the two rose trees with her, and they were planted in front of her window and every year bore the loveliest of roses, white and red.

THE MASTER THIEF

One day an old man and his wife were sitting in front of their rather shabby cottage having a little rest from their labours. Suddenly, there came towards them a magnificent carriage drawn by four black horses and a richly clad gentleman alighted from it. The peasant stood up, went up to the gentleman, and asked what was his pleasure and in what way he could serve him. The stranger shook hands with the old man and said, "I have no other wish than for once to enjoy a simple country dish. Prepare me some potatoes the way you are used to have them. Then I will sit down with you at your table, and will be delighted to eat them."

The peasant laughed and said, "You must be a count or a prince, or even a duke. Noblemen sometimes have such fancies. However, your wish shall be fulfilled."

The wife went into the kitchen, and started to wash and cook the potatoes to make potato cakes with them. While she was at work, the peasant said to the stranger, "Come into my garden for a while, sir, I still have some work to do there." He had dug holes in the garden, and wanted to put in some trees.

"Have you any children," asked the stranger, "who could assist you in your work?"

"No," answered the peasant. "To be sure, I had one," he added, "but he went out into the wide world a long time ago. He was an undutiful boy, clever and deep, but he wouldn't learn anything, and was always up to some kind of trick. At last he ran away, and I haven't heard anything of him since."

The old man took a young tree, put it in its hole, and drove a pole into the ground beside it. And when he had shovelled enough earth and stamped the soil around it, he tied the tree fast to the pole, below, above, and in the middle, with a rope of straw.

"Tell me," said the gentleman, "why don't you tie the crooked knobbly tree which lies in the corner there bowed nearly to the ground to a pole like this so that it may grow straight?"

The old man smiled and said, "Sir, you speak as it appears to you. It's plain to see you haven't such experience with gardening. The tree over there is old and crooked, it's too late now to make it grow straight. You must train trees while they are young."

"It's the same with your son," said the stranger. "Had you trained him while he was still young, he wouldn't have run away on you. Now he, too, will have become hard and crooked."

"Of course," answered the old man, "it's now a long time since he ran away. He will have changed."

"Would you know him if he were to stand before you?" asked the stranger.

"Hardly by his face," answered the peasant, "but he has a mark on him, a mole on the shoulder which looks like a bean."

When he said that, the stranger took off his coat and showed the peasant the mark.

"Dear Lord," cried the old man, "you are my true son," and love for his child stirred his heart. "But how can you be my son," he added, "you have become a great gentleman and live in wealth and abundance. How did you come by it all?"

"Alas, father," replied the son, "the young tree was not tied to a pole and has grown crooked. Now it's too late, it will never become straight again. How did I come by all this? I am a thief. But don't be alarmed, I am a master thief. There's neither lock nor bolt that I cannot open. Whatever I desire is mine. Don't think for a moment that I steal like a common thief. I only take the surplus riches of the wealthy. Poor people have nothing to fear from me. To those I rather give than take anything from them. Neither do I touch what I can have without effort, cunning and skill. Those things don't tempt me."

"Oh my son," said the father, "I don't like it all the same. A thief is a thief. I tell you you'll come to a bad end."

He took him to his mother, and when she heard he was her son, she wept for joy, but when he told her that he had become a master thief, tears of shame streamed from her eyes. In the end she said, "Even if he's become a thief, he is my son, and my eyes have rejoiced in seeing him once again."

They sat down at the table, and he once more ate with his parents the simple fare which he had not eaten for so long.

The father said, "When His Grace the Count up there at the castle learns who you are and what you do for a living, he won't take you in his arms and rock you as he did when he held you at the christening, but will have you swing on the gallows."

"Don't worry, father, he won't do that, for I know my profession. I'll go to him myself this very day."

As evening drew near, the master thief got into his coach and drove to the castle. The Count received him with courtesy, for he took him for a nobleman. However, when the stranger made himself known to him, the older man turned pale and was silent for some time. At last he said, "You are my godson, therefore I will temper justice with mercy and will treat you with forbearance. Since you boast you are a master thief, I will put your art to the test. If you can't prove your skill, you must marry the rope-maker's daughter, and the crowing of ravens shall be your wedding music."

"Your Grace," answered the master thief, "think of three tricks, as difficult as you possibly can and, if I don't fulfil the tasks, do with me as you think fit."

The Count reflected for a few moments, and then said, "Very well, first you shall steal my favourite horse from the stable. Secondly, you shall remove the sheet from under the Countess and myself without our noticing it and, in addition, take the wedding ring off my wife's finger. Third and last, you shall steal the parson and the sexton from my church. Take due note of this, for your neck is at stake."

The master thief repaired to the neighbouring town. There he bought clothes from an old peasant woman, and put them on. Then he coloured his face brown, and painted in wrinkles that made him look so old that no one would have recognized him. Finally, he filled a litle cask with old wine, and mixed a strong sleeping-draught in it. He put the cask in a basket which he carried on his back, and went with slow and tottering steps to the count's castle.

It was already dark when he arrived. He sat down in the courtyard on a stone, started coughing badly, and rubbed his hands as though they were freezing. Outside the stable door some soldiers were lying around a fire. One of them noticed the old woman and called out to her, "Come, granny, and warm your hands with us over here. You have nowhere to stay the night, and will have to take shelter wherever you find it."

The old woman tottered up to them, begged them to take the basket from her back, and sat down by them at the fire.

"What have you got in that cask, old lady?" asked one of the soldiers.

"A good draught of wine," she answered. "I make my living from trade, for money and kind words I'll be glad to give you a glass."

"Just push it over here, then," said the soldier, and when he tasted one glass he said, "When wine is good, I don't mind another glass," and he had another poured for himself, and the others followed suit.

"Hallo, comrades," shouted one of them to those who were sitting in the stable, "here is an old woman, she has wine that is as old as herself.

Take a draught, it will warm your stomachs better than that fire of ours."

The old woman carried the cask into the stable. One soldier sat in the saddle of the count's favourite horse, another held the bridle, a third had seized the tail. She poured out as much as was demanded till the cask was empty. Before long the bridle dropped out of the hand of the one holding it, he himself fell down and began to snore. The other who held the tail let go of it, lay down and snored even louder. The man who was sitting in the saddle remained sitting, but his head bowed down nearly to the horse's neck, he slept and blew out his mouth like a blacksmith's bellows. Outside the soldiers had fallen asleep long before, lay on the ground, and were as motionless as stones.

When the master thief saw that he had succeeded, he put a rope instead of the bridle in the hand of the one and a wisp of straw into the hand of the one who was holding the tail. But what he was to do with the one who was sitting on the horse's back? He did not want to throw him off, for fear he might wake up and raise an alarm. But he found a good solution. He unbuckled the girth, fastened a few ropes that hung in rings on the wall on to the saddle, and pulled the sleeping man along with the saddle in the air. Then he tied the rope round the post and made it fast. He soon had the horse unfastened from the chain, but had he ridden over the cobblestones, the noise would have been heard in the castle. So he first wrapped the horse's hoofs in old rags, led it out carefully, swung himself up, and rode off.

At the crack of dawn the master thief galloped on the stolen steed to the castle. The Count had just risen, and was looking out of the window.

"Good morning, Your Grace," he called out to him, "here is your favourite horse I was lucky enough to take from your stable. Just see how nicely your soldiers are lying asleep. And if you care to go into the stable, you'll see how comfortable your guardsmen have made themselves."

The Count could not help laughing. Then he said, "For once you have won the day, but things won't go so well for you the second time. And I warn you, if I catch you stealing like a thief, I will treat you like a thief."

When the Countess went to bed that night, she closed tight the hand with the wedding ring on it, and the Count said, "Everything is locked up and bolted. I will stay awake and lie in wait for the thief. But if he climbs up to the window, I will shoot him down."

Under cover of darkness the master thief went to the gallows, cut down an executed criminal who was hanging there by the rope, and carried him to the castle on his back. Then he placed a ladder at the bedchamber window, put the dead man on his shoulders, and began to mount. When he got as high as the window of the Count's and Countess's bedchamber, the dead man's head appeared in the window. The Count, who was lying in wait in his bed, fired a pistol at him. At once the master thief let the dead man drop down,

and himself jumped off the ladder, and hid in the corner of the grounds.

The night was so clearly lit by the moon that the master thief could see distinctly how the Count stepped from the window, and carried the body of the dead man into the garden. There he began to dig a hole in which to bury him. "Now," thought the thief, "the moment has come," and he sneaked nimbly from his hiding place, and climbed up the ladder straight into the Countess's bedroom.

"Dear wife," he said in the Count's voice, "the thief is dead. Yet he is my godson, and more of a rogue than a real villain. I will not expose him to public shame. Also I am sorry for his parents. Before day comes, I will bury him in the garden so that the thing is not noised abroad. Give me the sheet, I will shroud the body, and not bury him like a dog."

Then the Countess gave him the sheet.

"You know," went on the thief, "I have a generous heart. I will put your ring on the thief's finger. After all, the unfortunate man has staked his life on it, so he may as well take it into the grave with him." The Countess did not want to contradict the Count, and though none too happy about it, she slipped the ring off her finger and gave it to him. The master thief went off with both things, and arrived safely home before the Count had finished his grave digging.

The Count pulled a long face when the master thief came the next morning and brought him the sheet and the ring.

"Are you a magician?" he said to him. "Whoever got you out of the grave where I myself laid you, and brought you to life again?"

"It wasn't me that you buried," said the thief, "but a criminal from the gallows," and he described in detail how it all happened. The Count had to admit that he was a clever, cunning thief.

"But you are not through yet," he added, "there is still the third task to perform, and if you don't succeed, all you have accomplished shall be for nothing." The master thief smiled and made no reply.

When night fell, he came to the village church with a long sack on his back, a bundle on his arm, and a lantern in his hand. In the sack he had crabs, and in the bundle short wax candles. He sat down in the churchyard, took one crab out and stuck a little candle on its back. Then he lit the light, set the crab on the ground, and let it crawl. He fetched yet another out of the sack and went on till the last was out. Then he put on a long black garment which looked like a monk's cowl, and stuck a grey beard on his chin. When he was fully disguised, he took the sack in which the crabs had been, went into the church and went into the pulpit.

The tower clock was just striking twelve. When the last stroke had died down, he called out in a loud piercing voice, " Harken, harken, you sinners, the end of all things is at hand. Doomsday is near. Harken, harken. Whoever wishes to go to Heaven with me, let him crawl into the sack. I am Peter who opens and shuts the heavenly gates. Behold, out in the graveyard, the dead are roaming about collecting their bones. Come, come, and crawl into the sack, the end of the world has come!"

The voice echoed through the whole village. The parson and the sexton, who lived nearest the church, were the first to hear it, and when they saw the lights moving about in the graveyard, they realized that something extraordinary was going on, and came into the church. For a while they listened to the sermon, then the sexton nudged the parson and said, "It wouldn't be a bad idea if we used this opportunity and went to Heaven together in an easy way before Doomsday dawns."

"Exactly," replied the parson, "that's what I have been thinking too. If you feel like it, we can get ready to set off now."

"Yes," said the sexton, "but you, your reverence, have precedence. I shall follow you." So the parson went forward and mounted the pulpit where the master thief opened the sack. The parson crawled in first, then the sexton.

At once the master thief bound the sack fast, caught hold of it and dragged it down the pulpit steps. Whenever the heads of the two fools knocked against the steps, he called out, "Now we are going over the mountains." Then he dragged them in a similar way through the village, and when they went through puddles, he cried, "Now we are going through the damp clouds!" And when he finally dragged them up the palace steps he cried, "Now we are on the steps of Heaven and will soon be in the outer court." When they got upstairs, he threw the sack into a dovecote, and when the doves fluttered their wings, he shouted, "Do you hear how the angels rejoice and flap their wings?" Then he went off.

The next morning he went to the Count, and told him he had also accomplished the third task and kidnapped the parson and sexton from the church.

"Where did you leave them?" asked the Count.

"Why, they lie in a sack in the dovecote and imagine they are in Heaven."

The Count went up and convinced himself that the master thief had told the truth. When he had freed the parson and the sexton from their prison he said, "You are an arch-thief and have won your case. This time you shall get off with a whole skin, but take care you disappear from my country, for if you ever set foot in it again, then you can count on your place on the gallows."

The arch-thief said good-bye to his parents, went once more into the wide world, and was never heard of again.

THE DEVIL AND HIS GRANDMOTHER

There was a great war, and the King had many soldiers, but he gave them little pay, so little that they could not make both ends meet. So three soldiers got together and decided to run away.

One said to the others, "If we are caught, we shall hang on the gallows. What shall we do to avoid it?"

Another said, "See that big cornfield? No man shall find us if we hide there. The troops are not allowed to march across, and tomorrow they are to move on."

So they crept into the corn but the soldiers did not move on and remained all around it. The three sat in the corn for two days and nights, and were so hungry that they nearly died. But to come out would have meant certain death.

"What has our desertion gained us when we must die a miserable death here?" said one soldier in despair.

After a while, a fiery dragon came flying through the air, descended near them, and asked why they were hiding there.

They answered, "We are three soldiers and have deserted because we were badly paid. Now we shall starve if we stay here, or are sure to swing on the gallows if we leave."

"If you are willing to serve me for seven years," said the dragon, "I will guide you through the troops and no one shall catch you."

"We have no choice but to accept," the soldiers answered.

Then the dragon seized them in his paws, flew them over the troops, and put them down on the ground again far from the army. But the dragon was none other than the Devil.

He gave them a little whip and said, "Whip with it and crack it, and you will have as much gold as you can possibly desire. You can live like great lords, keep horses and ride in carriages. When the seven years have gone, you are all mine." Then he held a book open before them which all the three of them had to sign. "But first I will give you a riddle," he said. "If you can solve it, you shall be free and released from my power."

Then the dragon flew away. They went off with their whip, had plenty of gold, ordered themselves costly garments and travelled about the world. Wherever they came they lived a life of pleasure and magnificence. They rode on horses and in fine carriages, ate and drank well, but did no evil.

They found the time slipping by quickly and, as the seven years were very nearly over, two of them grew terribly scared and anxious, but the third made light of it saying, "Brothers, have no fear, I still have my mother-wit, and shall solve the riddle."

They went out into the fields, sat down, but two soldiers still had sullen faces. Suddenly an old woman came past, and asked why they were so sad.

"Ah, what does it matter to you?" they said. "You cannot possibly help us."

"Who knows," she replied, "just tell me your troubles."

Then they told her how they had been the Devil's servants for close on seven years. How they had been rolling in wealth, but they had sold their souls to him, and would fall prey to him if, after the seven years, they could not solve his riddle.

The old woman said, "If you are to be saved, one of you must go out into the forest. There he will come upon a dilapidated rocky wall which looks like a little house. This he must enter and there he shall find help."

The two miserable soldiers thought, "That will not save us." And sat on as before. But the third, the merry one, got ready to go, and walked far into the forest until he found the rock house. An ancient woman sat there, who was the Devil's grandmother, and asked the soldier where he came from and what was his business. He told her everything that had happened and, because she liked him she had pity on him and said she would help him. She lifted up a big stone lying over a cellar, and said, "Hide down there, you will hear everything that is said up here. Just sit still and do not stir. When the dragon comes I will ask him about the riddle. He tells me everything, so be careful to listen to his answer."

At twelve o'clock that night, the dragon came flying into the hut and asked for his dinner. The grandmother laid the table and brought food and drink to please him, and they ate and drank together.

Then they talked and she asked him how the day had gone and how many souls he had gained.

"Somehow nothing seemed to go well today," he answered, "but I seized three soldiers, nearly seven years ago. They are mine soon for certain."

"Yes, three soldiers," said she. "That's something worth having, but they may yet escape you."

The Devil said haughtily, "They are mine. I have given them a riddle which they will never be able to solve."

"What kind of a riddle?" she asked.

"I will tell you. In the great North Sea lies a dead dogfish, that shall be their roast meat; a rib of a whale, that shall be their silver spoon and an old hollow horse's hoof, that shall be their wineglass."

When the Devil had gone to bed, the old grandmother lifted up the stone, and let the soldier out.

"Did you take it all in properly?"

"Yes, thank you," said he, "I know enough, and will know what to do."

Then he went out secretly through the window and hurried to his comrades. He told them how the Devil had been outwitted by the old grandmother and how he had overheard the solution to the riddle. Then they were all merry and of good cheer, took the whip and beat out so much money for themselves that it hopped about all over the ground.

When the seven years had passed to the day, the Devil came with the book, pointed to the signatures, and said, "I will take you with me to hell, and there you shall have a meal. If you can guess what kind of roast meat you will get to eat, you shall be free and can keep the whip as well."

Then the first soldier spoke, "In the great North Sea lies a dead dogfish, that will surely be the meat."

The Devil was angry and muttered, "Hm, hm, hm!" and asked the second, "But what will be your spoon?"

"The rib of a whale, that is to be our silver spoon."

The Devil scowled, growled three times "Hm! hm! hm!" and said to the third, "And do you know what your wineglass shall be?"
"An old horse's hoof, that is to be our wineglass."

The Devil shrieked aloud, flew away, and lost his power over them. The three, however, kept the whip, whipped out as much money for themselves as they desired, and lived happily to the end of their days.

THE GRAVE-MOUND

A rich farmer was standing one day in his yard looking out across his fields and gardens. The corn was growing well and the fruit trees hung heavy with fruit. Last year's corn was still lying in such huge heaps in the loft that the beams could hardly bear it. Then he went into the stable, where stood well-fed oxen, plump cows and horses smooth-coated and polished like mirrors. Finally, he went back into his house and let his eyes roam along the iron chests where his money was kept.

As he was standing contemplating his wealth, all at once a violent knock was heard beside him. But the knock was not on the door of his house, but on the door of his heart. The door opened, and he heard a voice say, "Have you used any of this to do good to your relatives? Have you ever helped the poor? Have you shared you bread with the hungry? Were you satisfied with what you possessed, or did you desire more and more?"

His heart had no hesitation in answering, "I have been hard and have never done anything to help my relatives. If a poor man came, I turned my eyes away. I have never thought of the hungry, but only of how to increase my wealth. Had everything under the sun been mine, it still would not have been enough." When his heart had said this, the farmer got terribly frightened. His knees began to shake and he had to sit down.

Then another knock was heard, but this time it was on the door of his house. It was his neighbour, a poor wretch with many children for whom he no longer had enough to eat. "I know," thought the poor man, as he knocked at the door, "my neighbour is rich but he is equally hard of heart. I don't believe he will help me, but my children are crying for bread, so I'll risk it." He said to the rich man, "You don't give away lightly what is yours, but I stand here like a drowning man up to my neck in water. My children are starving, lend me four measures of corn."

The rich man looked at him for a long time, then the first ray of pity began to melt a drop of the ice of greed. "I won't lend you four measures, but will make you a present of eight," he said. "Only there's one condition you must fulfil."

"What am I to do?" said the poor man.

"When I am dead, you must keep watch at my grave-side for three nights."

The poor man had a very strange feeling when he heard this, but in the need in which he found himself he would have agreed to anything. So he accepted, and carried the corn home.

It was as if the rich man had foreseen what would happen, because three days later, he suddenly dropped down dead. No one knew exactly what had happened to him but there was no one who mourned him.

When he was buried, the poor man remembered his promise. He would gladly have disregarded it, but thought, "After all, he proved himself charitable. I have fed my children with his corn and even if it was not for this, I have made a promise and I must keep it."

When night came, he went to the graveyard and sat down by the grave-side. Everything was peaceful, only the moon shone, and sometimes an owl flew past, and gave out its sorrowful cry. When the sun rose, the poor man went home safe and sound, and the second night passed just as quietly as before.

On the evening of the third day, he was overcome by a strange uneasiness, and had a feeling of impending danger. When he got to the graveyard he noticed in the shadows of the graveyard wall a man whom he had never seen before. The man was no longer young, had scars on his face, and his eyes roved with a sharp and fiery glance. He was quite covered by an old cloak, and the only thing to be seen were his big riding boots. "What are you looking for here?" said the poor man. "Doesn't the lonely churchyard give you the creeps?"

"I am looking for nothing," answered the man. "Neither am I afraid of anything. I am nothing but a discharged soldier, and I intend to spend the night here, because I have no other shelter."

"If you're not afraid," said the peasant, "stay with me and help me stand guard over that grave-mound over there."

"Standing guard is a soldier's duty," he answered. "Whatever we encounter here, good or bad, we will bear together." The peasant agreed, and they sat down together by the grave.

All was quiet up to midnight, then suddenly a whizzing sound was heard in the air, and the two men standing guard recognized the devil standing in person before them.

"Clear off, you rogues," he shouted at them. "The man who lies in that grave is mine. I am here to fetch him, and I'll wring your necks if you don't go away."

"Sir, you with the red feather," said the soldier, "you're not my captain. I don't have to obey you and I haven't yet learnt to fear. You go your way. We are staying here."

The devil thought to himself, "Gold is the best to tempt these rogues with." He struck a softer tone of voice and asked if they wouldn't accept a sack of gold and go home with it.

"That sounds fine," answered the soldier, "but one little bag of gold isn't much. If you give us as much gold as will go into one of my boots there, we'll clear the field and withdraw."

"I haven't got that much on me," said the devil, "but I will fetch it. In the neighbouring town lives a money-lender, who is a good friend of mine, and he will be pleased to advance me that amount."

When the devil had vanished, the soldier pulled off his left boot, and said, "We will play a trick on that gentleman. Just give me your knife, comrade."

With that the soldier cut the sole away from the boot, and placed it in the tall grass on the edge of a partly overgrown pit. "Now we are ready, he said. "The devil can come."

They both sat down and waited and before long the devil came back with a little sack of gold in his hand.

"Just pour it in," said the soldier lifting the boot a bit, "but that won't be enough."

The devil shook the little bag empty but the gold fell through, and the boot remained empty.

"Stupid devil," cried the soldier. "That won't do. Didn't I say so? Turn about and bring more."

The devil shook his head, and an hour later came with a much bigger bag under his arm. "Just pour it in," cried the soldier, "but I doubt if it will fill the boot." The gold jingled as it dropped down, but the boot remained empty. The devil looked in himself with glaring eyes, and made sure that what he said was true. "You have damned big feet," he cried with rage and made a wry face.

"Do you think," retorted the soldier, "that I have a club-foot like you? Since when have you been so stingy? See to it that you fetch more gold, or our bargain is off."

The fiend trotted off again. This time he stayed away longer and, when he finally appeared, he was panting under the burden of the sack which was flung over his shoulder. He poured it into the boot, but it remained as empty as before. The devil was mad with rage, and was about to tear the boot out of the soldier's hand, but at that very moment the first ray of the rising sun pierced the sky, and he gave a loud shriek and fled. The poor farmer's soul was saved.

The peasant wanted to share the gold, but the soldier said, "Give my share to the poor. I will move in with you in your cottage, and with what is left we shall live in peace for the rest of our days.

THE BLUE LIGHT

Once upon a time there was a soldier, who had served his King and country faithully for many long years. When the war was over and the soldier, because of the many wounds he had received, could serve as a military man no more, the King said to him, "Go home. I do not need you now. No longer shall you receive any pay, for only he who is in my service receives money."

The soldier did not know how he would make out his living in the future, and went away in a wretched state. He walked about the whole day till in the evening he came to a forest. When darkness came, he saw a light in the distance. He approached it and came to a house where a witch was living. "Please put me up for the night," begged the soldier, "and give me something to eat and drink, or I shall starve."

"Oho," she answered. "Who is likely to give anything to a fugitive soldier? Yet I will have pity on you and take you in, if you will do what I ask."

"What is it you ask?" enquired the soldier.

"That you dig my garden tomorrow," said the witch.

The soldier agreed, and the next day he worked with all his might, but could not finish it by the evening.

"I see quite well that you can do no more today," said the witch. "I will keep you for another night, but in return you must chop me a cart-load of wood and split it small."

For this the soldier needed the whole day, and in the evening the witch suggested that he should stay yet another night.

"Tomorrow you shall do only a little piece of work for me. Behind my house is an old well, with no water in it. My lamp has dropped down there, it burns blue, and never goes out. This you shall fetch up for me again."

Next day, the old hag led him to the well, and let him down in a basket. He found the blue light, and made a sign that she should pull him up again. She pulled him up, but when he was near the edge of the well she reached down and wanted to take the blue light from him.

"No," said the soldier getting wise to her wicked intention. "I am not going to give you the light until I stand with both feet on the earth."

The witch flew into a rage, let him drop down the well, and went away.

The poor soldier fell on the wet ground without coming to grief, and the blue light burned on, but what help was it to him? He saw that he would soon die of starvation. For a while he sat there sadly, then by chance he put his hand into his pocket and found his pipe which was still half full of tobacco. This shall be my last pleasure, he thought. He pulled it out, lit it from the blue lamp, and began to smoke. When the smoke had curled out in the cavern, all at once a little black dwarf stood before him, and asked, "Master, what is your bidding?"

"What could I command you to do?" returned the soldier full of amazement.

"I can do anything," said the little man.

"All right," said the soldier. "First, help me out of this well."

The little man took him by the hand, and led him through an underground corridor, but the soldier did not forget to take the blue lamp with him. On the way he showed him the treasures that the witch had gathered and hidden there, and the soldier took as much gold as he could carry.

When he was above ground again, the soldier said to the dwarf, "Now go in, bind the old witch, and take her before the court."

Not long afterwards the witch came riding past him on a wild tomcat, shrieking like a whirlwind. Then the little man came back.

"Everything is done according to your command," he said, "and the witch now hangs on the gallows. Master, what do you bid further?"

"Nothing for the moment," answered the soldier. "You can go home but be on hand in case I need you."

"All you need do is to light your pipe from the blue light, and I shall appear before you instantly," said the dwarf. Then he vanished from sight.

The soldier went back to the town from where he had come. He went into the best inn and had some beautiful clothes made for him. Then he ordered the landlord to furnish a chamber for him with all possible magnificence.

When it was ready and the soldier had settled in, he called the black dwarf and said, "I served the King faithfully, but he sent me away and would have let me starve. I want to take revenge on him now."

"What am I to do?" asked the dwarf.

"Late in the evening when the King's daughter is lying asleep in her bed, bring her here. She shall serve me as a maid."

The dwarf said, "It's an easy thing for me, but a dangerous one for you, for if it becomes known you will pay dearly for it." Nevertheless, the dwarf obeyed his master.

As it was striking twelve, the door flew open, and he brought in the King's daughter.

"Ah, there you are!" cried the soldier. "Get down to work. Go, get the broom and sweep the chamber."

When she had finished, he made her sit opposite him in the chair, stuck out his feet toward her, and said, "Pull off my boots." Then he threw them in her face, and she was obliged to pick them up, clean and polish them. But she did everything he ordered without complaint, silently, and with half-closed eyes. At the first crow of the cock the dwarf bore her back to the royal castle and to her bed.

Next morning, when the King's daughter rose, she went to her father, and told him she had had a strange dream. "I was carried away through the streets with lightning-speed, and brought into the room of a soldier. I had to serve him as a maid and wait on him, and do all his menial tasks, sweep the room and clean his boots. It was only a dream, yet I am as tired as though I had really done all that."

"It may have been true, and no dream," said the King. "I will give you some advice. Fill your pocket with peas, and make a small hole in it. If you are carried off again, they will fall out and leave a trail along the street."

While the King was speaking thus, the little dwarf was standing nearby. He was invisible and heard everything. In the night as he carried the sleeping Princess through the streets, a few peas fell out of her pocket but they could leave no trace, for the cunning dwarf had strewn peas all over the streets beforehand. Once again the King's daughter had to do a maid's work until the cock crowed.

Next morning the King sent out his men to find the trail, but it was no use, for in the streets poor children were sitting and picking up peas, saying, "It rained peas in the night."

"We must think of something else," said the King. "Keep your shoes on, when you lie down in bed and, before you come back from wherever you have been, hide one of them there, I shall find it, I am sure."

The dwarf heard about the scheme and in the evening, when the soldier demanded that he should again bring him the King's daughter, he tried to change his mind saying that he knew of no means to thwart the cunning King. If the shoe were to be found in his room, things would be very bad for him.

"Do as I tell you," replied the soldier. So the King's daughter was brought again and had to work like a maid for the third night. However, before she was carried back again, she had hidden one of her shoes under the bed.

The next morning, the King ordered his men to look all over the city for his daughter's shoe. It was found in the soldier's room, and the soldier himself, who had, on the dwarf's entreaty, gone away through the gate, was soon caught and thrown into jail. During his flight, he had forgotten his most valuable possessions, the blue light and the gold, and he had just one ducat left in his pocket.

As he was standing weighted down with his chains near the window of his jail, he saw one of his former comrades going past. He tapped on the window, and when the other came to him, the soldier said, "Be so kind and bring me the little bundle that I left lying in the inn. I will give you a ducat in return."

The friend ran to the inn and brought the bundle. As soon as the soldier was alone again, he lit his pipe, and bade the little dwarf come to him.

"Fear not," said he to his master. "Go wherever they take you, and do not resist, only take the blue light with you."

Next day the soldier was put on trial, and though he had committed no crime the judge sentenced him to death. As he was being led out, he asked the King for a last favour.

"What is it?" asked the King.

"That I may smoke my pipe on the way."

"Three if you like," answered the King, "but do not imagine that I will spare your life."

The soldier then pulled out his pipe and lit it from the blue light. And scarcely had a few rings of smoke risen into the air than the dwarf stood there with a little club in his hand, and said, "Master, what is your bidding?"

"Strike the false knights here and their bailiffs to the ground, and do not spare the King either who has treated me so badly."

Then the dwarf rode like lightning, zigzag, here and there, and whomever he touched with his club fell down and dared not rise again. The King was terrified and begged the soldier for his life. To save it, he gave the soldier his kingdom and his daughter in marriage.

IRON JOHN

Once upon a time there was a King who had a big forest by his castle with all kinds of game running about. One day he sent out a huntsman to shoot a deer but the huntsman never came back.

"Maybe an accident has befallen him," said the King, and the next day he sent out two more huntsmen to look for him but these, too, stayed away. On the third day he bade all his huntsmen come to him and said, "Search through the whole forest, and do not give up till you have found all three." But none of these ever came home again, nor did anyone of the hounds they had taken with them.

Since that time, no one would venture into the forest, and it lay there in deep silence and solitude. Now and then only an eagle or hawk was flying over it. This lasted many years, but one day an unknown huntsman came to the King looking for work, and offered to go into the dangerous forest. However, the King would not give his consent saying, "The forest is haunted, and I fear you will not fare any better than the others."

The huntsman answered, "Sire, I will dare it at my own peril. For me fear is a thing unknown."

So the huntsman set out for the forest with his dog. Before long, the dog was on the track of some game, and was about to follow it. No sooner had he run a few paces than he found himself before a deep pool and had to stop, and a naked arm stretched out of the water, seized him and drew him down.

When the huntsman saw this, he went back and fetched three men who had to come with pails and drain off the water. When they could see the bottom, they saw a wild man lying there whose body was brown like rusty iron and whose hair hung across his face right down to his knees. He was known as Iron John. Then they bound him with ropes and led him to the castle. There Iron John was the cause of great astonishment, but the King had him shut up in an iron cage in his courtyard, and forbade anyone on pain of death to open the door. The Queen herself was given charge of the key. From then on the forest was a safe place for anyone to enter.

The King had an eight-year-old son. Once, when he was playing in the courtyard, his golden ball fell into the wild man's cage. The boy ran up and said, "Give me back my ball."

"No," said Iron John, "not until you open the door for me."

"That I will not do," said the boy, "the King has forbidden it."

He came again the second day and demanded his ball. The wild man said, "Open my door," but the boy would not do that. On the third day, the King went hunting and the boy came again and said, "Even if I would, I could not open the door. I haven't got the key."

Then the wild man said, "It's under your mother's pillow. You can go and get it."

The boy, who wanted very much to have his ball again, went to the Queen's chamber and returned with the key. The door was hard to open, and the boy jammed his finger in it. When the door was open, Iron John gave him the golden ball, and hurried off.

The boy was thoroughly frightened, and called after him, "Oh wild man, don't go away, or I will be thrashed!"

Then Iron John turned round, lifted the boy up on his shoulders, and walked with swift strides into the forest.

When the King came home, he saw the empty cage and asked the Queen how it had happened. She knew nothing about it and started looking for the key, but it was gone. She called the boy, but there was no answer. The King sent men out to look for him in the fields, but they could not find him. Then he guessed what had happened and the royal court was plunged into deep mourning.

When the wild man reached the dark forest again, he put the boy down and said to him, "You will never see your father and mother again. I will keep you with me, for you have given me freedom, and I should like to help you, in return. If you do everything I tell you, you'll be all right. Of treasures and gold I have enough, more than anyone else in the world."

Then he made a bed of moss for the boy, and the child went to sleep.

Next morning the man led him to a well, and said, "You see, the golden well is bright and crystal-clear. Your duty is to sit by it and mind that nothing drops into it, otherwise it will be spoiled. I will come every evening and see whether you have kept my order."

The boy sat down at the edge of the well. Sometimes a goldfish and sometimes a gold snake was to be seen there, and he took care that nothing should fall into the water. Once, as he was sitting there, his finger which he had jammed in the wild man's cage started hurting so badly that he unwittingly dipped it into the water. Quickly he pulled it out again, but saw it was covered all over in gold. No matter how hard he tried to wipe the gold off again, it was all in vain.

In the evening Iron John came back, looked at the boy, and said, "What has happened to the well?"

"Oh, nothing, nothing at all," he answered and kept his finger behind his back so that the man could not see it.

But Iron John said, "You dipped your finger in the water. This time we will let it go, but be on your guard that you never let anything fall in again."

At the break of dawn, the boy was sitting at the well keeping guard over it. Again his finger hurt, and he rubbed it on his head. Unfortunately, a hair fell into the well. Quickly he took it out again, but already it was gilded all over. Iron John came and knew at once what had happened.

"You let a hair drop into the well," he said. "Once more I will overlook it, but if something happens for the third time, then the well will be ruined and you can no longer stay with me."

On the third day, the boy was sitting at the well, and did not move his finger, no matter how badly it hurt. Gradually however, he got bored and he sat watching his face reflected in the water. And he bent lower and lower until his long hair slid down from his shoulders into the water. He pulled himself up quickly but his head and all its hair was already gilded and shone brightly like the sun.

You can imagine the fright the poor boy got. He took his handkerchief and tied it round his head so that Iron John should not see it.

When he came he knew what had happened and said, "Untie that handkerchief!" Then the golden hair tumbled out, and, apologize as he would, it did the boy no good at all.

"You have not stood the test, and cannot stay here any longer," said Iron John. "Go out into the world, there you will learn about poverty. But, as you are good at heart I wish you well and will allow you one thing. If you get into trouble go to the forest and cry "Iron John!" Then I will come and help you. My power is great, greater than you think, and I have gold and silver more than enough."

Then the King's son left the forest and followed beaten and unbeaten tracks until he finally came to a great city. He looked for some work there, but could not find any, neither had he learnt any skill by which to earn his living. At length he went into the palace and asked whether they would keep him there. The courtiers did not know what use they could make of him, but they liked his face and bade him stay. Eventually, the cook engaged him and said he might carry wood and water and sweep up the ashes.

One day, as there happened to be no one else about, the cook had him carry the dishes to the royal table. However, as he did not want anyone to see his golden hair he kept his cap on.

The King had never experienced anything like this before, and said, "When you come to the royal table, you must bare your head."

"Oh, Sire," he answered, "I can't. I have a bad wound on my head."

Then the King summoned the cook, reproved him and asked how he ever could have engaged such a boy. He ordered him to dismiss the boy at once. But the cook took pity on him and exchanged him for the gardener's boy.

Now the lad had to plant and water the garden, hoe and dig, in all kinds of weather. One day, in summer, when he was working in the garden alone, it was so hot that he took his cap off for the breeze to cool him a little. As the sun shone on his hair, it glittered and flashed so that the rays fell into the bedchamber of the King's daughter. She jumped up to see what it could be. Then she noticed the young lad and called to him, "Bring me a bunch of flowers, young man!"

In all haste he put his cap on again, picked some wild flowers and tied them together. As he was going up the stairs with them he met the gardener who said, "How can you bring the King's daughter a bunch of weeds? Hurry and fetch some others and mind you pick the best."

"Oh no," answered the lad, "the wild ones have the best scent and will please her better."

When he entered her room the King's daughter said, "Take your cap off, it is not right that you should keep your hat on in my presence."

Again he answered, "I must not. I have a wound on my head!"

But the King's daughter snatched at his cap and pulled it off and his golden hair rolled down his shoulders and it was a marvel to see. He tried to run away, but she held him by the arm and gave him a handful of gold coins.

He went off with them, but thought nothing of the gold, and brought it to the gardener and said, "Here's a present for your children, to play with."

The next day, the King's daughter again called to him to bring her a bunch of wild flowers, and when he came in with them she at once clutched at his cap to pull it off. But he held on to it firmly with both hands. Again she gave him a handful of coins, but he would not keep them, and gave them to the gardener as playthings for his children.

The same thing happened on the third day: she could not take off his cap, and he would not keep her gold.

Not long after this a war swept over the kingdom. The King gathered his

people together, but did not know if he would be able to resist the enemy who was too powerful and came in with a great army.

Then the gardener's boy said, "I am grown up now and wish to go to the war. Just give me a horse!" The others laughed and said, "When we have gone, find one for yourself. We'll leave you one in the stable."

When they were gone, he went into the stable and led the horse out. It was lame in one foot and hobbled along. None the less, he got up on it and rode off into the dark forest. At the edge of it he shouted "Iron John!" three times so loud that it echoed through the trees.

At once the wild man appeared, and said, "What is your wish?"

"I want a strong steed, for I will go to the war."

"You shall have it," said Iron John, "and even more than you demand."

The wild man went back into the forest, and before long a groom came out of the forest leading a charger that was hard to keep in check. And behind him followed a great host of warriors, all in armour and their swords glittering in the sun. The youth handed over his three-legged horse to the groom, got into the saddle of the other and rode at the head of his troop.

When he approached the battlefield, he saw that a great many of the King's men had fallen, and before long the others would have had to retreat. Then the youth rode up with his warriors, flew like a tempest over the foe, and struck down everything in his way. The enemy tried to flee, but the youth fought them until not a single man was left. Then, instead of riding to the King, he led his troop back into the forest, and called for Iron John.

"What is your wish?" asked the wild man.

"Take back your steed and your troop, and give me back my three-legged horse."

Everything was done as he wished, and he rode home.

When the King returned to the castle, his daughter came out to meet him, and congratulated him on his victory.

"It was not I who won the day," said he, "but an unknown knight who came to my aid with his troop." The daughter wanted to know who the unknown knight might be, but the King didn't know and said, "He fought the enemy and I never saw him again."

Then the King's daughter asked the gardener about his young assistant, but he said laughing, "He's just come home on his three-legged horse."

The others were poking fun at him and crying, "Here comes our Humpety-Hump back again." They also asked, "Which hedge were you lying asleep behind?" But the boy said, "I did my best, and things would have gone badly without me!" Then he was laughed at even more.

The King said to his daughter, "I will give a great festival. It shall last three days and you shall throw a golden apple. Perhaps the unknown young man will come along."

When the festival was announced the youth went out to the forest and called Iron John.

"What is your wish?" he asked.

"That I catch the Princess's golden apple."

"It's as good as yours already," said Iron John. "You shall also wear red armour, and ride a proud chestnut mare."

When the day came, the youth came galloping on a proud chestnut mare and took his stand among the knights. He was recognized by no one. The King's daughter stepped forward, and threw a golden apple towards the knights, and he alone caught it. Yet the moment he had it, he rode off.

On the second day, Iron John fitted him out as a white knight and gave him a white horse. Again he alone caught the apple but did not stay a single moment, and rode away with it.

The King was angry and said, "This must not happen again. He must appear before me, and give his name." He gave an order that if the knight who caught the apple rode off again, he should be pursued and, if he wouldn't turn back to kill him.

On the third day Iron John gave him a suit of black armour and a black horse and the youth caught the apple again. As he was galloping away with it, the King's men pursued him and one got so near that he wounded him in the leg. Still he managed to escape but his horse jumped so violently that his helmet fell off his head, and they could see his golden hair. They rode back and reported everything to the King.

The next day the King's daughter asked the gardener about his boy. "He is working in the garden. He was out at the festival, and didn't come back till yesterday evening. He also showed my children three golden apples he had won."

The King summoned him to appear before him, and the youth came and again he wore his cap. But the King's daughter went up to him and took it off, and then his golden hair fell over his shoulders, and it was so beautiful that they were all amazed.

"Are you the knight who came every day to the festival, and who caught the three golden apples?" asked the King.

"Yes, and here are the apples," he said pulling them out of his pocket and handing them to the King. "If you wish yet further proof, you can see the wound that your men gave me when they were pursuing me. But I am also the knight who helped you to win a victory over your enemy."

"If you can perform such deeds, then you are no gardener's boy. Tell me who your father is."

"My father is a powerful king, and I have plenty of gold as much as I desire."

"It's plain to see, I owe you a debt of gratitude. What can I do in return?"

"Give me your daughter's hand in marriage," answered the youth.

The maiden laughed and said, "He is very outspoken, but I've seen from his golden hair that he is no ordinary gardener's boy."

His father and mother came to the wedding and were overjoyed, for they had given up every hope of ever seeing their dear son again. And as they were sitting at the wedding feast, the music suddenly stopped, the doors flew open, and a proud king walked in with a grand suite. He went up to the young man, embraced him and said, "I am Iron John and was turned into a wild man by a spell, but you have set me free. All the treasures I possess are now your own."

THE BOOT OF BUFFALO LEATHER

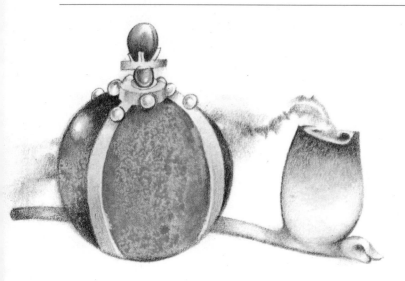

A soldier who is afraid of nothing is concerned about nothing as well. One such fellow had received his discharge from the army, and as he had learnt no trade and could earn nothing, he wandered about and begged good people for alms. All that was left to him was an old great-coat, and a pair of riding boots of buffalo leather.

One day he walked on without looking where he was going further and further into the fields and finally came to a forest. He did not know where he was, but saw a well-dressed man in a green huntsman's coat sitting on a fallen tree. The soldier shook hands with him, dropped down onto the grass beside him, and stretched out his legs.

"I see you are wearing fine, brightly polished boots," he said to the huntsman, "but if you had to wander about like I do, they wouldn't keep their lustre long. Look at mine, they are of buffalo leather and have already served me a long time, though they go through thick and thin."

The two travellers talked awhile, then the soldier stood up and said, "I can't stay any longer, hunger is driving me on. But, brother Shiny-Boots, where does this road lead to?"

"I don't know either," said the huntsman, "I've lost my way in the forest."

"Then you are in the same plight as I am," said the soldier, "birds of a feather flock together. Let's stay together, and try to find our way."

The huntsman gave a little smile and they joined company and walked on till night set in.

"We won't get out of the forest now," said the soldier. "But in the distance I can see a light. We should find something to eat there."

They found a house built of stone, knocked at the door, and an old woman opened it. "We're looking for a night's shelter," said the soldier, "and a little lining for our stomachs, for mine is as empty as an old knapsack."

"You can't stay here," said the old woman, "this is a robbers' den. The best thing for you to do is to set off again before they come home, for if they find you, then you are doomed."

"It won't be as bad as that," answered the soldier, "I haven't had a mouthful for two days now, and whether I perish here, or starve in the forest is all the same to me. I am coming in."

The huntsman was loth to follow him into the house, but the soldier pulled him along by the sleeve. "Come, dear brother, they won't kill us easily."

The old woman took pity on them and said, "Crawl behind the stove. If there is anything left when the robbers have gone to sleep, I'll slip it to you."

Hardly had they sat down in the corner when the twelve robbers came storming in. They sat down at the table, which was already laid and clamoured for food. The old woman brought in a big roast joint, and the robbers fell upon it with great relish.

As the smell of the food reached the soldier's nose, he said to the huntsman, "I can't stand it any longer. I'm going to sit down at the table, and eat with them."

"You will get us both killed," said the huntsman putting his hand on the other's arm. But the soldier suddenly started coughing. When the robbers heard this, they threw down their knives and forks, sprang up from the table, and discovered the two behind the stove.

"Oh ho, your lordships," they cried, "sitting in the corner? What are you looking for here? Have you been sent out as spies? Just wait, you shall learn to fly on a dry bough!"

"Pray, be merciful," said the soldier, "I'm hungry. Please give me something to eat and then you can do what you like with me."

The robbers stopped short, and the leader said, "I can see that you are not afraid. Very well. You will get some food, but after that you must die."

"We shall see about that," said the soldier as he sat down at the table and began to attack the joint in good heart. "Brother Shiny-Boots, come and join me," he called out to the huntsman. "You are sure to be as hungry as I am, and you will certainly get no better roast at home."

But the huntsman would not eat.

The robbers watched the soldier in astonishment and said, "The fellow makes no bones about it."

After a while, the soldier said, "I have eaten enough, now bring some good drink as well!"

The leader was willing to oblige the soldier in this, too, and called to the old woman, "Fetch a bottle from the cellar, and mind it is of the best."

The soldier pulled out the cork so that it popped, took the bottle to the huntsman, and said, "Pay good heed, brother, you are in for a great surprise. I am going to toast the whole clan." Then he swung the bottle over the robbers' heads, and cried, "The health of you all! But with your mouths open and your right hands up!" and he took a hearty draught.

Scarcely were the words out of his mouth than they all sat motionless as if made of stone with their mouths gaping open and their right arms stretched upwards.

The huntsman said to the soldier, "I see you can still do tricks. But now come, and let's go home."

"Oh no, dear brother, that would mean leaving the field too soon. We have beaten the enemy, and now we must take our reward. They are sitting here, with their mouths gaping wide in amazement, and they can't move until I say so. Come, eat and drink."

The old woman fetched another bottle of the best wine, and the soldier did not get up from the table till he had eaten enough for three days.

Finally, when daylight came, he said, "Now it's time to break camp, and so that we may have a short march, the old woman shall show us the shortest way to the city."

When they arrived there, the soldier went to see his old comrades, and said, "Out in the forest I've found a nestful of gallows' birds. Come with me and we shall clear it out."

The soldier led them back to the robbers' house and said to the huntsman, "You must come in with me and see how they tremble when we seize them by their feet." Then they went into the house and the soldier placed his men around the robbers. He took a bottle of wine, drank a draught and swung it over their heads, and cried, "Long life to you all!"

The robbers immediately started to move again, but were overpowered and bound hand and foot with ropes. Then the soldier ordered them to be thrown on to a wagon like so many sacks and said, "Now drive them straight to prison."

But the huntsman took one of the soldiers aside and gave him another commission and sent him into the city.

"Brother Shiny-Boots," said the soldier, "we have been lucky enough to overpower the enemy, and have been well fed. Now we will walk behind quietly."

When they were approaching the city, the soldier saw a crowd of people pouring through the city gate shouting loudly and waving green branches high in the air. Then he saw that the whole of the life-guards were marching towards them.

"What does it mean?" he said to the huntsman in utter amazement.

"Don't you know," he replied, "that the King has been away from his kingdom for a long time and is returning home today? They are all coming out to meet him."

"But where is the King?" asked the soldier, "I can't see him."

"Here he is," replied the hunstsman, "I am the King, and have sent news of my arrival ahead." Then he opened his hunting coat for the soldier to see his royal garments.

The soldier was alarmed, fell on his knees, and begged the King's forgiveness for having treated him as an equal and addressing him with such familiar names without knowing who he really was.

But the King took his hand and said, "You are a gallant soldier and have saved my life. You shall never again suffer from want, and from now on you will be under my protection. And, if ever you wish to eat good food, just come to the royal kitchen. But, any time you want to drink a toast, you must first have my permission!"

THE HEDGE-KING

In olden times each sound still had its sense and meaning. When the blacksmith's hammer resounded, it was crying, "Forge me! forge me!" When the joiner's plane snarled, it was saying, "There it goes! there it goes!" If the mill wheels began to rattle, they were saying, "Help, Lord God! Help, Lord God!" And if the miller who set the mill going was a cheat, the wheel would ask slowly, "Who is there? Who is there?" and then answer quickly, "The miller, the miller!" and finally, "He steals brazenly! He steals brazenly! Three quarts from a bushel!"

In those days birds, too, had their own speech which everybody understood. Nowadays it sounds like twittering, screeching and whistling and, with some, like music without words.

One day it occurred to the birds that they should elect one from among themselves to be King. Only one of them, the lapwing, opposed it. Free he had lived and free would he die, and he withdrew into lonely and unfrequented marshes, and never showed himself again among his kind.

Now the birds wanted to talk the matter over and, on a fine May morning, they all gathered together from wood and field; eagles and chaffinches; owls and crows; larks and sparrows. How could I name them all? Even the cuckoo came, and the hoopoe, and a very tiny little bird which, as yet, had no name also mingled with the crowd.

The hen, who by some oversight had heard nothing of the whole matter, was astounded at such a great assembly. "What, what, what a to-do?" she clucked, but the cock calmed his beloved hen by saying, "Just the rich make the ado!" and told her what all the birds were up to.

It had been decided that the one who could fly the highest should be elected King. Hearing that, a tree-frog sitting in the brushwood cried a warning, "Wet, wet, wet, wet!" because he thought many tears would be shed on account of it. But the crow said, "Nonsense, caw, caw! Everything would pass off in peace and quiet."

Since it was a fine morning, the birds thought they should start flying right away, so that nobody could say later on, "I could have flown even higher, but night came on." Thus, on a given signal, the whole flock rose into the air. Dust blew up from the field, there was a mighty swishing and beating of wings, and it looked as if a black cloud were flying across the sky.

Before long, the smaller birds were left behind, and dropped back to the earth again. The larger birds flew much higher, but none could match the eagle, who rose so high that he could have pecked out the sun's eyes. When he saw that the others could not follow him, he thought, "Why should I fly any higher? I am King anyway," and began to descend again.

The birds below all called to him at once, "You must be our King, no one has flown higher than you!"

"Except me," cried the little nameless fellow who had crept in among the eagle's breast feathers. And as he wasn't tired, he rose up so high that he could have seen God sitting on his throne. When he got that far, he folded his wings, and drifted down and down crying with his fine, piercing voice, "I am King! I am King!"

"You our King!" cried the birds angrily. "You flew so high by trick and cunning!"

So they made another condition. The bird that could bury himself deepest into the earth should be their King. How the goose with her broad breast smacked against the earth. How quickly the cock scraped a hole! The duck got the worst of it, when she jumped into a ditch, sprained her legs, and waddled off to the nearby pond crying, "Dirty work, dirty work!" But the nameless little bird found himself a mousehole, slid down into it, and cried out in his piping voice, "I am King, I am King!"

"You our King!" cried the birds even more angrily than before. "Do you think your tricks are going to count?"

Then they resolved to keep him in his hole and let him starve to death. The owl was placed on guard in front of it and was not to let the trickster out, if she valued her life. When evening came and the birds, feeling very tired after all their exertion, went to bed with their wives and children, the owl alone remained standing at the mousehole, gazing steadfastly into it with her big eyes.

Eventually, she too, got tired and thought to herself, "I can easily shut one eye, and stay awake with the other in order to keep the little scoundrel in his hole." So she shut one eye, and with the other she stared steadily into the mousehole.

The little fellow put out his head and peeped and was about to slip away, but the owl at once stepped forward, and he drew his head back again.

Then the owl opened the one eye again and shut the other, intending to shut them in turns like that all night. But when she shut the one eye she forgot to open the other, and the moment both eyes were shut she fell asleep. The little chap inside the hole soon noticed that and slipped away.

Since that very day the owl may no longer be seen by day, for fear the other birds may tear at her coat. She flies only by night and hunts for mice because they make such crafty holes. Nor is the little bird too keen to show himself, for fear it might cost him his life if he were to be caught. He hops about in the hedges, and if he is quite safe, he calls from time to time, "I am King!" And that is why the other birds call him mockingly the "Hedge-King."

THE HUT IN THE FOREST

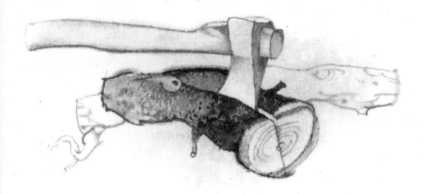

A poor woodcutter lived with his wife and daughters in a little hut on the edge of a lonely forest. One morning when he was ready to go to work, he said to his wife, "Have my midday-meal brought into the forest by our eldest daughter, otherwise I shall not finish all the work I must do today. And so that she may not lose her way," he added, "I will take with me a bag of millet and strew the grain along the way."

Now when the sun was high in the sky above the forest, the girl set out with a pot full of soup. However, the tree-sparrows and wood sprarrows, the larks and finches, blackbirds and tomtits had eaten the millet, and she could not find the way.

So she went on and on this way and that till the sun set and night set in. The trees rustled in the dark, the owls hooted, and the girl began to feel frightened. Then she noticed a light in the distance gleaming among the trees. "There should be someone living there who will put me up for the night," she thought, and went towards the light.

Before long she came to the house with the lighted windows. She knocked, and a rough voice from within called, "Come in." The girl stood on the door step, and knocked on the door of the room. "Come in," cried the voice, and when she opened the door she saw an old grey-faced man sitting at the table, resting his head on his arms, and his white beard flowing down below the table, nearly to the floor. In front of the fire, three animals were lying, a hen, a cock, and a brindled cow. The girl told the old man what had befallen her, and begged shelter for the night. The man said,

"Pretty young hen,
Pretty young cock,
And you pretty brindled cow,
What do you say now?"

"Duks!" answered the animals, which must have meant, "That's all right with us," for the old man said, "Here's everything in abundance, go out to the stove and cook us some supper."

In the kitchen the girl found everything in plenty, so she cooked a good meal, but forgot the animals. She carried the full bowl on to the table and sat down beside the old grey-haired man. When she had eaten, she said, "But now I feel tired. Where is there a bed in which I can lie down and sleep?"

The animals answered,
"You have eaten with him,
You have drunk with him,
You had no thought for us.
Now find your own place
To spend the night."

Then the old man said, "Go upstairs, there you will find a room with two beds in it. Shake those up and cover them with fresh linen, then I will come, too, and lie down to sleep."

The girl went upstairs, and as soon as she had shaken up one bed, and covered it with fresh linen, she lay down in it without waiting for the old man to come up.

Some time later, however, the man came, held a light over the maiden, looked at her, and shook his head. And when he saw she was fast asleep, he opened a trap-door and let her drop down into the cellar.

Meanwhile, the woodcutter came home late in the evening, and scolded his wife for letting him go without food all day.

"It's not my fault," she answered. "Our daughter went out with your dinner. She must have lost her way. She is sure to come back tomorrow."

Before daybreak, however, the woodcutter got up to go to the forest again, and asked that this time the second daughter should bring him the food. "I will take a bagful of lentils," he said, "the grains are bigger than millet, the girl will see them better and can't lose her way."

At noon the second girl set out with the meal, but the lentils had disappeared. The birds of the forest had pecked them up as on the previous day. The girl wandered about in the forest till night came, and she too found her way to the old man's hut, was called inside, and also begged for food and shelter for the night. Again the man with the white beard asked his animals,
"Pretty young hen,
Pretty young cock,
And you pretty brindled cow,
What do you say now?"

Once again the animals answered, "Duks," and everything happened as on the day before. The girl cooked a good meal, ate and drank with the old man, but did not think of feeding the animals. And when she asked where she could spend the night, they answered,

"You have eaten with him,
You have drunk with him,
You had no thought for us.
Now find your own place
To spend the night."

When she had fallen asleep, the old man came, looked at her, shook his head and then let her down into the cellar.

On the third morning, the woodcutter said to his wife, "Today send out our youngest child with the food, she has always been good and obedient. She will keep to the right path, and not run about like her sisters."

The mother did not want to, and said, "Am I to lose even my dearest daughter?"

"Don't worry," he answered, "the lass will not lose her way, she is too clever and sensible, besides, I'll take peas and strew them along the path. They are larger still than lentils, and will show her the way."

However, when the youngest daughter came out with the basket on her arm, the wood-pigeons had already eaten the peas and she did not know which way to go. She was very worried, and her mind was troubled about her father starving and her dear mother's sorrow if she should fail to return.

Finally, when it grew dark, she espied the little light and came to the forest hut. She begged very politely if they would put her up for the night, and once again the man with the white beard asked his animals,

"Pretty young hen,
Pretty young cock,
And you pretty brindled cow,
What do you say now?"

"Duks," they said. Then the maiden stepped towards the fireplace where the animals lay, caressed the hen and the young cockerel by stroking their smooth feathers, and scratched the brindled cow between the horns. And when she had prepared some good soup, and the bowl was standing on the table, she said, "Am I to have my fill, and the dear animals have nothing? There is food in plenty outside, first I will feed them."

So she went and fetched some barley and sprinkled it in front of the hen and the cock, and then brought sweet-smelling hay, a whole armful of it, to the cow. "Eat it up, and enjoy it, dear animals," she said, "and, if you are thirsty, you shall have some fresh water to drink."

Then she brought in a pail of water, and the hen and the cock sprang up on to the edge, dipped their beaks in and held their heads up the way birds do when drinking, and the brindled cow also took a hearty draught. When the animals were fed, the girl sat down at the table beside the old man, and ate what he had left. Before long the hen and cock began to put their little heads under their wings, and the brindled cow blinked its eyes. Then the maiden said, "Shouldn't we go to bed now?"

"Pretty young hen,
Pretty young cock,
And you pretty bringled cow,
What do you say now?"

The animals answered,
"You have eaten with us,
You have drunk with us,
You thought of us, too.
We wish you a good night!"

Then the girl went upstairs, shook the feather-beds and put on fresh linen, and when she was ready, the old man came and lay down in his bed, and his white beard reached down to his feet. The girl lay in the other bed, said her prayers, and fell asleep.

She slept quietly until midnight, then there was so much noise in the house that she woke up. Things started to shake and rattle, and the door was flung open so violently that it hit the wall. The beams rumbled and shook as if they were being torn out of their grooves, and it looked as if the stairs were falling down. Finally there came a thundering crash as if the whole roof were collapsing. Then it got quiet again, and the girl having suffered no harm, stayed lying, quietly in her bed, and fell asleep again.

But when she woke up in the morning in the bright sunshine, what did she see? She was lying in a great hall and round about everything shone in regal splendour; on the walls golden flowers grew on green-silk background, the bed was of ivory, and the cover of red velvet. And on a chair by its side stood a pair of pearl-embroidered slippers. The girl thought it was a dream, but three richly clad servants came in and asked what orders she had for them.

"Please go away," answered the girl, "I will get up in a moment, and make the soup for the old man and then feed the pretty hen, the pretty cockerel, and the pretty brindled cow."

She thought the old man must have already risen, and looked round for his bed, but he was not lying there, instead there was a strange man. And when she looked closer and saw that he was young and handsome, he awoke, raised himself up, and said, "I am a Prince and had been enchanted by a bad witch to live in the forest like an old man. No one was allowed to attend me but my three servants in the shape of a hen, a cock and a brindled cow. The spell would not be broken until a maiden of good heart should come and be kind not only towards humans but also towards the animals. And that was you. At midnight we were disenchanted, and the old hut in the forest changed back into my royal palace."

And when they got up, the Prince told the three servants they should go and fetch the maiden's father and mother to the wedding festival.

"But where are my two sisters?" asked the girl.

"Those I have shut up in a cellar, and tomorrow they shall be led into the forest to serve as maids to a charcoal-burner till they have mended their ways, and are no longer selfish."

BRIAR ROSE

Once upon a time there lived a King and Queen who said every day, "Oh, that we only had a child!" But they never had one.

And it happened that as the Queen was bathing one day, a frog crept out of the water on to the bank and addressed her saying, "Your wish shall come true. Ere a year passes, a daughter shall be born to you."

What the frog had said came to pass and the Queen gave birth to a little girl. She was so beautiful that the King was beside himself with joy and gave a grand feast. He invited not only his relations, friends and neighbours, but also the fairies, that they might pour out their blessings on the child.

Now there were thirteen fairies in his kingdom, but the King had only twelve golden plates for them to eat from, and so one had to stay away.

The feast was celebrated in all splendour and, when it was over, the fairies bestowed on the Princess their wondrous gifts. One gave her virtue, another beauty, a third riches, and so on, in fact everything that her heart could desire.

When eleven of the fairies had given their blessings, the thirteenth suddenly burst in. She had determined to take her revenge for not having been invited and, without a word of greeting, or looking at anybody she cried out, "When she is fifteen years old, the King's daughter shall prick her finger with a spindle and fall down dead." And without another word, she turned and left the hall.

They were all terror-stricken. Then the twelfth fairy, who had not yet given her gift, came forward and unable to lift the curse but only moderate it, said, "The King's daughter shall not die but fall into a deep sleep lasting a hundred years."

The King would fain have saved his beloved daughter from the impending disaster, so he commanded that every spindle in the kingdom should be burnt.

Meanwhile, all the fairies' gifts to the maiden were fulfilled. She grew to be so beautiful, modest and wise that to see her was to love her.

Now it happened that on the very day when the Princess became fifteen, the King and Queen were not at home and she was left all alone in the palace. She wandered about all over the place, looking into rooms and chambers as she pleased and finally came to an old tower. She went up the narrow winding staircase until she came to a little door. There was a rusty key sticking in the lock and, when she turned it, the door sprang open. There, in a little room, sat an old woman with a spindle and busied herself with spinning her flax.

"Good day, Granny," said the King's daughter, "what is it you are doing?"

"Spinning," said the old woman nodding her head.

"What sort of thing is it that skips about so merrily?" asked the maiden and took the spindle wishing to spin as well.

No sooner had she touched the spindle than the spell came true and she pricked her finger with it.

At that very moment, she fell down on a nearby bed and lay in a deep sleep. And this sleep spread over the whole castle.

The King and Queen, who had just returned and had stepped into the hall, fell asleep and the whole royal household with them. The horses went to sleep in the stable, the dogs in the yard, the doves on the roof, the flies on the wall; yes, even the fire flickering in the fireplace stopped and went to sleep and the roast meat stopped sizzling. The cook, who was about to box the ears of the young kitchen boy for having done something amiss, let go of him and went to sleep. The wind dropped and not a leaf stirred on the trees around the castle.

A hedge of briar roses soon began to grow up round the castle growing higher every year. Finally they enveloped the whole castle so that nothing could be seen of it, not even the flag on the roof.

A story soon spread about the land of Briar Rose, as the King's daughter came to be called and, from time to time, kings' sons came and tried to break through the briar-bush into the castle. But they found this impossible. The thorns stuck fast together as if they had hands, and the young men remained hanging there unable to free themselves again and so died a miserable death.

Many, many years had passed before a Prince came to that country again and heard an old man tell of the hedge of briars that hid a castle behind it. Of a Princess of wondrous loveliness called Briar-Rose who had been asleep there for a hundred years, and with her the King, Queen and the whole royal court. The old man also knew from his grandfather that many kings' sons had already tried to force their way through the hedge of briars, but had got trapped inside and died a pitiful death.

Then the youth said, "I am not afraid. I am resolved to go, and find Briar Rose."

In spite of all the good old man could do to dissuade him, the Prince would not heed his words.

It happened that just then, the hundred years had passed and the day had now come when Briar Rose was to wake up again. When the Prince

approached the thorny hedge, it turned into beautiful flowers, which parted to let him pass, then closed again into a briar bush behind him.

In the castle courtyard he saw the horses and dappled hounds lying asleep. On the roof he saw the doves with their heads tucked under their wings. And when he entered the house, the flies were asleep upon the walls, the cook was still holding up his hand as if to seize the boy, and a maid was sitting with a black chicken about to be plucked.

He went on and in the spacious hall he saw the whole of the royal court lying asleep and, above, near the throne, lay the King and Queen.

He pressed on still further. Everything was so quiet that he could hear his own breathing. At last he came to the tower and opened the door of the little room where Briar Rose was asleep. There she lay and looked so beautiful that he could not take his eyes from her, and he bent over and kissed her on the lips. The moment his kiss touched her, Briar Rose awoke, opened her eyes, and looked at him lovingly.

Then they went down together and the King and the Queen awoke and all the courtiers, and looked at each other with their eyes wide open. The horses in the courtyard stood up and tossed their manes; the hounds sprang up and wagged their tails; the doves on the roof pulled their little heads from under their wings and flew off into the fields. The flies on the walls crawled about again; the fire in the kitchen burned up, flickered and cooked the meat; the joint began again to sizzle; the cook boxed the boy's ears till he screamed and the maid finished plucking the fowl.

Then the wedding of the Prince and Briar Rose was celebrated with all splendour and they lived happily ever afterwards.

Once upon a time there was a Princess, and in her castle, high up under the battlements, was a big hall with twelve windows which looked out on all the four quarters of the globe. So when she went up and looked out of these windows she could see all over her kingdom. Out of the first she could see more clearly than anyone else, out of the second still better, out of the third even more distinctly, and so on until the twelfth, where she could see what was above and below the earth, and nothing was hidden from her.

However, as she was proud and would not submit to anybody, and wanted to reign alone over her kingdom she proclaimed that no one should become her husband who could not hide so well that it was impossible for her to find him. Whoever tried and was discovered would have his head cut off.

At this time there were already ninety-seven heads of dead men stuck on stakes in front of the castle, and for a long time no one came forward. The Princess was highly pleased and thought to herself, "Now I shall stay free as long as I live."

Then three brothers appeared and announced they would try their luck. The eldest believed himself to be safe if he crept into a lime-pit, but she espied him from the very first window, had him pulled out and his head cut off. The second crept into the cellar of the castle, but this one, too, she spotted from the first window and his fate was sealed. Then the youngest came before her and begged that she would grant him one day's chance, and for her to be gracious enough to give him twice a second chance should she discover him. If he failed for the third time, then he wouldn't like to go on living anyway.

As he was so handsome and asked so earnestly, she said, "Yes, I will agree to that, but you will not succeed."

The next day he meditated a long time how he was to hide himself, but in vain. Thereupon he took his gun and went out hunting. He saw a raven and took aim at it. He was just about to fire when the raven cried, "Don't shoot, I will repay you if you spare me." He put his rifle away, went on and came to a lake where he surprised a big fish which had come from the depths up to the surface. When he took aim, the fish cried out, "Don't shoot, I will repay you if you spare me!" He let it dive under water, went on, and met a fox which was limping. He fired but missed it, then the fox cried, "Better come here and pull the thorn out of my foot." He did so, but all the same he wanted to kill the fox and skin it. The fox said, "Don't do it, I will repay you if you spare me!" The youth let it free and, as it was evening, he turned homewards.

The next day he was to go in hiding, but no matter how he racked his brain, he did not know where to go. He went into the forest to the raven and said, "I spared your life, now tell me where I am to hide so that the King's daughter shall not see me." The raven dropped his head and was lost in thought for a time. At last he croaked, "I've got it!" He fetched an egg from his nest, separated it into two parts, and shut the youth inside it. Then he made it whole again and sat down on it. The King's daughter stepped to the first window and could not discover him. Nor could she see him from the second window and she was beginning to feel uneasy. But at the eleventh window she spotted him. She had the raven shot, the egg fetched and broken in two, and the young man had to come out.

She said, "You have been spared once, but if I find you next time, you're lost."

The next day he went to the lake, called the fish and said, "I spared your life, now say where I am to hide so that the King's daughter will not see me!" The fish reflected and at last cried, "I've got it! I will hide you in my belly!" It swallowed him and swam down to the bottom of the lake. The King's daughter looked through her windows, and this time even from the eleventh she did not see the young man, and was dismayed. Yet at the twelfth she discovered him. She ordered the fish to be caught and killed, and the youth appeared. Anyone can imagine how he felt. She said, "Twice you have been spared, but your head will certainly adorn the front of my castle."

On the last day he went with a heavy heart into the fields and met the fox. "You know how to find the remotest places," he said. "I spared your life, now advise me where I am to hide so that the King's daughter won't find me." "A hard proposition," answered the fox and looked thoughtful. At last it cried, "I've got it!" The youth went with it to a spring. The fox dived in and came out dressed like the keeper of a pet shop. The youth also had to dive into the water, and was turned into a little monkey. The shopkeeper came to town, and displayed the clever little animal. Crowds of people came running to see it. At last even the Princess came, and as she found much pleasure in it, she bought it and gave the shopkeeper a lot of money for it. Before he handed it to her, he said to it, "When the Princess goes to the window, creep quickly under her plaits."

Now the time came for her to look for the young man. She stepped from the first to the eleventh windows in order, and could not see him. When even through the twelfth she could not see her quarry, she was filled with fright and rage, and slammed it so violently that the glass in all the windows split into a thousand pieces and the whole castle shook.

She drew back and felt the little monkey under her plaits. She grabbed it, threw it on the floor, and shouted, "Get out of my sight!" The monkey ran to the shopkeeper and they both ran to the spring, where they plunged in and changed back to their true form again. The youth thanked the fox and said, "The raven and the fish are stupid compared to you, you know the right tricks, there is no denying it."

The young man went straight into the castle. The Princess was already waiting for him and reconciled to her fate. The wedding was celebrated, and he was now King and ruler of the whole kingdom. He never told her where he had hidden the third time and who had helped him, so she believed he had done it all on his own and held him in high esteem.